THE FLIGHT OF THE UNICORNS

THE FLIGHT OF THE UNICORNS

ANTHONY SHEPHERD
Foreword by MAURICE A. MACHRIS

ABELARD-SCHUMAN
NEW YORK

For Sarah who had
to stay at home

© Anthony Shepherd 1965

Library of Congress Catalog Card Number: 66-25006

First published in Great Britain 1965 by Elek Books Limited

Published in the United States 1966 by Abelard-Schuman Limited
6 West 57 Street, New York 10019

CONTENTS

ILLUSTRATIONS

Grateful acknowledgement is made to Bini Malcolm for permission to use the photographs facing pages 16, 17 (top), 32, 64 (top), 81, 96, 97.

FOREWORD

It is particularly pleasing to be able to write a few words for Anthony Shepherd's *The Flight of the Unicorns*. At the time I first learned of the expedition to collect a herd of wild Arabian Oryx, I was president of the Shikar-Safari Club International, an organization of big game hunters, mostly American, who are particularly dedicated to conservation and the preservation of threatened species.

News of the expedition brought to mind a particularly rewarding conversation I had several years ago, on a trip to Africa, with Colonel Jack Vincent, who at that time was head of the Natal Parks Board and is now connected with the International Union for the Conservation of Nature (Switzerland). I will always remember his statement that too many people interested generally in conservation seem to confuse the two distinctly separate issues of conservation and preservation, especially as the terms apply to wildlife.

In an attempt to arrive at the simplest possible definitions, we agreed that *conservation* encompasses all those efforts needed to guarantee that the total environment of plant, animal, soil, rainfall, watershed, and other natural geographic conditions remains in the same balance as created by nature. It implies, ideally, that man's role as a conservationist is to prevent man himself from upsetting the balance of nature, especially in those areas set aside for wildlife, such as the great national parks.

Yet we agreed also that an ideal situation seldom exists and that conservation has come to include whatever steps are necessary for man to restore to a given area a balance of nature, once this balance has been upset drastically either by natural disaster or by increasing pressure from man himself.

Our definition of *preservation*, on the other hand, is far more limited. As a term applied to wildlife, it should generally be confined in its use to those efforts needed to guarantee the survival (even if only as a scientific curiosity) of vanishing species of rare animal forms, plant life, birds, and such individual landmarks or individual living natural specimens as face extinction without man's help.

There is, of course, a bridge between preservation and conservation. Sometimes the rigid protection afforded a certain species in an all-out effort at preservation is so successful that this species makes a phenomenal comeback and is again able to compete in the balance of nature. Such a species would then, technically, no longer need preservation and would be subject only to the overall efforts for conservation in whole areas.

Preservation almost always involves rigid protection of the threatened species; even if this means transplanting that species to a more favorable environment, which may be one in which that species never before existed. The new environment may be miles or, in some cases, continents away. The real danger, in my opinion, lies in confusing preservation with conservation, especially when preservational thinking is applied to whole areas such as the national parks. There are too many variables having to do with animal population explosions, prolonged droughts, animal migration, etc., to say flatly that every living thing within a national park should be rigidly preserved.

Yet the case for preservation is a vital one. Research shows that in the last 150 years, approximately 40 species of animals and birds have disappeared under an avalanche of changing forces to which they could not adapt. Unless immediate and drastic steps are taken to preserve them, another 78 species face extinction in the next few years.

The Shikar-Safari Club International, like the World Wildlife Fund, the Fauna Preservation Society of London, the African Wildlife Leadership Foundation, and the Conservation Foundation of the United States, is vitally interested in both preservation and conservation. Furthermore, as in my own case, it is only natural that the game hunters of the world should be so, for as avid sportsmen it is to their own advantage to see that those areas in which they hunt will continue to abound in game for all the foreseeable future. In fact, it is the game hunter, familiar with wildlife problems, who channels the greatest amount of money into preservation and conservation projects everywhere. By and large, it is the veteran hunter who gives the most publicity to wildlife problems, who is among the first to admit that certain species are actually endangered and should be singled out for preservation.

The Arabian Oryx makes an excellent case in point. There are others, like that of the white rhino of South and East Africa, the axis deer, and Nene Goose of Hawaii, but the saving of the Arabian Oryx is probably the most outstanding example of a pure preservation attempt in recent years. It was extremely gratifying, therefore, for the Shikar-Safari Club International, like other large conservation groups, to play an important and continuing part in this project. Through combined efforts, the plight of the Arabian Oryx was brought to the attention of American wildlife enthusiasts, and dozens of newspaper and magazine articles were written on the subject. These began to appear as early as 1960, when it was reported that the species was being systematically exterminated by desert tribesmen, who felt that killing an oryx endowed them with virility and the ability to live for long periods without water.

It is interesting to note that in the case of the Arabian Oryx, neither the animal nor its habitat has been a customary target for European or American hunters, so it must be assumed that this preservation attempt stemmed solely from a genuine concern over a threatened species rather than from a selfish desire to see the animal listed as one of the world's big game trophy animals.

In the summer of 1962, I did some research to discover if any similar effort had been made in recent years to enlist cooperation for such a project on an international scale, and I was surprised to learn that there had been only one such case, and that dated back to the turn of the century. In 1901, Britain's Duke of Bedford organized a drive to save the Père David's deer from almost certain extinction.

This exotic Chinese deer was first brought to the attention of the Western world in 1865, when Père Armand David, a French missionary, saw several of them as he stole a look over the wall of the Imperial Hunting Park outside Peking. In subsequent years, a few of these deer were, through diplomatic channels, brought out of China for display in European zoos. These few animals became the only surviving specimens when, in 1900, the Boxer Rebellion brought about the final and complete extermination of those remaining in China.

The Duke of Bedford, through foresight and a will to save the species, influenced the European zoos to give up their individual animals so that they could be put together in one breeding herd in a concerted last-ditch effort to increase their number. Altogether, he was able to acquire 20 head, which he took to Woburn Abbey in England to begin the survival program. In 20 years, the herd had increased to 47 adults and 17 fauns. By 1935, it had grown to approximately 200. Today, there are between 450 and 500 Père David's deer in various places in Europe and the United States.

It was logical to reason that the same thing could be done for the Arabian Oryx. The difficulty was that there were so few of the animals in captivity, and these were mostly in the hands of Arabian royalty. There were all kinds of barriers to overcome, both in language and diplomacy, before the release of the animals for a world pool could be obtained; then a proper place to keep them had to be found, and adequate funds for their transportation, housing, quarantine, and upkeep provided.

Yet today, a world pool of the Arabian Oryx is a reality. The Phoenix Zoo in Arizona is becoming famous in its own right because visitors know when they stop by the spacious pens that enclose the animals that they are looking at some of the rarest antelopes in the world. Zoologists are equally impressed by the record of this relatively new zoo in being able to breed the animals in captivity so successfully; so impressed, indeed, that the Phoenix Zoo was awarded the 1965 Rare Animal Propagation Trust's Award.

The fact is, however, that the choice of Phoenix as the home of the world pool for the survival of the Arabian Oryx in captivity was no chance decision. It was the result of careful consideration by responsible conservationists in just *one* phase of what can now be termed the most important example in history of international cooperation to save a single species of animal from extinction. The intent was to establish the Arabian Oryx in a location as similar as possible to its natural habitat, yet in a place where it would be so sure of long-term protection that it would have an ideal chance to breed prolifically and increase its total number to a point that might some day make it feasible to reintroduce the animals into the wilds of their native Arabia.

Australia and the American Southwest had been considered for the home of the world pool, because each is free of hoof-and-mouth disease and rinderpest. Phoenix was finally chosen in a joint decision of the Fauna Preservation Society, the World Wildlife Fund, the London Zoological Society, and the Shikar-Safari Club International. The choice was made only after Major Ian Grimwood, leader of the expedition described in this book, had personally surveyed a number of the possible sites and reported that the climate and terrain of Phoenix were ideal.

The Flight of the Unicorns is the saga of the almost incredible hardships involved in capturing the first three animals for the world pool of the Arabian Oryx. With the completion of the expedition, "Operation Oryx," as it came to be known, began to develop into the truly remarkable international preservation effort it has become. In addition to those mentioned above, there were numerous others who aided the effort from its inception or who joined the project as it gained momentum. Foremost among these were the East African Wildlife Society, the International Union for the Conservation of Nature in Switzerland, the Kenyan government, the United States Department of Agriculture, and Arabian government, the government of Kuwait, the British Royal Air Force, the Arizona Air National Guard, and the Naples Zoo in Italy.

The world pool in Phoenix now comprises fifteen animals. In addition to the three whose capture is described in this book, one was transferred from the London Zoo, four were made the gift of H.R.H. King Feisal of Arabia through the efforts of Mr Sherman Haight of New York, and another was donated by H.E. Sheikh Jabir Abdullah al Sabah of Kuwait.

These original nine animals have now produced six offspring, evidence that the effort to place the animals in their new home was worth all the necessary time and expense. It is even possible that others will be added to the pool from other sources, until eventually a second location for the animals will be possible. The important thing, however, is that had it not been for the daring, determination, and stamina of the men like Anthony Shepherd, who wrote this book, and all the others who made up the expedition, very likely the Arabian Oryx would be extinct today.

The saving of the oryx has, in the past five years, become a shining example of what can happen on an international scale when conservationists, preservationists, and just plain wildlife enthusiasts pool their efforts. It is proof-positive that private conservation societies and even private individuals can work in harmony with governments to accomplish worthwhile projects on a worldwide basis whenever there is a just and logical reason to do so.

Maurice A. Machris
Los Angeles, California
June 1966

INTRODUCTION

This book is the diary of an expedition into one of the last great areas of the world unchanged by Man's civilisation—the deserts of Arabia, "the land which has stolen so many wits away".

Many expeditions have gone into the wild places seeking lost cities, buried treasure, tombs—some have gone merely to kill the animals roaming there in their ancient freedom. Thus, in some cases, yet one more animal has become extinct.

People have argued that all this butchery is a cruel part of evolution, that only the fittest should survive. They do not stop to ask why the earth has lost—and is losing—so many of its mammals. They do not realise that the law of the survival of the fittest has been Nature's way of ensuring that the best specimens of each type of animal thrived. But Nature did not intend this to be at the expense of another species. It is Man, with his gun, his car, his aeroplane and his bombs, who has begun to wipe out many kinds of life in the animal world.

It is only recently that we have woken up to what is happening. At last men are beginning to discharge their duty to weaker species whose backs are to the wall. Societies in various countries are now financing expeditions to save these animals and birds. The Fauna Preservation Society of Great Britain is one of these societies.

Our expedition, on their behalf, was to save one of the most graceful animals on earth, the Arabian Oryx, now facing extinction.

I am proud that I took part in such an expedition. To rescue an animal from the fate unthinking men have set for it is a worthy cause that should appeal to everyone. I hope that my readers

7

will find some way, financial or otherwise, to pay their debt to the species which are dying out. So my book is written for all who strive to save.

Our quest for the oryx took us into some of the least known parts of a still comparatively unknown country. There we found traces of ancient civilisations, destroyed by God for their disobedience, or their disbelief. We came across their roads, their ruins, their graves—all the things which would be left if God chose to destroy our civilisation.

But above all my book is a narrative of an adventure—sometimes grave, sometimes gay—with an aim. The rescue of something of great beauty. We need such beauty in our world. An earth where everything that moves will be driven by an engine will be a sad, mad place. We must not have a world where the open spaces, the wide skies are just empty, where there are no black rhinoceros, no Mongolian wild horses, no Kashmir stags, where the cheetah will have vanished with the Giant Panda. For all these may not survive much longer.

Dead as a Dodo is a familiar phrase. We are determined that Dead as an Oryx shall not become equally so.

ADEN

PART I

THE ARABIAN ORYX

"His glory is like the firstling of his bullock, and his horns are like the horns of Unicorns: With them he shall push the people together to the ends of the earth."

Deuteronomy xxxiii. 17

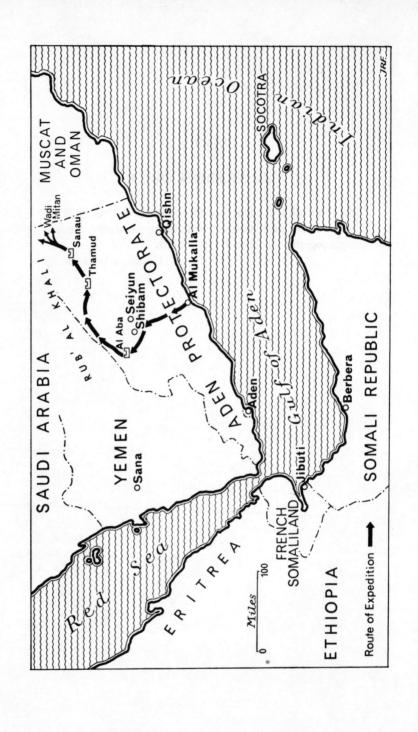

CHAPTER I

THE ARABIAN ORYX

" 'She might indeed be said to resemble a little cow. "Uktub-ha"! Write, that is portray her,' exclaimed the Emir."

Doughty

The Arabian Oryx is one of four species, and the only one to be found outside Africa. Its full name is the Beatrix Oryx, or Oryx leucoryx. The three species in Africa are known as the beisa, found in Somaliland, Kenya and Tanganyika; the gemsbok in South Africa, and the white, or scimitar-horned—the Oryx algazal—which inhabits the plains and deserts from Senegal to the Sudan.

The Oryx leucoryx is the smallest of the four. It is a medium-sized antelope, standing about forty inches at the shoulder. Its horns are twenty-two to twenty-nine inches long, those of the female being longer than the male's. It is white, the same white as the adult rim gazelle and the South Arabian bedouin's goats. The legs are darker and it has black patches on the nose, in front of the horns and in 'tear' stripes under the eyes. The young are fawn coloured.

Until the last century the Arabian Oryx lived throughout the Middle East. Then it began to be hunted with firearms, which meant it could be stalked and killed from a distance. This new way of hunting caused its steady retreat from Jordan, Syria, Iraq and the Sinai Peninsula. It became scarce in the north of Arabia itself. As long ago as 1864 Carlo Guamani noted that its last refuge in the North was at Tubaiq.

The motor car greatly accelerated the slaughter. By 1914 there were very few oryx outside Arabia. By 1930 the retreat had become a rout, leaving only two populations, one in the Nefud of northern Saudi Arabia, the other in the south in the Rub'al Khali, "the Empty Quarter". By the end of the 1950's the northern population had become extinct as a result of hunting drives by the Saudi Arabian sheikhs and by the oil companies' employees, shooting from fleets of motor cars. The southern group alone was left alive.

Shooting from vehicles, the oryx is easy to hunt. Its track is unlike that of any other animal in the desert; it roams the steppes and gravel plains, which surround its food areas, and on these, unfortunately, it can be easily overtaken by a fast vehicle.

It is the summer heat which drives the beast out from the trackless sands, where it is comparatively safe, on to the steppes. When chased it runs in a straight line for the sheltering sands, but, if they are a long way off, it cannot hope to outpace a car. Exhausted, it turns at bay and is easily shot down.

Left to itself it is a harmless creature. During the day it lies up wherever it can find shade, under a bush or in a recess in the side of a hill. It is said to dig itself a trench with its forefeet if no other shelter is available. At night it browses in the wadis—river bed valleys in which the water has either completely or partially dried up. It seeks out fresh vegetation where rain has fallen, or grubs up tubers and other desert growths which retain water.

In the past the oryx would be hunted only by the best hunters of a tribe, men capable of existing for long periods on dried meat and the milk of their own camels. Mounted on the tribe's best camels they would trail the oryx for days, hoping to manœuvre close enough to use their primitive weapons. More often than not they were unsuccessful. It was dangerous work. A true story related to H. R. P. Dickson, and repeated in his book *The Arab of the Desert*, tells of a bedouin who set out to look for his brother who had been gone for four days on an oryx hunt. He knew the area where his brother was likely to be, and where oryx were plentiful. There, on the ground, he found his brother's hunting weapons. A trail of blood led away from them. The brother followed this and came up with the herd of oryx. One of the animals had something on its back. The Arab saw that it was his brother hanging with his head over the animal's tail, his arms round its belly, his thigh impaled on one of the horns.

The bedouin was unable to fire for fear of hitting his brother, so he made a wide detour and laid two daggers down among the choicest grazing, praying that the animal would feed towards it. It did. The injured man managed to pick up one of the daggers and stab the oryx with it. After he had recovered the man told how he had risen from his hide after, as he thought, killing the oryx with a shot from his crude firearm. The animal had sprung into life and charged him. Hunters didn't always have it their own way.

The oryx appears to rely on its very sensitive hearing to keep out of danger, but there is no doubt that its sight and sense of smell are also highly developed. Its chief protection, however, is the country in which it dwells. Cheesman, who explored Arabia after the First World War, noted that:

> The oryx owes its continued existence in Arabia to its ability to live in places that are inaccessible to the bedouin on account of their waterless character. The hunters of the oryx, indeed, have to depend on camel's milk, and the extent of their journey is limited by the time that their camels can exist without water.

The Rub'al Khali is the last of those inaccessible places, but even it can no longer be said to be unfrequented. The quest for oil has taken cars and aeroplanes into places where the bedouin of old would not willingly travel in summer. If only the oryx could last out the summer in the sands, they might stand a chance, but they cannot. There is no food for them there and no shade. Like the bedouin, they are driven on to the steppes, where they can find some relief from the torturing sun.

The history of the *Arabian Oryx* is an interesting one. It is generally believed to be the *Unicorn of fable*, and it is easy to see why. An oryx seen sideways appears to have only one horn. It may be, although there are no reports of this, that some of the animals have lost a horn in battle, or through some mischance—

indeed there may have been cases when an oryx has been born with only one—but this is conjecture and no more. Certainly the passage from *Deuteronomy* with which this part of the book commences indicates that the animal had more than one, but in *Le Besteare Divin de Garillaume, clerk de Normandie* written in the thirteenth century, we find that:

> The unicorn has but one horn in the middle of its forehead. It is the only animal which ventures to attack the elephant, and so sharp is the nail of its foot, that with one blow it can rip the bellies of that beast. Hunters can catch the unicorn only by placing a young virgin in its haunts. No sooner does he see the damsel, than he runs towards her, and lies down at her feet, and suffers himself to be captured by the hunter.

The Fauna Preservation Society regrettably did not provide our expedition with a virgin. Some light-hearted inquiries were made at cocktail parties, but the vacancy was unfilled. We had to employ other stratagems.

We find the first mention of the unicorn in classical literature in the writings of Ctesias in the fourth century before Christ. Since that day the mythology has grown, investing the animal with powers far removed from those it really possessed. In addition to elephants it was alleged to be a match for lions. Spenser in *The Faerie Queene* writes:

> Like is a lion, whose imperiall poure
> a proud rebellious unicorn defyes.

The Arabian Oryx only received its official name in the eighteenth century. The first traveller to record seeing what was probably an oryx in Arabia was Ludovic Vathema in 1503. He saw two.

A few years later a Portuguese called Antonio Tenreiro described it as follows:

> The cow had a silvery very shining coat and hindquarters like a horse, which are white and shining looking like silk. The head was like that of a horse with horns right on top (standing straight up).

We have a record of another sighting in 1656, this time in Muscat, where a Carmelite friar, Vincenzo Maria, was rightly impressed by what he saw.

The animals I particularly admired in the locality were certain animals as large as stags, similar to them in the shape of the head and body, except that they are purest white ... with coat the same all over silken and so clean that nothing more graceful was ever seen. They all have two horns, two or three cubits high at the root about as thick as the circumference of a crown, at the tip extremely thin, straight, even and black, divided into equal nodes, as though they were screw-turned. I myself believe these creatures to be those which some writers describe as the Unicorn, some of which, it is said, were to be found in olden days in Mecca, but as a matter of fact they are not Unicorns.

The good friar obviously wasn't one for legends and sounds a precise man. His description was exact and painstaking, and there is no doubt that the animals which he saw were indeed oryx.

In 1777 Pallas felt certain enough of his facts to distinguish the Arabian Oryx from its brothers. He called it Oryx leucoryx. Pennant confirmed the name in 1781, when he showed a picture of one in his *History of Quadrupeds*, published in that year. The picture was drawn by Sir John Lock, of the East India Company, at Isfahan where he found two in the park owned by Shah Sultan Husayn.

A muddle followed when in 1827 Lichenstein transferred the name leucoryx to the scimitar-horned oryx of the Sudan. However, the now anonymous oryx was rescued from this unhappy position thirty years later when a Captain John Shepherd (it would be nice to know if he was a relation) presented a pair to the Zoological Society of London. He, too, belonged to the East India Company, and the animals had been sent to him from Bombay. Unfortunately the female did not survive the long sea journey, and the male, which did, succumbed to the English climate a short while later. Nevertheless they were renamed Oryx beatrix by Sir John Edward Gray after the princess of that name.

In 1903 Oldfield Thomas righted the wrong done to the unicorn and the scimitar-horned oryx was renamed 'Algazal'. The Arabian species was now free to reassume its original name, but such confusion had occurred that it was decided to call the Arabian oryx by both names, Leucoryx and Beatrix, and so it is today.

The London Zoo received another live specimen in 1872. This had been obtained by the Resident at Bushire, Colonel Pelly, from Muscat. Six years later a Commander Burke sent another animal which he had got from Jeddah. Oryx were thus being obtained from the east and west of Arabia at the same time, although in neither case would they have been resident on the coastal strip itself.

It is inevitable that Doughty should have a good deal to say about the oryx. His descriptions are accurate, but tend to be a little romantic as well:

"Her horns," he says, "were like sharp rods set upright, the length I suppose of twenty-seven inches. I saw her about five yards off, less than a small ass. The hide was ash coloured going over to a clear yellow. There was a slight rising at the root of her neck and no hump, her smooth long tail ended in a bunch. She might indeed be said to resemble a little cow; but very finely moulded was this creature of the waterless wilderness, to that fiery alacrity of their wild limbs."

He relates that he treated the animal with circumspection.

But look yonder, where is a better, and that is the cow. "Stand back for fear of her horns!" the courtiers said about me. "Do not approach her!"

Doughty also mentions the Rub'al Khali, perhaps the first writer to give it that name, and he mentions it in connection with the oryx.

The wild oxen are in their country (the Qahtan Bedouin) which they also called Wothyhi.

Now that is the name which is given to them today by the South Arabian bedouin, and the more usual spelling is Wudhaihi.

I approached Mukalla from the air. The houses climb,
wherever they can find footing, along the spurs of the sharp
red mountains which back the town.

Mukalla waterfront—a ribbon of isabelline houses follows the line of the shore.

"The Unicorn of Fable." Side view of an oryx which appears to have only one horn.

This is the word that Philby used, and the name which the expedition found wherever it travelled. It is suggested that it may come from the Arabic word meaning white—"Abyadh, Baidha". In the Oman they are called Busola or Bausolah and in North Arabia—Maha. The young are known universally as Deray.

In another reference Doughty says:

> The animal has the mouth of a gazal, a cow's foot, the tail of a cow but shorter.

Another visitor to Arabia in 1879, Lady Anne Blunt, saw three in captivity in Hail, where Doughty had seen his cow. After giving the usual description of the animal, this expert in horse flesh notes that "These wild cows were less tame than the rest of the animals, and the slaves were rather afraid of them, for they seemed ready to use their horns which were sharp as needles."

In this century Douglas Carruthers stands out as the authority on the oryx. He hunted them in 1909 and 1910. He travelled in the north in the days when there was still a fair number of them, and his description of his first sighting of the animal is worth repeating.

> I found, not as I expected, one solitary oryx, but a whole herd, bulls and cows and their little ones running beside them. It was a weird and ghostly sight in the gathering dusk. They seemed to be phantom beasts moving in a silent and supernatural world.

Lucky Carruthers. He saw a sight which none of us are likely to see. He killed four for science, and left the rest roaming in big herds of twenty and thirty strong.

Carruthers drew attention to the camouflage effect of their white coats which "appeared glistening white in certain lights and showed up clearly at a great distance, but at other times with a change of light they were extraordinarily difficult to see, so well did they merge with their surroundings".

The Unicorn was a creature of fable to the European, who used its horns for detecting poison in the courts of France as late as 1789. The beneficial results which accrued from the killing of an oryx were even more fabulous to the Arabs. A sign of how difficult they were to catch in the past perhaps. The bedouin considered that a man who did catch an oryx took on its virtues, which were those of courage, strength and endurance. By eating it he became bursting with those desirable qualities. There were other reasons for killing them, however, and Philby records that a properly cured carcase would fetch up to £20 sterling in the markets.

Few animals can be said to be as useful as the oryx—when dead. The bedouin on his camel pursuing the oryx can be admired not only for his pertinacity, but also for his refusal to waste the smallest part of his victim. The uses were legion. The fat, blood and water were all said to be good for snake bite, and the bedouin kept the mixture wrapped with salt in the creature's own intestine. People suffering from aching joints or from wind used the fat, which is either burnt and inhaled or rubbed on the affected parts. The gastric juices of the animal were drunk. One of Philby's companions, Ali Juhman, had spoken of "squeezing out the liquid contained in the tripe of the animals, if the party went short of water".

The solid contents of the paunch were given to camels. The flesh was used for exorcism as well as for meat. The skin was used for leather and the face skin was prized as a cover for a rifle butt. The horns were made into the pipes on which the shepherd boys played their plaintive airs.

Life has always been hard for the Arabian Oryx and this is reflected in the animal itself. It is smaller and less ferocious, but at the same time shyer than its African cousins. Philby found many traces of its fight for survival, when he crossed "the Empty Quarter". He came across the carcases and skeletons of many which had died of starvation in the years when the rains failed and the vegetation died. After his crossing he spoke in prophetic terms of the plains over which they roamed, looking for food and shade.

A better speed track than these vast plains of light gravel could scarcely be conceived and I thought with a shudder, as I rode on, that perhaps some day, after just such rains as we had had, this strange wilderness may be visited by motoring parties in search of gazelle and oryx.

How right he was!

The oryx has survived to the present day—just. The ostrich has now gone down, and the tahr and ibex are growing much more rare. We believe there are not more than nine oryx left in the Eastern Aden Protectorate. We saw their tracks. They may already have died. There are, we think, more in Dhofar along the edge of "the Empty Quarter", though we have no proof of this. It is difficult to see how the few remaining can survive the normal annual depredations of the bedouin, looking for food. They may linger on for a year or two, but, unless action is taken by the governments concerned, the Arabian Oryx will exist only in captivity. It is a sad end to the Unicorns: their courage and their endurance have availed them nothing. They cannot match the motor car and the rifle.

We hope that some survive—in their own country where they belong. I should not like to be the last to be able to write about the Unicorns at large.

CHAPTER 2

BIRTH OF THE EXPEDITION

"Will the Unicorn be willing to serve thee, or abide by thy crib?

Canst thou bind the Unicorn with his band in the furrow? Or will he harrow the valleys after thee?"

Job xxxix. 9–10

The expedition was really the result of two quite separate events. The first of these was the inclusion of the Arabian Oryx in Lee Talbot's book *A Look at Threatened Species*. This publicised the serious state of the oryx population. The second was the posting of Michael Crouch, a member of the Fauna Preservation Society, to the Northern Deserts Area of the Eastern Aden Protectorate as Assistant Adviser. Michael happened to meet Colonel C. L. Boyle, the secretary of the Fauna Preservation Society, in the summer of 1960, and he noticed that the Society's tie featured an oryx head motif. Michael told Colonel Boyle that he had seen some oryx in the Northern Deserts in the Wadi Mitan area—after this meeting he returned to his lonely outpost at Thamud, where he was the only European in the area, and, indeed, the only one north of the Wadi Hadhramaut.

That winter two expeditions set out after oryx. One was planned by the Adjutant of the Hadhrami Bedouin Legion, hereafter referred to as the HBL in this book. He took two guides, Tomatum and Mabkhaut bin Hassana, and he caught two oryx. Unhappily one of the oryx, already suffering from gunshot wounds, died on the way back. The other, a pregnant female, died a few days later.

The other expedition set out in December 1960 from Qatar

in the Persian Gulf. It was led by members of the ruling house of that country—a Qatari tribe.

The expedition crossed five hundred miles of desert in a concourse of motor vehicles. This was no amateur effort. The oryx were to be massacred to provide sport for sheikhs with too much money to spend on their new craze of hunting from cars, too much spare time and too little respect for their own heritage. The expedition was a complete success—from the viewpoint of the Qataris. They shot down at least twenty-eight oryx, as well as an unknown amount of anything else that moved.

Michael Crouch informed the Fauna Preservation Society of this massacre on 9 January 1961, and received an early reply asking for further details. Attention was drawn to the disaster in the Press, and the Foreign Office was asked to intervene. Unfortunately nothing occurred to stop further raids by the same people. Michael suggested that an effort be made to save some of the oryx and to move them to a place of safety, mentioning Kenya as a possibility.

There was a further Qatari raid in January 1961 which killed a further score or so of oryx. It was estimated that only thirty-five were left alive. These had to withstand the normal attentions of the bedouin as well as the natural annual loss caused by vagaries of the climate.

In the space of two months the damage had been done, and the position of the oryx was desperate. As a race we are inclined to wait until things are desperate before acting, thus making things much more difficult for ourselves.

The Fauna Preservation Society and the Survival Service Commission of the International Union for Conservation of Nature and Natural Resources now began to act. Towards the end of July 1961 the first meeting took place to discuss the possibility of sending an expedition. It was estimated that it would cost £6,000. Its charter would be to catch sufficient animals to start a breeding herd of Arabian oryx in some place where they might survive. A daily newspaper promised to give £6,000 to finance the expedition, in return for the exclusive rights to the story, and it was expected that one of their reporters and a photographer would accompany the expedition.

Ian Grimwood, the chief game warden of Kenya, was invited to lead the party. There could not have been a better choice. Luckily he had some leave due and could take it in the early summer of 1962. Early summer is the optimum period for hunting the animals for, at the start of the hot season, the oryx come out from the sands on to the steppes. And it is on the steppes that one can catch them.

Michael Crouch was asked to be deputy leader, and this was another splendid choice. He knew the country and the language, besides having all the necessary contacts among the Colonial Office departments in Aden and the Protectorate. There was some initial difficulty as he had been transferred from the Northern Deserts to be Assistant Adviser to the Wahidi State. The State was about to join the Federation of South Arabian States and it was a busy time. Nevertheless Michael was given leave by the sympathetic British Adviser—a most generous gesture.

During 1961 and early 1962 the files grew bulkier and bulkier as the correspondence between the Secretary of the Fauna Preservation Society in London, Ian in Kenya, and Michael in Wahidi grew more and more voluminous. There was a great deal of discussion about the method which should be adopted for catching the animals. There is a trapper in Kenya who catches all his prey from a horse. Ian wanted to know if the Northern Deserts were suitable for horses. They had to be ruled out because of the climate, lack of fodder and the nature of the ground. Dogs were suggested, but this idea was turned down for the same reasons, with an additional one—the dislike of the Arabs for any dog other than a saluki. Saluki would not have been any good with an animal as large as an oryx, although they are very adept at catching hares.

Sorting out possible catching methods was not made easier by the fact that Ian had not seen the country, and could only work from his African experiences. Eventually it became apparent that what was wanted was a catching car, a vehicle which would be able to travel over all sorts of terrain, have very quick acceleration, a good lock and a wide field of observation from the catching platform. It soon became apparent that it would have to be specially built. The right sort of chassis was obtained and the vehicle built in Kenya to the specifications of Peter Whitehead, whom Ian had invited to come as the catcher.

The result of Peter's design was an 'Emett' type of vehicle, which looked as though it were a cross between an abandoned Afrika Corps reconnaissance car and the sort of thing which usually pulls trailers in circuses. Beneath its unlovely bonnet was a powerful V8 engine, which would provide the necessary acceleration and overcome the fact that the car had two-wheel drive. Small wheels and a long wheelbase helped to give it the turning circle of a London taxi. Some scaffolding was placed overhead, against which the catcher could lean as he stood poised for action. An awning could be put over this as a protection against the sun. There were no other comforts. The vehicle looked stark, but Peter was sure that it would be effective.

The problem of catching method was only one of many. How were we going to get the animals out of the desert, if we caught them, and where were they to go to anyway? Suggestions for new homes included Kenya, Australia, California, parts of Arabia, Kamaran Island and an Israeli zoo. The last was not considered very politic for an animal from Arabia and was dropped. After all the pros and cons had been weighed it became clear that the Northern Frontier District of Kenya was the most suitable place, at least as a temporary refuge. Ian put in hand the building of a compound at Isiolo where the climate would be similar to that of the Northern Deserts.

The problem of getting the animals out was even more difficult. Various air charter firms were approached. Some would not countenance the carriage of animals in case they dirtied their nice aeroplanes. Others asked such exorbitant rates that they could not even be considered. Finally it seemed that Aden Airways would provide the best and the cheapest service.

It was also decided to try to interest the RAF, who sometimes flew in the area, and might therefore be able to help.

But before you can catch an oryx you have to find it. Ian was very keen on a spotter plane, but this in turn raised the problems of a pilot, fuel supplies, navigation aids and so forth, but it was known that an aircraft had been used by Locust Control successfully some years earlier in much the same area. The East African Wild Life Society heard of Ian's difficulties and offered the loan of their Piper Cruiser, just the sort of plane Ian had had in mind. This was a generous gesture—for it was obvious that the plane might come in for some rough treatment.

Other members of the expedition were enrolled. Michael Woodford, an expert on roe deer who is a member of the Fauna Preservation Society, wrote to the Secretary, asking if he might join as Veterinary Officer. After the experience of the previous year, when two oryx had died after capture, his offer was accepted with alacrity. The RAF kindly offered to fly Michael, with his equipment, to Aden.

Don Stewart of the Kenya Game Department joined the party as biologist with the task of studying the ecology of the oryx. It might be the last chance anyone would have of so doing.

A pilot had to be found to fly the plane. Both Ian and Don could fly, but they already had jobs which would keep them fully occupied on the ground. Mick Gracie, a member of the Aero Club of East Africa, heard that a pilot was wanted, threw up his job in Kenya and volunteered.

I was asked after David Harrison, doctor, author and expert on bats, had put my name forward. I was collecting mammals for him, and in return for some (to me) unpleasant specimens of Rattus rattus (the common ship rat), he managed to get me included in the expedition. It was thought that my knowledge of Arabia and Arabic might be helpful. I doubt if it was. I certainly felt very unqualified.

This is a good place, I think, to describe the full team, so that readers can identify more easily the personalities involved in the adventures that follow.

Major Ian Robert Grimwood, B.Sc., ARCS, was born in Surrey in 1912. He studied at the Imperial College of Science and Technology, where he read biology for four years and did research for one. In 1935 he joined the Indian Army, being commissioned into the Frontier Force Regiment. He served on the North-West Frontier until the war, and it was there he learned to go without food and water for long periods, while walking considerable distances in very high temperatures. He says he enjoyed his service, and it served him in good stead when he fought the Japanese in Malaya. He was taken prisoner while trying to escape by swimming the Straits to Singapore. He laboured for three and a half years on the 'Death' railway in Siam and Indo-China. He commanded the regiment for some years, then resigned and joined the North Rhodesian Game Department as a biologist. In 1960 he became Chief Game Warden in Kenya.

Since then he has taken part in one other expedition to Angola and Barotseland, and has also driven his family car, a Rolls, across Africa from west to east. He is married with one child and two stepchildren. His hobbies are travel, fishing and ornithology. He has a number of birds named after him. The Press is apt to call him lean and wiry. He is certainly that. I envy him his hair, and he looks at least ten years younger than he is. He is certainly ten years fitter than he should be.

The deputy leader, Michael Armstrong Crouch, MA (Cantab.), was born in London in 1935. His father was at one time Court Physician to the Dowager Empress of Ethiopia, and was later the Assistant Director of the Sudan Medical Service. Michael is very proud that he was one of four boys at the Limuru girls' school. Being an 'old girl' entitles him to have the school choir sing at his wedding. After further schooling in Kenya, he went to Oxford (Lincoln) and, for good measure, Cambridge (Downing) as well. All this qualified him to become a lead smelter in Canada, a Roman sewer explorer in North Africa—he believes that an unsavoury, but ancient, underground passage has been named after him at Cyrene—and later a waiter in the restaurant at the

London Zoo, where he saw a cigarette being stubbed out on a fried egg at ten in the morning and left. He joined the London Electricity Board and was the first Limuru old girl to work in a road gang. He transferred to the Aden Civil Service in 1958 and served for two years as Assistant Adviser in the Northern Deserts, where he learned to speak truly fluent Arabic.

Michael's hobbies are archaeology and fauna preservation. He claims that the idea of the expedition originated with him. Michael looks intense but isn't. He wears spectacles and has a round face, which is inclined to beam. He cannot be prevented from singing at the parties he holds.

Peter Whitehead was born in Shanghai thirty-nine years ago. His father was an English merchant there. Peter went to school at the Perse school in Cambridge, and says that he was a notoriously dull scholar. At the age of fourteen he took himself to Australia under the assisted immigrant scheme and worked on the land until he was sixteen, when he became self-employed as a contractor breaking horses. He did so in two days—or rejected the horse. At nineteen he joined the remount section of the Australian Army Supply Corps and continued to break horses until one rejected him in a rodeo—breaking him considerably in the process. Peter was in hospital for six months before he was fit enough to join the Royal Australian Air Force. He ended up as a gunner in Liberators, flying over fifteen hundred missions against the Japs, ending the war as a flight lieutenant.

Peter then decided to continue his education and attended the Dookie Agricultural College. He followed that with two years studying veterinary science, but failed his exams as a result of driving a taxi every night in Sydney to make enough money to pay for the course. He became a seaman and worked his way to England, where he was offered the job of Agricultural Extension Officer in Nigeria. He took the job and set up a cattle breeding station there before falling out with the Director on the way to run it. Following this he was a game ranger in Northern Rhodesia, Tanganyika and Kenya. He is now general manager of a large safari firm in Kenya. He is married, and has a daughter and four stepchildren. His hobby is animals, and he took two years' entitlement of leave so that he could join our party.

Peter is six foot one, has blue eyes and what is usually described in the film world as a craggy face. He gives the appearance of great competence and toughness, and, except when faced with fried spam, has a great sense of humour. His hair is grey and when I asked him why, he attributed it to years of limitless fear. He hopes eventually to return to Australia to farm.

Donald Robert Milton Stewart, B.Sc., was born in 1933 in London. He was educated at Canford and Reading University, where he studied Natural Sciences. He did his National Service with the twenty-sixth battalion of the King's African Rifles in Mauritius, then joined the Northern Rhodesia Game Department as a biologist and game warden. Later he went to Kenya as a biologist. He is married, suitably, to a botanist. His hobby is fishing.

Don was asked to join the expedition by Nature Conservancy, who are responsible to the Privy Council, in order, as I have said, that he could study the ecology of the oryx. While on the expedition he won a thousand pounds from Premium Bonds, which shows that it can be done. Unfortunately we were not in a position to celebrate at the time. Don was seldom seen without a battered jungle hat and a large polythene bag into which he put samples of all the plants. He was probably the tallest member of the party and managed, against small opposition to appear the youngest—and also the most knowledgeable.

Michael Henry Woodford, MRCVS, was born in Berkshire in 1924. He was educated at Blundells School and the Royal Veterinary College, London, where he studied until 1946. After qualifying he went into a veterinary practice at Wells, Somerset, before starting his own practice near Yeovil. He is the Secretary of the British Falconers' Club and author of *A Manual of Falconry*, the standard work on the subject. His hobbies are research into roe deer and rifle shooting. He is a member of the Fauna Preservation Society. He is married with three children. His stories of his attentions to various animal patients were the cause of considerable hilarity. Michael was collecting forms of desert cucumbers for Kew Gardens, and he and Don worked as a team in filling the polythene bag.

Christopher Kaye Macaulay Gracie, AFC, our pilot, was born in Ealing in 1914. Mick was educated at Clayesore and in 1931 he went into pest control in connection with shipping. He joined the Royal Air Force at the outbreak of war and became a bomber pilot flying Wellingtons in the Middle East with 70 Squadron.

After the war he went back to pest control and worked for the same firm in Kenya. He had kept up his flying with the Aero Club of East Africa, and as I have said, gave up his job to join the party.

Mick boxed for Belsize Park, played rugger and was a cross-country runner for Blackheath Harriers. He claims that his hobbies are games and "red-heads with large bank balances". Perhaps the two go together. He is of medium height, very thin and also very fit. His magnificent moustache was greatly admired by the Arabs.

These were the members of the expedition besides myself. All very different people, but all with the same desire—to save the oryx. I doubt if there has been a happier expedition ever, and I never heard a cross word between members. This must have been due to Ian's example, but was also helped by the sense of humour which we all shared.

On 2 January 1962, *The Times* reported that there had been a further raid by a Qatari tribe and sixteen more oryx had been killed. We began to fear the expedition would be too late. From Sanau fort in oryx country it was reported that the raiders had remained in the area for two months and the smaller total of their kills reflected the increasing rarity of the animals. It was decided that it was even more necessary that the expedition should start as soon as possible.

We were all set with members and equipment organised and ready when disaster struck. An American called Setzeder, who had been a member of the Smithsonian Expedition, and who was working on rodent surveys in the Protectorate, was told that the last oryx had been killed. Unfortunately this reached the ears of the Press and the newspaper backing us promptly withdrew its support, but left its deposit, which had already been spent on the car.

A flurry of telegrams and signals followed. The expedition was frozen, while the position was considered. It was suggested from London that Ian should carry out a reconnaissance to see if there was any truth in the report. He replied that it would cost almost as much and require nearly as great an administrative backing as the real thing.

Many people believed the report to be unduly pessimistic. Further, a statement like that could only be verified by considerable research, and it was known that that had not been done.

Then came a telegram from the Governor of Aden who, acting on information signalled by Michael Crouch, said that he believed that the expedition should go on. Colonel Boyle agreed. The money would be found from the Preservation Society's own resources. At worst the expedition would furnish proof of whether or not the oryx still lived.

In Kenya, Ian, Peter and Don began to practise with the catching car, using Beisa Oryx and zebra as targets. The car seemed most successful and after the initial snags had been ironed out, they found themselves catching with ease, even over rough lava flow. Peter cracked some ribs during the practice, when he got in the way of one of the ropes on which an animal was being played, but recovered before he left Kenya.

Messages were then sent out for the expedition to assemble at Mukalla, a town on the South Arabian coast, on 19 April. Ian arranged to spend a month there before the rest of us joined him, so he could complete the organisation on the spot, and meet all the people on whose help we were going to have to rely. He also hoped to get the Piper aircraft there in time for him to do some reconnaissance.

We had one great stroke of good fortune when Pat Gray, the Commandant of the HBL, offered to provide the expedition with transport and communications. This offer was of inestimable value. Looking back I don't really know how we could have managed otherwise. Certainly it would have cost the Society a great deal more to have hired the necessary lorries and wireless equipment. The wholehearted support of Arthur Watts, the Resident Adviser of the Eastern Aden Protectorate, also did a great deal to smooth out the various snags. Indeed we couldn't have hunted the oryx in the Eastern Aden Protectorate without the support of Watts and all the other Colonial Office officials from the Governor downwards and including many members of the Secretariat in Aden—Archie Wilson in particular—who acted as hosts and a clearing house for numerous telegrams and signals. The Qa'iti state were most co-operative in offering to let equipment and stores into Mukalla without the usual Customs tax. The Air Ministry had also agreed to help—if it didn't involve spending public money—and the RAF responded magnificently.

Ian and Mick Gracie left Nairobi on 22 March. The RAF were flying them and the dismantled Piper in a Beverley to Aden. During a stopover at Mogadiscio the expedition nearly suffered another disaster when Mick was arrested as a spy for carrying a camera while stepping over a strand of rusty barbed wire. The wire, which was probably a relic of the Italian occupation, was apparently considered an important military installation. It took a lot of smooth talking to avoid having a casualty before the trip had even begun.

In Aden they were told that the Beverley was not going on to Riyan, Mukalla's airfield, as was hoped, and the Piper and the stores were unloaded. Aden Airways who share the same airfield with the RAF agreed to reassemble the Piper. In fact Mr Smail and his men had the plane together in no time. It looked airworthy, but, of course, there was only one way to find out—fly it.

So Ian and Mick took off, avoiding as best they could the screaming jets, which were the more usual customers at the airport. The left wing showed an alarming tendency to droop, but otherwise all was well, so they set course for Riyan, where they landed safely.

Then Ian and Mick left for Mukalla to meet Michael Crouch. This they did, but only just, because on the thirty-first Michael was flown out to hospital in Aden with malaria. He was in no fit state before he left to discuss details with Ian. The fates had dealt us another harsh blow. More were to come.

The petrol ordered for the Piper had not arrived so the plane was grounded. This left Ian and Mick virtually stranded in Mukalla, unable to do any of the things Ian had planned, except meet the people who were to be so helpful when the expedition finally got under way.

Difficulties continued to assail Ian, as he languished in Mukalla. The shipping line, which was to bring the catching car to Mukalla, announced that it couldn't do so after all. On 4 April Ian learned that only nine drums of aviation fuel had been sent from Aden, which meant the total would be two hundred gallons short.

Somehow the expedition struggled into life. On the seventh Peter wired from Nairobi that the RAF had agreed to lift the catching car and that it should arrive on the next day. I was asked to meet it in Aden. There were signals and counter-signals, saying that the car was on its way, then it wasn't and so on. Finally I received a telephone call to say that it had arrived at the airport. I have already described the appearance of the car. I looked at it with some apprehension. It looked very odd indeed. I filled it with water, and then refilled it because the first lot ran out on to the road through a cleverly hidden drain tap. The petrol tanks appeared to hold about forty gallons. I gave it two. Fortunately I put them in the right tank. There were a number of complicated switches which enabled one to change tanks and I had no idea how they worked. I connected the battery and located the starter. The engine started with a roar at the first attempt and several aircraftmen came out to see what aircraft was taking off.

After some experiment I found what appeared to be the lowest gear. Very gingerly I drove off. The horn shorted and stuck at full blast. This ensured that I had a clear right of way. The car had Kenyan number plates, and I suspected that it wasn't insured.

As quickly as possible I got it to my garage and parked it, covering the evidence with a tarpaulin.

Michael Crouch recovered sufficiently to come and view the catching car. Then he brought friends to see it and my garage was full of disbelieving people.

Ian flew in from Mukalla and his arrival was an excuse for a large and happy party at the airport restaurant, the best place to eat in Aden. "Old Macdonald had a Farm" was sung noisily in Arabic to the delight of the Lebanese waiters. The expedition was well and truly launched, and it was a shame that the other members hadn't arrived.

Yet it seemed to me as the exciting day approached when I was to fly to Mukalla, that it was a sad thing that we were about to do. We were assembling to take an Arabian animal out of Arabia in order that it could survive. In the Arab states neither rulers nor individuals had done anything towards preserving a very fine part of their splendid heritage. Seven Europeans were going into Arabia to rescue the oryx so that sufficient might be bred to enable the species to be reintroduced into its own country. It is to be hoped that the Arabs will have learnt by then the value of preserving their own diminishing fauna.

Somali flock passing decayed mansion on Mukalla waterfront.

The harbour: men have sailed from Mukalla to make their
fortunes all over the world.

PART 2

"And now come down to Arabia we
are passing from known landmarks."
Doughty

CHAPTER 3

MUKALLA

"And upon him who dwells in Mukalla it is incumbent that
his gifts should be fiery steeds or beautiful maidens."
The Christian bishop of Najran
in the seventh century

Mukalla is usually described as a jewel, and almost every writer
on South Arabia has produced an enthusiastic description to prove
it. The town has great charm, particularly for those used to the
modern monstrosities of Aden, Bahrein or Kuwait. Half of its
charm is that it is unspoilt—or nearly so. A ribbon of isabelline
houses follows the line of the shore against which the monsoon
breakers push and swell during the summer. The town is backed
by sharp red mountains, showing traces of old fortifications
along the peaks and ridges. Below them the houses climb,
wherever they can find footing, along the spurs.

By the western gate there is the Sultan's palace, his guesthouse
and the British Residency. They stand out whiter than the rest,
flying their different flags and overlooking, outside the gate, the
caravan halt, where camels in their hundreds chew the cud,
despising everything and everyone they see. Then comes a wadi
mouth, separated from the sea by a narrow belt of sand on which
piles of fish lie drying, too slowly for those who have to bear
the smell. Beyond the wadi an untidy suburb huddles on the
further bank. It is called Sherij Ba Salam and used to house the
less fortunate inhabitants of the town. Now it has grown respectable, but only slightly so.

At the eastern end of the town there is a small promontory on
which the old palace, now used for government offices, the

customs house and other administrative buildings stand among a jumble of houses of different sorts. The old palace stands above them all on a rise and looks down on them with the complacency born of old and happy decay. Further east still, there are more houses, some lime kilns and unlovely petrol tanks under the cliffs.

Turtles peer wisely out of the sea and small fish leap and scud above the breakers as they avoid the attentions of their larger relations. In June, when a cold current hits the coast, sea snakes, jelly fish and sting rays crowd the shallows, making bathing an uncomfortable experience. Above the town Arabian kites and fan-tailed ravens spiral hopefully, the kites making a harsh, keening noise not unlike the English buzzard, the ravens croaking mournfully in lower keys.

Mukalla should be approached from the sea if the visitor really wishes to appreciate its beauty. I approached it from the air. The plane in which I was travelling carried an official cargo of pilgrims *en route* for Riyadh and the Haj, and also an extra cargo of thirty cases of beer, the extremely generous gift of Ind Coope to the expedition. Aden Airways were equally kindly moving it without charge, two favours for which the expedition was deeply grateful.

I was worried about the 23 per cent import tax which I might have to pay—if the beer was allowed in at all for the Qa'iti state is 'dry'. I knew the import of alcohol was forbidden, but I hoped to get it in as a member of the Forces, and I had asked the RAF at Riyan to stand by to receive me and my valuable cargo.

The airstrip for Mukalla is at Riyan, fifteen miles east of the town. It is a small untarmac'd airfield used only as a staging post, though Aden Airways call there regularly and so does the RAF on their way to airfields further east. It is a lonely spot and there is nowhere outside the rash of bleak huts where the airmen can go off duty.

As we circled before landing I could see the expedition's small plane like a freshly painted toy below. It looked frighteningly small.

Our aircraft landed smoothly and taxied towards the huts.

Then there was a pause. The steps which were produced were far too short. The pilgrims sweated a little and the two English air hostesses looked out unexcitedly at the reception committee of RAF men clad only in shorts. The RAF looked up with more animation. White women—I could almost hear the excited buzz going round the camp.

Eventually a precipitous ladder was produced, and the pilgrims, remembering no doubt how blessed it is to die on the Haj, climbed gingerly down. I identified myself to the RAF men who said that they were expecting me and my cargo. I could leave it to them. The customs men, in ill-fitting khaki, sniffed suspiciously as case after case bearing the red hand of Allsopps was unloaded and whisked into a waiting RAF truck. Then Ian arrived in an HBL Land-Rover to take me and my kit to the hut which served as the RAF Officers' Mess. Ian painted a rather gloomy picture of the state of the expedition. He had arrived the previous morning after driving the catching car from Aden. The car only had its top gear left and was now being stripped by the HBL fitters in their workshop. The petrol for the expedition plane had only just been off-loaded, and it was still undecided whether it could be imported free of tax. Its quantity was, as I have already mentioned, considerably less than that ordered and that needed. The worst disaster of all was that the other three members of the expedition were not on the plane with me as Ian had expected. Where were they? I didn't know. I had made innumerable visits to the RAF at Aden to try to find out when they were arriving, but no one had had any idea, and after several false alarms I had given up meeting planes. Ian took the disappearance of half his expedition quite philosophically.

We stayed for an hour in the mess while Ian fixed up various details with the RAF, and then, still breakfastless, went to visit the HBL headquarters at Dis, near Mukalla, where Pat Gray, the Commandant of the HBL, welcomed us in his office. He was a large, kindly-looking man with a big grey moustache and sparse grey hair. He looked what he was—a father figure running a force on strictly paternalistic lines. We discussed plans for the convoy which was going up country, led by Pat himself, and to which we would be attached.

Afterwards we went to look at the catching car. "Tubby" Dawson was in charge of a superbly equipped workshop, which could undertake almost any major repair, except the grinding of crankshafts. Even so, Tubby was worried now. He had diagnosed the touble. The agents in Nairobi, who had overhauled the gearbox before the car had left Kenya, had omitted to replace an important part. In the next few days Tubby and his fitters assembled and took the gearbox apart three or four times. They bought another gearbox which had belonged to a derelict car and they tried to make one good one out of the two. They cut new teeth and filed old ones. They welded and brazed and cursed. All through the Easter holiday they worked and twice the car was tested and each time something new was found to be wrong. The fitters loved their machines and their work, but they didn't love the catching car by the time the convoy left.

That morning we left them hard at it and I went to meet Mick Gracie for the first time. He turned out to be a delightful chap, spare, hard and, as I have said, enormously moustached. The Arabs quickly christened him 'Father of Moustaches'. Mick was supervising the packing and loading of our stores. He had plenty to do so we drove away to the Residency rest house in Mukalla, where the expedition had set up headquarters.

The rest house was an extension, built on top of the flat roof of the Residency offices. It consisted of two small rooms, but it boasted electric light, fans and a refrigerator. Other huts built on to the roof served as the kitchen, bathroom and chemical lavatory.

I walked around the roof, looking at the view. We were only a few hundred yards from the sea. I noticed that concrete pens divided the bathing places of the two sexes. Nearby the Sultan's palace stood gleaming white and constructed of a mixture of architectural styles, mostly hideous. It resembled more closely than anything a second-class Mediterranean hotel.

A cook brought us some coffee. It was nearly midday and I

had lost my taste for breakfast. Our own staff were in the process
of taking over the responsibility for feeding us and they did not
appear to be very experienced. In the meantime the Residency
cook provided the coffee, while the others bickered around the
kitchen in the kind of pained vacuum in which servants without
orders find themselves, when they are anxious to impress but
haven't the initiative to do so.

Ian remembered that he had to get to the solitary bank before
it closed, and I decided to go with him to see something of
Mukalla. We drove almost the whole length of the town down a
long, unpaved, shop-lined street which ran parallel with the
shore. In many of these shops—appropriately for the Incense
Coast—incense was being burnt and the sweet smell filled the air.
It was crowded with a pleasing mixture of almost naked bedouin,
Mahra tribesmen, and effete-looking Hadhramis in ankle-length
futahs. The futah is a garment rather like a kilt, worn at different
lengths in different districts; the hill bedouin have the shortest
and the Hadhramis of the trading class the longest. The Hadhramis gazed in a superior fashion at the other road users. The
bedouin had about them the proud air of men looking, one felt,
for insults to be quickly avenged. The really poor and the aged
looked at the ground, hoping perhaps to find something to their
advantage there. Running in among the more leisurely pedes-
trians were coolies of a uniform ebony black. Musclebound and
unintelligent-looking they moved everywhere at a sharp trot,
talking together in their own incomprehensible dialect, a mixture
of their old African and their new Arabic. They may not have
been legally slaves, but they were certainly slaves to an existence
which can have been little more than animal. Fishermen pushed
their way through the crowd, bearing their catches hung from a
pole across their shoulders. They looked wiry rather than
muscular and moved with a flat-footed shuffle.

We saw women dressed in yellows and reds. Most of the
women were veiled, except those too old to bother. These latter,
dressed in torn, dirt-stained, black dresses as old as themselves,
crept along the walls, neither looking nor being looked at.

Street vendors hawked cold water from brightly coloured vacuum flasks.

In the barbers' shops the Indian barbers crouched, round-faced and sweaty, over their bearded customers. Butchers stood by their stalls, unmoved by the spectacle of flies hanging in black moving masses over their wares. Fruit sellers exposed equally fly-covered split melons. Goats of many colours and one grotesque giant sheep wandered haphazardly about, chewing cardboard, string or, as a luxury, a banana skin or a melon rind.

Cars and lorries hooted their way through, and only the scraggy, wild-eyed, brown dogs seemed to get run over. The goats seemed to have an instinct for self-preservation, or perhaps they relied on divine intervention to save their lives, until it was time for them to be killed with a quick knife slash across the throat, before taking their places on the butchers' slabs among the flies. The nanny goats wore modest brassieres over their teats to preserve their milk for their owners. They looked absurdly overdressed.

We drove past a mosque, then past the Customs, where dhows swung creakingly at anchor under the lee of the promontory, waiting to unload or pick up cargoes. Coolies pulled and pushed enormous loads on narrow two-wheeled trolleys. It was a scene of the most enormous bustle and confusion, and, to add to it all, no one spoke at less than a shout.

We parked below the old seven-storey-high palace and went into the bank. This appeared to be a small dark room packed with Arabs, their hands full of hundred-shilling notes. One or two ceiling fans did little to disturb the atmosphere. There were no other comforts for the hot, hard-worked bank staff, whom we could just see through the crowd. It was a little time before we managed to get close to the counter, and even then we were ignored. Old men, wearing only a beard and a sarong, pushed past, their hands clutching more money than I am ever likely to see in a month. Some counted it on the floor and others seemed to have started their own banks.

At last a European, sitting at a table under one of the fans behind the counter, spotted us, and we were allowed to escape from the babel and to sit primly on chairs at his table. I sweated and waited for Ian to complete the financial arrangements for the trip. It was a relief to get back into the sunlight again.

We drove back to the Residency, avoiding the fishermen, the goats, the other vehicles, etcetera, and there we found Mick, who had returned from his labours for lunch. We joined him and tried to eat our way through some of the toughest meat I had ever encountered. My teeth ached for days afterwards. There were also some bullet-like potatoes which added nothing to the meal. We took an immediate dislike to the cook. It appeared that the expedition had suffered another disaster, for we knew of nothing more likely to upset morale than an incompetent cook.

That afternoon Michael Crouch arrived from Wahidi. He brought with him his Pick-Up, which looked like a moving piece of salvage, and a Land-Rover. Both were heavily loaded with what appeared to be a not inconsiderable amount of kit. In addition to his stuff there was an old blind man and a very small boy. They could surely not be part of a political officer's retinue? A procession began to stagger up the steps, bearing huge bundles. A light green tent was erected on a flat part of the roof and pegs were hammered in with complete disregard for anyone below. It became rapidly obvious that the political officer of today travelled in more comfort than in the old days. The tent had two compartments—a bedroom and a bathroom. A fly-sheet made a shady veranda on which various camp chairs were erected. Cases of gin and whisky appeared.

Michael was a great asset to us. Not only did he speak Arabic excellently, but he was understood in the Eastern Protectorate; I wasn't. Also he knew Mukalla very well indeed, and seemed to be acquainted with half the inhabitants of the town. After the settling-in process, the blind man stood patiently in the sun. The little boy was packed off to the bedouin boys' school. I gathered it was the first time he had left home, but he was entirely self-possessed and not at all intimidated by his surroundings. Even after his departure Michael's staff seemed to outnumber the expedition. We discovered that Michael had brought his own cook, Mohammet, a bearer called Omar, who was a corporal in the Wahidi tribal guard, a driver called Qassim and a garage boy whose name I never discovered. He didn't appear to be altogether with us; a thin black man in dark overalls, he was usually to be found leaning sadly against the side of the Pick-Up with a bemused look.

After an evening swim in the sea we opened the first of Messrs Ind Coope's gift and discussed the situation. We now had the majority of the expedition in one place—four out of seven. We had the aeroplane, and, we hoped, some petrol for it. We had the catching car in pieces and we had a dubious staff. There was good news in a signal later that night telling us that Peter Whitehead and Don Stewart had arrived in Aden. They, at least, were now in the same continent. We thought that the vet, Michael Woodford, might also have arrived, for I had heard rumours before I left Aden that another member of the expedition had been seen at a cocktail party. With any luck some or all of them should be with us the following day. We made plans hopefully, ate an unappetising supper and went early to bed. Ian and Mick slept on the two rest house beds in the second room. I put up a camp-bed under the fan in the dining room, and Michael retired to his tent.

I woke up suddenly in the middle of the night. Flashes of lightning illuminated the bare white walls of my room. There was the urgent drumming of rain on the roof. Most of Michael's kit was stacked in the open outside, and I got up to put it under shelter. As I got out of bed the door flew open and Michael himself appeared with his arms full of Saudi Arabian rugs. Mick was also up and together we carried all the boxes and bundles into my room. Only Ian, as befitted the leader, slept undisturbed throughout the storm, but he, too, had to get up later when the roof in his room demonstrated its porosity. The rain fell torrentially, and I lay comfortably in bed and listened to the sounds of furniture being moved next door amid claps of thunder, curses and the flapping of Michael's tent. The roof over my room with-stood the rain and soon I slept.

Mukalla after rain is not an attractive place. The streets had turned to liquid mud in which was mixed all the dirt and other forms of animal unpleasantness. The Arabs, however, were cheerful as only Arabs can be after rain, and their songs and shouts woke me in the early morning. The schoolboys were as excited as are English ones after snow.

After breakfast Michael and I decided that something would have to be done about the staff, over whom I had nominal charge. The foreman was an effeminate Hadhrami with a great deal of Javanese blood in him. He was a townsman and a pleasant fellow, but quite incapable of giving orders. Furthermore we thought that he would be likely to go to pieces when faced with the conditions we expected to meet in the desert. The same went for one of the bearers, who might have been the foreman's brother. He wore blue jeans and avoided work like the plague. They would have to go, as would the cook. We decided to seek out the local contractor who had chosen them for us, and get him to replace them.

The contractor lived near the harbour and we drove down to see him. By reputation he was a good contractor. He appeared to be on first name terms with Michael, who said that he was the only man in Mukalla who could have fitted us out. After seeing his idea of suitable servants I kept quiet. Even Michael had to agree later that he hadn't taken much care or shown much interest in us. There was no doubt that there wasn't much money to be made out of us, and with oil companies looming on the horizon, he had other, bigger fish to catch. His carelessness over the petrol might have been very serious indeed.

His office was near the customs building. It was a long, clean room in which one or two clerks bent dutifully over their ledgers. We were asked what we would like to drink. Michael wisely asked for a Coca-Cola, but I, forgetting where I was, accepted the offer of an ice cream. I expected it to arrive hygienically wrapped in its paper. Not a bit of it. It came in a glass bowl into which a spoon had been stuck. Michael and I looked at one another. I tried it. It was delicious.

Michael suggested various changes that should be made among the staff and the contractor agreed. Mohammet, Michael's own man, would be foreman and chief cook. The cook the contractor had hired for us and who was a hard worker and willing—though no cook—would become a bearer. The two willowy Hadhramis would disappear altogether. It was the kindest thing we could have done for them. After mutual protestations of good will we left.

It was, we realised, Good Friday, and the Residency staff were on holiday. We went to see John Weakley, the Assistant Adviser Coastal Areas, and found him in his house, nursing a poisoned knee. We drank squash and cadged the use of his Land-Rover from him for the evening swim. When we got back to the rest house we found that the catching car had arrived. It sat importantly outside the door, and then proceeded to drop a vast quantity of oil on to the ground from the area of its gearbox. Sadly Tubby Dawson drove it away, and prepared to spend the rest of the Easter holiday working on it. It would have to be stripped right down again.

That evening the Residency was showing the weekly film in the open air on the roof, but we had been asked to drinks by the Sergeants' Mess at Riyan.

The mess was a cheerful place and we were welcomed to the bar by Sergeant Cracknell, our ally there, who was taking a personal interest in our Piper aircraft. He gave us bad news. The airstrip was under water and it would be several days before planes could land. It appeared that we were cut off from the other members of the expedition who would not be joining us after all. We were getting used to disasters, but this seemed a particularly unkind one in a country where one hardly expects rain to upset one's plans.

When the rains had broken the previous night Sergeant Cracknell's first concern had been for the Piper, which he had fully expected to find afloat. It was safe, but it, too, would be grounded until sufficient of the strip dried out to allow it to take off.

We forgot our sorrows in the cheerful company. Mick particularly was in his element back in an RAF mess. His moustaches drooped lovingly round a tankard. When we left we went to the store where the beer was being kept and took the rest of it back with us.

When we got back to the resthouse, we moved all the kit into my room again as a precaution for lightning was again flickering over the sea. We had another storm in the night, but its centre missed us and only a few drops of rain fell, although a gust of wind had Michael out of his tent and asking for help to tether it more firmly.

We were beginning to feed quite well now that Mohammet was cooking and we started the day well. The sky remained grey and forbidding, and the sea a dark threatening green as we paddled around Mukalla doing our last bits of shopping, while, at the same time, anguished signals flashed between us and the half of the expedition in Aden.

In the evening we motored to Dis and dined with Edith and Pat Gray, who lived in a solidly built house on a hill above the chance of floods.

We ate a delicious Crayfish Thermidor and Tubby Dawson and his wife, who were also there, seemed to have forgiven us for ruining their holiday.

We now expected the rest of the expedition to fly into Raudah the following day, and we sent a signal asking the Federal Regular Army to meet them. Otherwise they would have found themselves stranded in a completely strange country among people who spoke no English.

There was no more rain that night, which was encouraging because Edith Gray had told us that about a year earlier when there had been similar rains they had been marooned on a piece of ground, which had suddenly become an island, for two weeks.

On Sunday, our last day in the town, there remained a lot to be done. The contract was finally signed with the contractor, and the appropriate Government Minister agreed to allow the aviation fuel in free of duty. While Ian and Michael were in the old palace negotiating this concession, Mick and I stayed outside, watching the hustle of Mukalla on a working morning. The court was in session and scruffy members of the Mukalla Regular Army and of the police stood, sat and lay on guard outside. A grinning prisoner was guided in. He looked as though he was enjoying himself hugely. Wild tribesmen, wearing the briefest of futahs, but carrying huge daggers in their belts, waited for the court. Their daggers were curved and studded, and the handles were made from rhinoceros horns, to Ian's annoyance, for they were obviously poached since his department dealt with the legal export. One old man in particular caught my eye. He was fuzzy-headed and almost naked. He trailed what must have been his grandson by the hand. Both were liberally stained with indigo, which the tribesmen believe keeps out the cold. The old man had a pointed grey beard and wild, hard eyes. He dragged the boy after him, and the child, who cannot have been more than seven, showed all the fear of an untamed animal first confronted with civilisation. He clutched his grandfather's futah firmly and buried his face in it. Occasionally huge scared eyes peeped out, but the sight was always too much and the boy hid his head, which was covered by a bush of indescribably matted hair.

The coolies passed by incessantly, pushing and pulling their two-wheeled carts and chanting their private songs. Some sat in a coffee house and their uncouth tongues chattered without dignity, and without apparent point.

When Ian had finished his business we drove eastwards again, hoping to take some better photographs of the town. Mukalla is fantastically photogenic, for, in addition to the beauty of the town itself, there are the many different types and tribes to watch. Something is always going on, and when we were there it was nearly always something colourful.

Mukalla is very ancient. It has been suggested that it is the Greek Mykale. This is very likely because Periplus mentions a Greek community on Socotra. Besides the reference which heads the chapter, there is another seventh-century one, which can be attributed to the poet Ajjay, who wrote in the second half of that century:

> I journeyed from the utmost lands of travel,
> From the hills of Shihr and the environs of Maukala.

Ptolemy mentions it as well. Nevertheless it was never a very important port as was Qana (Bir Ali), but it is entitled to its own antiquity. It remained in decent obscurity until the British came looking for a naval base in 1829, but no Resident was appointed until 1937, and it still remains today outwardly uninfluenced by any outside Power.

If Mukalla and the Qa'iti state, whose capital it is, owe anything to anyone it is to their own expatriates. Men have sailed from Mukalla to make their fortunes all over the world, but most particularly in what is now Indonesia. Not only do the people travel, but they make money, a great deal of it, and a good proportion of that comes back to the country, for the Arabs return to live out their old age in their country.

We have had treaties with the state since the 1880's, but it was not until fifty years later that we began to accept our responsibilities in the area, and to act as a protecting power. No Hadhrami could complain of the British colonial yoke. If he complained at all, as many did, particularly during the bad famine of the war years, it was because they felt that Britain was not taking enough interest in the Protectorate, and, regrettably, I feel that they were right.

Mukalla was fascinating enough, but neither Ian nor I were sorry that we should be leaving the next day. Ian had been in the town for a month off and on and the expedition did not seem to him to have got very far. We were itching to be off. We had drinks that day with more of the small European community, and we found Tubby Dawson there, still discussing ways of making the gearbox work. He told us that it would be touch-and-go whether the catching car would be ready in time, and even if ready, whether it would last.

Michael Crouch's Pick-Up, which was one of the most dilapidated vehicles I have ever seen, was not as bad as it looked. It had recently had a new engine fitted but, even so, after five years of continuous cross-country work, it didn't fill one with confidence. Nevertheless it was decided to do what we could to fit it up as a reserve catching car, and, when we had done so, it looked even more peculiar. A hole was cut in the roof of the cab, and a rough wooden frame fitted in the hole. Through this the catcher could stand upright, if necessary. We hoped that we would never have to use it, because the catcher, standing on the passenger seat, had very bad vision to the driver's side of the car, while the driver couldn't see the catcher's side at all. The catcher's position was quite dangerous as well because of the lack of decent support for his body. Michael took the 'new look' with fortitude. We hoped that his department would be equally obliging.

Ian decided that he and I should leave the following day, 23 April, come what may. Michael and Mick Gracie were to follow us in the plane some days later, when we had reached a place called Husn al Abr. A routine HBL convoy had swollen enormously in size and seemed to be composed entirely of vehicles carrying our kit. Unfortunately, although Mick knew which crates were where, he didn't know what most of them contained, and we had no idea what was in the contractor's mountain of boxes, sacks and cartons. We hoped that it was sufficient food for six weeks. The truck's springs groaned under the weight.

We had six tents lent by the RAF in Riyan and some camp furniture on loan from the Residency. One truck was almost completely loaded with timber to build the crates for the animals —crates for them to travel in and crates for them after capture. There was wood for the stalls, which we hoped to build for them at the fort at Sanau, and a carpenter was going with us to do the work. Some of the crates were prefabricated and he practised on those before we left. Later it was discovered that our helpful contractor had changed carpenters at the last minute, and the man who came with us knew nothing about the crates at all, and had to be taught from scratch.

Pat Grey was coming with us, taking the opportunity of visiting some of his distant outposts, and we hoped that he would smooth the way for us and ensure that his own spirit of co-operation was matched by the officers and men of his outlying garrisons. Edith, who was accompanying him, was hoping that, after her previous experience of being stranded by floods, the recent rains were not going to have the same result. Reports from up-country differed. Some reported rain, but the tracks were apparently still fit for motors.

The plan was for the heavy trucks to set off first at eight in the morning, while a faster convoy of Land-Rovers and Pick-Ups would follow at eleven, catching the first convoy up. It meant a fairly early start for us, because most of the camp kit and the staff would have to go with the trucks.

That night it didn't rain—perhaps in answer to our prayers—but we learned that the other members of the expedition had not arrived at Raudah as expected. We found out later that Aden Airways had refused to take all the luggage, and Peter and the others had wisely decided not to make confusion worse by getting separated from their belongings.

Perhaps perversely Ian and I felt a lifting of spirits. Surely nothing else could go wrong. Most important, we were all set to start. Neither of us knew the country inland over which we would be travelling for a week on our way to our base camp, and the whole journey promised to be full of interest.

Monday the twenty-third dawned clear and sunny. We saw the sun rise as we helped to pack the stores. Ian disappeared early to Dis to collect the catching car, which we hoped would be ready, and Michael went with him to film the start of the first convoy. Mick and I remained behind to supervise the packing. The staff seemed quite excited, and carried the boxes down the stairs with us, while the Residency cook hovered around, making sure that we weren't stripping the resthouse of its few pieces of furniture. When we had finished loading the Pick-Up, it drove away. Nothing remained but the few boxes that would go on the catching car, if it turned up.

We sat in the sun on the roof, waiting for Ian to return, and watched the Mukalla Regular Army changing guard outside the palace over which the Sultan's flag flew bravely in the light wind. The guard mounting was far from the ceremony of tradition. The palace guard were dressed in very ill-fitting khaki shirts and shorts. Some wore shoes and some did not. They wandered about in front of the palace, or lay on the steps, waiting for their relief. An old lorry drove into the courtyard without being challenged, and the new guard scrambled out. There was much shouting and laughter. A proportion of the old and new guards formed up in two lines opposite each other and presented arms shakily. Then began a general mêlée. Two of the men played at soldiers, pretending to fire at one another from behind a balustrade, clicking their bolts, and shouting "bang", or something like it. It was delightfully informal. I wondered whether the Sultan was at home.

When the first British Resident in 1937 had brought in the Colonel commanding the Aden Protectorate Levies to reorganise the army, the Mukalla Regular Army had been almost entirely composed of mercenary Yafa'is from the Western Protectorate, with a sprinkling of Indian officers and NCOs. Now there were many tribesmen in it as well, and no British officers to supervise. During the winter before our visit it had suffered a reverse, when it had been ambushed by tribesmen and suffered heavy casualties. The HBL had been called out to go and bring the remnants in. The attacking tribesmen had been most distressed when they learned that the bulk of the casualties had been suffered by the local members of the force and not by the Yafa'is. Perhaps it was unfair of me to overlook their antics from the Residency roof, but it did not seem that any reforms initiated by the first British Resident had lasted.

I watched the HBL changing the guard on the Residency, and this was very different. To start with they looked smart in their red headcloths and white skirts with their polished bandoliers. The guard changed smoothly, with much slapping of rifle butts.

Although the British Army has seldom received much praise

for the way it has trained numerous colonial forces, it is a record the Army can be proud of, and this HBL efficiency seemed to me to be a fair example of the increased efficiency which the employment of British experience brings to growing forces.

My thoughts were disturbed by a commotion in the yard. Ian rattled up in the catching car, looking very pleased with himself. We ran down the stairs to look. "A bit of a whine in the first two gears, otherwise all right," Ian said. We examined the ground underneath the car. There was no apparent leak. Ian added that Tubby had given no guarantee with the car. On the contrary he had been doubtful if it would do a thousand miles, but it might just last out. We said some unkind things about the Kenyan people who were supposed to have overhauled the gearbox, and started to load the rest of the luggage.

When that was done Ian and I looked at one another. "Come along," he said. We jumped in, said goodbye to Mick, and bowled merrily out of the courtyard and through the town gateway, where somebody laughed and the camels looked singularly unimpressed.

The car only had three forward gears, and the top gear was the only one which sounded healthy. Ian kept it in top as long as possible. The pinking which had been so noticeable in Aden had gone. Tubby had tuned the engine properly and it sounded sweet.

Ian told me that the trucks had got away on time and the rest of the convoy was ready to move as soon as we arrived. We struggled up the hill into the camp, leaving the gear changes to the last moment. I saw a pleased-looking Tubby ready to see us off. It really looked as though he was going to get us off his shoulders. He couldn't have done more. He had fitted a fearsome horn to the car, and he had stopped the radiator cap from coming off every mile and deluging the passengers with boiling water. He had managed to cure the habit the rear lights had of remaining on, when everything else was switched off, and he had finally welded up the gearbox.

The vehicles which were going with us were drawn up in a line.

Over them HBL men swarmed, looking for places to put one more parcel, or one more person. It looked as though there were far too many men for the number of trucks, but in the end they all found places, and we took Musellim, one of the bearers, in the back of the catching car, where he was able to lie flat and keep an eye on the kit, which was piled so high that it looked in imminent danger of falling off.

Michael's Pick-Up was having new tyres fitted, and in a fit of temper it blew one noisily, so that they had to start again. It stood rustily on jacks, and seemed to grin sardonically at our preparations. Pat decided it wasn't worth waiting for it, and that it would have to catch us up. Ian and I hoped sincerely that it would. After all it was carrying most of our supplies, as well as the cook.

Michael stood with his camera poised. Edith and Pat climbed into their Land-Rover and signalled to us to follow. Ian gingerly engaged first gear, and we were off. Tubby waved cheerfully at us. A sentry saluted, though whether at us or at Tubby's handi-work we couldn't tell.

Ian was dressed in what soon appeared to be his expedition uniform of jungle hat, khaki shirt and green trousers. On his feet he had a pair of brand new hockey boots—he called them his co-respondent shoes—and he had, inevitably, a cigarette in his mouth.

We followed Pat's car down the hill through the village and past the stark naked small boys who also saluted us, and along the track towards Riyan. Then we turned north up what is called the West road to the Hadhramaut and the deserts. We let out a great sigh of relief. Two members of the expedition and all the stores were on the move.

CHAPTER 4

THE JOL

"The Jol has usually been dismissed by travellers as a piece of dull dreariness, a plateau where heat and cold are alike unbearable, where food is quite, and water almost, non-existent, a hard, inhospitable, flat expanse."

Freya Stark

Almost as soon as we had turned north, we began to climb steadily. We were grateful for the recent rains. We had no windscreens, and had Pat's Land-Rover left the usual plume of dust behind it we would have been very uncomfortable. As it was, the hot air rushing by was invigorating, and, after we had quickly left the coastal humidity behind, it was cooling as well. When we splashed through puddles, mud was thrown up by the front wheel over our arms. It dried at once, and fell off. As we motored Ian deftly lit one cigarette from the stub of the last. I offered to help him, because the track was not the sort on which I would recommend people to drive one-handed, but Ian was used to it and declined any assistance.

Ian told me that once on a trip in Kenya in a closed Land-Rover he had smelled burning. He and his African companion had got out, but neither of them could discover where the smell was coming from until the African let out a squawk. One of Ian's stubs had fallen into his trouser pocket.

I looked back at Musellim, who grinned cheerfully as he lay spreadeagled on the bedding, but, behind him I could see no sign of any other vehicle. Pat stopped at the top of a rise, and we got out and looked for oil leaks, but everything appeared to be holding out. I did notice, however, that one of my canvas

53

chaguls (water bags) had already fallen off, which was a bad start. When the rest of the convoy caught up I asked the drivers if they had seen it, but they hadn't. Fortunately I had another, and the contractor had sent several with us, but it was a stupid loss, entirely due to my bad knot tying.

We drove on again. The hills on either side were a dark brown colour and there was a good deal of scrub on them, but that was all; they were far too rocky to allow any cultivation. We saw no sign of any human being, not even a shepherdess.

We continued to climb, but rounding one of the many bends, had to halt. Ahead of us was a line of trucks. They were the trucks which had left three hours before us. They hadn't managed to get very far. One of them had a broken spring. They had stopped by a village, if a few bare huts with rush roofs is worthy of the name. The trucks had stopped on the road and were blocking the way, so a civilian truck coming the other way had also been forced to stop. Nobody minded. The village contained at least one coffee shop, and there were bananas on sale. I was not sorry that we had stopped. The view on our right was a magnificent one. A fertile wadi fell away to the east. Below us palms and banana trees made a beautiful dark green carpet, which was very restful after the browns and greys of the track. Red winged starlings flew noisily from tree to tree and sunbirds flickered among the bushes like high-speed black bees. Edith said that the place, which was called Nuwaima, had a bad reputation for snakes, and I don't doubt it. There was enough water and dank vegetation to attract all the animals—pleasant and unpleasant—from the surrounding area.

While Pat stirred the convoy drivers into some sort of activity, Ian and I decided to have some lunch. Mohammet had prepared a vast quantity of ham sandwiches, and we were feeling very hungry after our early breakfast. I told Mohammet, who had caught up in Michael's vehicle, to buy some of the bananas. They were the last fresh fruit we would be likely to see for some time.

We left the trucks preparing to move again, and managed to

squeeze by the civilian vehicle and on to the track. We began to climb steadily. An HBL Pick-Up was travelling behind us and this showed an annoying tendency to travel only a few yards from us. The noise of its engine was added to the noises which our own car was making, and to which both Ian and I were listening apprehensively. Apart from the noise in the first two gears the car was going well, and I was becoming quite attached to a vehicle which gave such good visibility and a comparatively cool ride. Later its low clearance gave us trouble, but it rode well, if bouncily, over the road. It was far too light at the front, and would have benefited from having jerry-can holders on the front bumper. The rear of the vehicle was weighed down with our kit, but there was nothing but the engine to do the same for the front wheels.

The road must have been a considerable feat of surveying. From the air the Jol looks like a gigantic jigsaw puzzle, none of the pieces of which were interlocking, and some of which were only touching. It looked as though surveyors might struggle for years trying to find a route which didn't end suddenly in nothing.

Still climbing gently the convoy made good time. The hills were now made more colourful by bushes of Adenium, the desert rose, called the Dhala rose in the Western Protectorate. This flower, which grows on a strange bulbous branch, is the colour of almond blossom, and the flash of colour here and there was most striking and very satisfying. Whenever there was a halt we had some more sandwiches, but we never stopped for long because Pat was anxious to press on to a place called Molar Matar, where there was a resthouse, where we could spend the night.

In the middle of the afternoon we came to a particularly vicious series of hairpin bends, which looped over and over above and below us up the steep side of the mountain. At the bottom of the slope we could see that the Pick-Up had stopped for some reason, but before we could give it much attention the catching car decided to break down as well—and on one of the steepest parts of the road.

For some time the electric petrol pump had been rattling like a machine gun, and only the mechanical pump had kept the engine supplied with fuel. Now that, too, failed. It was probably only petrol evaporation—the curse of travel in any hot climate— but it was enough to worry us. Anything out of the ordinary in the catching car filled us with apprehension. It had become a sort of fetish with us. The catching car must get there. We just couldn't allow it to break down after all Tubby's labours.

Musellim leapt out and stuck rocks behind the rear wheels. Well below us other vehicles had stopped, either with troubles of their own, or to give us a clear run. We opened the bonnet, and looked at the silent engine. It told us nothing.

Musellim picked up a hard stone and we carried out the first action for a defective petrol system. We hit all the parts of it which we could get at with the stone. For good measure we took off the filters and cleaned them. Ian climbed back into the driver's seat and pressed the button. Silence! The ignition system had passed out as well. We carried out the first action for a defective ignition system. We hit it with a stone. After we had hit the condenser hard several times, the engine roared into life.

Then I looked under the car. A steady trickle of oil was coming from the region of the gearbox. We examined it sadly. "Perhaps the box was overfilled," Ian said hopefully. We got in and Ian started to coax the car up the hill. Several times it stalled, and, each time Musellim was out of the car and there were rocks behind the wheels before Ian had even got the hand brake on. The engine was having the greatest difficulty in finding enough power to pull the car up so steep a slope. Somehow we inched our way upwards, listening fearfully to the noises from the gearbox. There was no alternative to using the doubtful first gear and that first gear was beginning to protest.

At last we managed to creep up to the top of the pass, where Edith and Pat were comfortably waiting. There we took up the floor boards, and checked the level of the oil. It seemed to be all right. The other vehicles ground their way up the hill until everyone was at the summit. There was no sign of the other convoy, which was, by now, well behind us.

We were between five and six thousand feet up, and we reached the real Jol. Only isolated peaks and ridges reared to a greater height—perhaps to seven thousand feet. The tableland remained at a fairly constant height between three and five thousand feet. We had an altimeter attached to the car and whoever was not driving found himself constantly asked what it was reading.

The Jol (pronounced like pole) is unlike any other country in the world. It consists of a flat plateau, which shelves imperceptibly northwards until it loses most of its height and merges with the sand of "the Empty Quarter". It appears to be completely flat as though it had been sliced sideways by a sharp knife, but it is intersected by deep ravines and steep, fertile valleys, some of them lying a thousand feet below the surrounding Jol. The best known of these valleys is the Hadhramaut.

The Jol is a monotonous brown colour. There are few villages and only sparse vegetation grows on the tableland, but in the valleys there are villages, date gardens and fields of wheat and millet. From the road it was impossible to get more than a glimpse of the life that went on in this different world hundreds of feet below us. Philby was not impressed with the inhabitants. He wrote, on a very short acquaintanceship:

> Unpleasant people they seemed to me, but it is probably wrong to judge them by any human standards. They stand out in my memory as animals, bestial in every detail, but often as amusing as monkeys.

As we drove on and the afternoon wore on the country became tedious in its monotony. It is all very well travelling on what seems to be the ceiling of the world, but it gets boring if it is impossible to see the floor. Sometimes we came across sacks of charcoal, stacked by the side of the road. No one was looking after them, but they would be quite safe, and eventually they would be collected by a truck going to Mukalla. The charcoal burners are a menace, and should have been controlled years ago. What little timber there is in this bare country is being systematically burnt and the country is becoming even more stark. Very occasionally we came across some scattered houses, hunched by the track and primitive in the extreme. Their inhabitants looked out at us apathetically, or took no notice at all. It was very difficult to imagine what they did with their lives, which must have been as drab as their homes. We could see no signs of any cultivation, although some may be hidden away in the valleys, and we couldn't guess how they supported themselves.

The convoy was twice forced to halt behind unconcerned shepherds, who were driving their flocks along the track, oblivious of the horns blaring behind them and determined not to budge until they felt like it. In one case the soldiers ran forward and began shepherding the shepherd, who stared at us with something approaching contempt for our mode of travel. He was a skinny old man, with a wild straggling beard, and it was quite likely that he was walking the length of the Jol with his charges, living on the milk, which they gave him, and carrying the kids or lambs, which they dropped. We left him throwing stones at his scattered flock—a happy, independent old man—and I felt a sense of guilt at having disturbed his travels.

As the day drew on Ian and I watched hopefully at each bend for a sign of our objective, but there was nothing. Just the grey ribbon of the road stretching interminably up and down, winding up the slight rises, skirting the deep ravines and, in places, doubling back on itself.

Eventually about 5 p.m. Musellim pointed out Molar Matar ahead. All we could see was a small white dot, backed by a high ridge of rock. We were at about the highest point and the altimeter was reading five thousand six hundred feet. It was some time before the dot grew any larger, and sometimes we seemed to be going away from it. Ian had been driving all day, but didn't seem at all tired. I was beginning to learn how tough he was.

At last we passed the police post at Molar Matar. It was, as far

as I could tell, the only other building except the resthouse, and
was itself merely a shabby hut with an aerial above it. We
bounced over a rough track and stopped in front of the resthouse,
a small white bungalow, with a flat roof and a verandah. We got
out stiffly and investigated. There were two cell-like rooms, large
enough to sleep in, and four other rooms little larger than cup-
boards. In one of them was a tap. It didn't work. The Grays
took over one of the larger rooms, and Ian and I the other. Our
staff, with Pat's flooded into the small rooms, and soon there was
a pleasant smell of cooking.

The view from the resthouse was superb. We looked back over
the track along which we had come; a few yards away from the
verandah the ground fell away steeply into a winding wadi, where,
among the rocks, there were scattered sparse clumps of plants.
Except for the high ridge, which cut off our view in one direction,
there was no limit to the distant horizons of flat, brown, bare rock.

Molar Matar, as a resting place, is very old indeed, probably
pre-Islamic. There is a tomb there, which is an object of pilgrimage and veneration to the bedouin. It may have been a place
of rain worship in much earlier times, for Matar means rain in
Arabic, and it is a place of rains, high up among the clouds and the
winds. The ground is too harsh and stony for the rains to produce
anything more than the scattered plants on the hillside, but the
water drains away and brings life to the hidden villages in the
clefts and valleys far below.

As we stood that evening on the verandah there was a most
peculiar yellow light in the sky across which pale grey mists were
rolling. The sun sank quickly and the yellow faded to a matchless
pale violet. It was a sight that left us silent and wondering. Clouds
scudded by below us and then the light was gone. It became very
cold. After Aden and Mukalla I found it almost insupportable.
We put on what warm clothing we possessed and shut the doors
and shutters. A pressure lamp gave a bright light and a little
warmth.

The height and the solitude would have been a marvellous
tonic, if only it hadn't been so cold. Ian had announced that he

would be sleeping outside, but he soon changed his mind. Mohammet brought us tea and we opened a bottle of whisky to combat this unexpected chill. I wondered if it was likely to freeze, and, if so, whether we should drain the radiator of the catching car, but I concluded that half the trouble was probably in my own thin blood. In fact, after dark, the wind dropped, and it became much less cold.

The wireless operator contacted Mukalla without difficulty. We tried our portable wireless and found the BBC broadcasting a programme by Victor Sylvester, and later we were able to hear the news. Pat and Edith joined us for a drink and were amused to find me wrapped in my sleeping bag. We had supper, more whisky and felt much better. We went to sleep with the door wide open and the fresh mountain air swirling about us.

We could hear the HBL soldiers singing to help to keep themselves warm as they huddled behind the hut for shelter, crouched round a fire, drinking tea. I don't think that any of them got much sleep that night. They were equipped for sleeping in the desert, where even one blanket can be too much.

We were up at dawn. It was much warmer, and the air was completely still. The sun was just climbing into a clear, unclouded sky when we finished packing up and were ready to move. We were sorry that we hadn't longer to explore this mysterious and exciting place. Somewhere we heard a shepherd calling to his flock. The land was not as empty as it looked. With a few more warm clothes Ian and I would have enjoyed some weeks exploring.

The truck convoy had caught up during the night, and we left before them this time. As we drove off we missed having a windscreen: the icy blast was far too invigorating. Ian and I wrapped what we could find about us. We looked more like a polar expedition than one through Arabia in early summer. Later we saw a Sakar falcon. I was driving so Ian was able to have a good look at the first bird of any sort we had seen since leaving Molar Matar, where a cluster of ravens had visited to scavenge after we left. We passed a village and some fields; an unusual sight for they were on the surface of the Jol, not tucked away in a valley.

About eight we stopped so that the wireless operator could call
Mukalla, and we were able to thaw out over some coffee. There
was the cheerful sound of flocks of sheep in the nearby valleys, and
a shepherdess came over and passed the time of day with the
soldiers. In the distance we could see others, moving like small
blackbirds across the brown hill sides, and on a well-defined
camel track other people were moving purposefully. It was very
pleasant after the emptiness of the previous day, and it was a
relief to see movement and colour again.

We motored all morning. The chill of the early hours was
quickly forgotten, and we travelled in the minimum of clothing,
keeping well behind the dust which was now being thrown up by
Pat's vehicle. Behind us the convoy was strung out over several
miles. Occasionally we stopped to allow the rearmost trucks to
catch up, and each time we had a look at the underside of the
gearbox. There was nothing worse than a smear of oil.

At midday we reached the HBL post at Jahi, a minute two-
room fort, which looked more like a dolls' house than a real fort.
The post was manned by a section, and an unpleasant duty it
must have been. The ground was devoid of any vegetation,
except for a plot, a few feet square, of millet which the soldiers
had been growing. The ground was rocky and reflected the
fierce heat of the sun in one depressing, shimmering glare. There
was no shade except in the fort and one tent.

But the place was well chosen for it stood at the top of the road
down into the Wadi Do'an, and none could come up from the
valley, or come down from Molar Matar, without passing by.
The post's links with civilisation were a wireless and one Land-
Rover, and relied on the HBL convoys, passing through to the
garrisons in the north, to provide supplies.

Pat and I sat in the little wireless room while the operator called
Mukalla and the other HBL stations. For a change we heard
good news. The three members of the expedition who had been
stranded in Aden had flown the previous day to Ghuraf in the
Wadi Hadhramaut and a vehicle had already left Husn al Abr to
pick them up. I broke the good news to Ian, and good news it

really was, because it looked as though the others would get to al Abr before us after all. And, as our plane was also due there the following day, we might all be united at long last.

It was very hot indeed, and I was content to sit gasping with Edith who seemed quite unaffected by the heat. She looked as spruce as when she had started, and cheerfully plied me with life-giving tea. We had lunch and looked forward to moving again, when the breeze would rescue us from the oppressive stillness of that barren spot. Pat sent the garrison's Land-Rover down the pass first to stop any vehicle trying to come up while the convoy was descending. The trucks had caught up, and when everyone was ready Pat gave the signal. We started to descend a thousand feet from the Jol to the Wadi below.

CHAPTER 5

THE WADI DO'AN

"This subtle unexpected pleasure, this very salt of life, is the reward of those who, after crossing the Jol, stand on the lip of the cliff and look down into Wadi Do'an."

Freya Stark

Slowly, very slowly, we began to descend. Ian had taken over the driving and I was grateful to him. We moved so slowly that I was able to get out and walk. I don't know who was responsible for the particular engineering feat in creating the road but he must have had no idea of the length, or breadth, of the trucks which were likely to use it. One of the trucks was forced to stop at each hairpin bend, reverse more than once and then creep cautiously around the lip of the road to the shouted advice of all the passengers, who were wisely standing. The HBL Pick-Up behind us was also having trouble, but this was due to the impetuosity of the driver. His passengers walked.

Freya Stark was quite right when she described the pleasure of the contrast between the Wadi and Jol in such glowing terms. The Wadi is a fascinating sight, and a complete change from the horizontal features of the Jol. The contrast took our breath away as we drove down, the Wadi running away to our left and right, three-quarters of a mile across. In either direction we could see lush green fields, and from our great height above them, they looked like a lawn, with above them the darker blobs of the date palms. There was standing water in places in the Wadi bed, shining green and cool in the sun. Huddled at the foot of the cliffs were villages composed of tall mud-coloured houses, which merged so closely with the background of the cliffs that I often missed seeing them at first glance. Some were whitewashed, and they stood out clearly, and there were castles with towers and turrets. They looked as though they had been well maintained, and, indeed, it was not so many years ago that they were used in the bitter feuds which had made this valley, like all the others, a place of hate and fear.

The Wadi has been inhabited as long as history records. There is a theory, never disproved, that it was the Thabane of Ptolemy and the Thoani mentioned by Pliny. There are Himyaritic remains, which were first discovered by the Bents in the last century. One can only conjecture how long ago it must have been when the valley was cut to its present depth and no one can say when it suffered its last disastrous floods, the traces of which can still be seen on the cliffs. The inhabitants still recall Noah and his ark as though his floods had happened yesterday.

There is a wonderful feeling of peace in the Wadi these days. Both Ingrams, the first British Resident, and Freya Stark noted the feeling of tranquillity which pervades the valley. Perhaps it is something to do with the feeling of having walls about one after the openness of the Jol. Perhaps the people of the valley are a gentler race than those who have to make their living out on the harsh tableland among the winds and endless brown horizons. We, like those illustrious travellers who had gone before us, dropped the thousand feet into the valley as though we were entering another world.

The inhabitants of the Wadi have generally emigrated to the Red Sea area, not to the Far East, and many have become rich. Nearly always they have returned to their valley to end their days there, spending their money on their houses and on improving the land. Not for gain, only for the pleasure of making the valley even more beautiful.

However, today, this feeling for the quiet but lasting pleasures of life is not so strong as it used to be. The modern world has reached as far as the Wadi Do'an and the tempo of life has increased. It is no longer quite the peaceful backwater it was in the thirties. There is almost a go-ahead feeling about it, and it has

Bedouin camel train crossing the Jol—"a hard, inhospitable, flat expanse."

Wadi Do'an, a fascinating sight and wonderful relief after crossing the harsh tableland of the Jol.

A moment of tremendous triumph—the capture of the cow
oryx.

The expedition in the Wadi
Shu'ait.

Our guides: Mabkhaut
bin Hassana and
Tomatum.

lost its sleepiness. Perhaps this has not improved it. Some of the houses show too much foreign influence and resemble the worst sort of seaside architecture, but the quiet date gardens, which surround most of the secluded houses, remain. The old men can still wander among their carefully tended gardens, and can still listen to the trickle of clear water, the best sound any Arab can hear, for it is one of the features they are promised in paradise along with dusky houris and gliding servant youths.

As Ian drove the catching car slowly down the hill, a nasty smell of burning developed. It was coming from the brakes, but there was nothing that we could do about it. Ian did not dare to drive in a low gear because of the risk to the gearbox. The only alternative was a steady pressure on the brake pedal, and the brakes were protesting. We must have taken half an hour over the descent, and we both breathed a sigh of relief when we reached the bottom without anything serious happening to the car. The altimeter showed that we had dropped nine hundred feet.

Ian was able to rest the gears and the brakes at the bottom, and after that it was easy work over the flat Wadi bed in top gear. The track wound through villages and humped and dipped over watercourses. It was mid-afternoon and there were few people about to watch us pass. The trees were full of birds and the Bulbul loudly announced our passage. We soon came in sight of two buildings. They were large and looked exactly like seaside hotels —rather seedy ones. We christened them the Metropole and the Norfolk.

The water here was pumped and piped and Michael's Pick-Up stopped to fill up at a tap, but Pat signalled us to keep going and we followed him closely, or as closely as his dust would allow.

In places the track crosses the Wadi bed where Ilb trees grew, large, shade-giving trees, which produce the Dom fruit (like tasteless cherries) and which grow all over Southern Arabia. They provide both a generous amount of shade and an edible berry, and are fairly widespread in both the East and West Protectorates. We saw more and more birds of different varieties, including the beautiful green and blue bee-eater, and twice Ian stopped so suddenly that I was afraid that the HBL Pick-Up, which, as usual, was following far too closely behind us, would crash into us, not seeing that we had halted because of the dust. After one near escape they learned to keep their distance.

We pressed on all afternoon, passing fortified towns and villages. The houses seemed to hide under the towering cliffs, which were surmounted by watch towers, and each village had its fort, situated on higher ground. In places the cliff had fallen away and there were lumps of rock, or earth, the size of the houses themselves, lying on the ground close to the settlements. Later we were to see the same in the Hadhramaut. Children were working in the fields. Some were busy and others were not. I remember one small girl, weeding among the wheat, who took her duties so seriously that she didn't even raise her head as we went by.

Sometimes we passed groups of men asleep in the shade. Not for them the mid-afternoon labours of the children. They lorded it under the trees, their faces covered from the flies and none of them woke to watch us. Only one man, working high up in a palm tree which he had climbed in much the same way as men climb telegraph poles, with a safety rope, waved to us.

There was no monotony about that afternoon's drive. Every mile was packed with interest, and there was life and colour to satisfy us all. We followed the Wadi as it widened steadily, and we seemed to be running north-west for most of the time, although the many bends in the valley made direction deceptive. Occasionally the Wadi branched, or tributaries joined the main trunk. By four o'clock we were approaching Hajarain, an imposing village built like a citadel on a hill at the junction of the main Wadi and a subsidiary one.

We stopped below the rocks on which the village was built. Pat said that it would be our last opportunity to fill up with really sweet water, and we didn't want to miss that opportunity. Pipes ran along a wall and every few feet there was a brass tap. Men and girls were standing on the concrete surrounds filling their waterbags. As we climbed out of the trucks, more and more donkeys came galloping down from the village with their empty water skins. One came out of control with its owner running and shouting behind it, the donkey gaining impetus but managing somehow to keep on its feet. It was luckier than the man. Everyone cheered, and someone captured the runaway. The donkeys all had little wooden saddles, of a type I had not seen elsewhere, and, on these, the full water skins were fitted, the weight being distributed equally on either side. They looked like the pillion bags on a motor cycle.

The crowd drawing water was a colourful one. There were half-naked men, grinning, wet and boisterous. There were shy, serious-faced boys and even shyer young girls. One of these caught my eye. She was dressed in a bright red dress that came down almost to her feet. On the back of the dress was worked a pattern in gold. The pattern was of crosses—a most unusual form of Muslim decoration. She was a very difficult subject to photograph, and I was afraid of upsetting the men if I was too obvious about it.

Previous travellers have commented unfavourably upon the dirt of the village. We had no means of checking this for we hadn't the time. From the outside it was certainly imposing, and very well sited, both for defence and for avoiding floods. The money for the water pumps, pipes and taps had been provided by an expatriate, living in Saudi Arabia, who had wanted to do something with his wealth for his old town. When we left, our waterbags and jerry cans were full of the water which was, as Pat had told us, beautifully sweet.

After Hajarain the Wadi broadened considerably, and the villages no longer nestled under the shelter of the cliffs, but stood bravely, dotted about the valley on mounds, or on the flat among the cultivation. The pebbly Wadi bed gave way to sand, and the cultivated portions were separated by areas of low sand dunes; these we had to cross, not without difficulty. I was driving now, and in my anxiety to conserve the gears, got stuck. We were quickly pushed out by a dozen men and no damage was done, but it was a foretaste of what we were going to have to cope with. The gears had been protesting more loudly as the day had worn on, and Ian and I were feeling less optimistic. Nevertheless, we hoped that it would at least get us to Husn al Abr, where Peter would be able to see what had happened to his brainchild.

It was not to be. Just short of Qadha we came on another area of sand, covered in tall green shrubs though which we had to weave our way with care. Without warning there was a frightful clank from the gearbox and that was that. We were left with top gear again, but nothing else. It was a sad moment. We knew that we would have to abandon the car. Tubby had done all that could be done, but a new gearbox would be the only answer, and there was no hope of one here. Slowly I drove it up to the village, where Pat had stopped to wait for us. We tried to force it into another gear, but it was quite hopeless. There was no chance of taking it on to al Abr, although that place was only a few hours further on, for there was a belt of sand dunes to be crossed, and the car would never make it. We stopped for the last time and discussed the situation with Pat.

Qadha is an interesting place. Ingrams had had great difficulty in persuading the inhabitants to sign the general truce. The village had been the capital of the Nahd, and it had taken all his powers of persuasion to make the tribe sign, and he remarks with feeling:

> Nahd are a distinctive tribe, well-built, not small of stature, and their many elders all seem to have enormous bellies and resonant voices.

When the truce had been signed the people appeared. Some of them had been besieged in their homes for years. There was one who hadn't left his house for eighteen years, and another who hadn't seen his sister for twenty although she lived almost next door. And all this was due to fear. This was the peace which Ingrams brought to replace the horror of what had gone before. The peace came at the beginning of 1937 and has existed since. No book about the area should fail to give Ingrams credit for what he did. There can be few men who have been able to look at so

great a lasting monument to their labours, and, yet, outside
Arabia, his work is hardly known. Perhaps because we are
ashamed of the fifty years' neglect which preceded the peace.

There was little sign of the past quarrels at Qadha, when we
stopped. We were immediately surrounded by a group of
inquisitive townsmen, most of whom seemed to know one or
other of the HBL soldiers, and there was a great deal of hand
shaking and smacking of lips. Pat agreed that there was no
alternative to abandoning the car. Luckily the Mukalla Regular
Army had a post in the village fort, and we would be able to leave
the car there safely until its future was decided.

An immediate problem, however, was how we were going to
fit ourselves and all our equipment on to the other already over-
loaded vehicles. Somehow it was done and bits and pieces were
parcelled out among them after as much argument as though the
trucks had been camels. Ian had the doubtful honour of driving it
in top gear to its resting place. It was an unhappy ending and
Tubby Dawson's efforts over Easter deserved better.

I found myself allotted the front seat in a closed Land-Rover.
There was already a sergeant and the driver—and two four-
gallon cans of aviation fuel on the seat—which didn't leave me
much room. Somehow I managed to get my legs over the cans,
and travelled in acute discomfort with my feet pressing against
the windscreen. At the first halt the sergeant took pity on me and
changed places. His knees seemed used to the contortions necessary, and he appeared unaffected by his position. There was a
nauseating smell of dried fish coming from the back of the car.
Also I was conscious of the fact that one or other of my companions had not made use of the washing facilities at Hajarain. I
missed the open-air feeling of the catching car.

The breakdown had delayed us and it was dark before Pat led
the way off the track and on to a flat gravel plain, where we
halted. We were near the village of Khasha, where we were to
spend the night. It had been a long, hard day and there was
nothing to be gained by attempting to go on to Husn al Abr that
night.

We had no sooner unpacked the cars than a very strong wind got up suddenly, and we had great difficulty in erecting one of the tents, but before long Mohammet produced an excellent warm supper. The gale soon passed us by with a patter of raindrops, but nothing worse.

After the tumult of the wind, the stillness which replaced it was breathtaking. I pulled my bed outside the tent. The temperature was perfect. Against the dark sky I could just see the darker outlines of the cliffs. Around us scattered acacia trees housed various birds rustling themselves into their positions for the night. In the village a dog barked, and one or two lights twinkled in the distance. It was very different from Molar Matar, and the silence was not the silence of empty mountains, but rather the silence of a world resting, complete, but more friendly. Later in the night I woke to find the camp bathed in a pale moonlight almost as bright as day.

We started early again, just as dawn was breaking, and the sky was still an innocent light blue, waiting for the arrival of the hostile sun. The acacias were outlined sharply and their topmost branches held grey shrikes preparing for their onslaught on the day's crop of insects. Bedouin fires smoked in all directions. The pale blue columns of their smoke rose vertically until they merged in the breathless sky.

This time I travelled in greater comfort. The sergeant had decided to travel in less cramped quarters, and we rearranged the petrol cans so that there was room for my feet at their proper level. The Land-Rover still seemed stuffy after the catching car, and the hot air from the engine was no tonic at all. After the first few miles across the sand, which presented no obstacle to us in the cool of the morning, we found ourselves running over a flat gravel plain. We halted for the usual early morning wireless call, and heard that the others had reached al Abr safely the previous night. We were no longer in the vanguard. If the plane took off on time, it would be with us at midday and the expedition would be complete.

The cars sped on in line abreast across the wide plain, no longer shut in by the two lines of hills, but following the northern edge of the Wadi. We were out of the Do'an and in the open. The driver pointed at four flat-topped hills and said, "al Abr". They were miles away across the plain, but we were driving at such speed that the distance quickly narrowed. The line of hills on our right grew softer and more rounded. Vegetation appeared on the plain and herds of camels grazed amongst it. They lifted their heads and galloped clumsily away, their feet hobbled. An occasional bedouin raised his hand in greeting. We waved back cheered by the speed and the nearness of our goal.

CHAPTER 6

HUSN AL ABR

"Think in this batter'd caravenserai
   Whose portals are alternate night and day,
How Sultan after Sultan with his pomp
   Abode his destin'd Hour, and went his way."
                              Rubyiat
                              Edward Fitzgerald

It is said that the four flat distinctive hills of Husn al Abr can be
seen seventy miles away. They stand up like islands in a yellow
sea, and are a useful landmark for the desert traveller. In the quite
recent past, I was told, hyenas, ibex and other animals lived on the
summits. A precarious existence it must have been.

Husn al Abr is an important place. It has been called the key to
the Hadhramaut for there are tracks radiating from it in all
directions, most of which are motorable. There is a track to
Shabwa—still a forbidden place because of frontier disputes—and
one to Najran, used by thousands of pilgrims. There is a track to
Thamud—along which we proposed to travel, and another going
in the opposite direction towards the Western Protectorate.
Strangely no town has grown up at so important a centre, but
the place is important enough with a fort and the busy customs
post which lies beside it, the first south of the Saudi border.

It contains the last water before the Yemen forty miles further
west, or before Saudi Arabia to the north. The bedouin, as well
as the pilgrims are dependent on it, and there is sufficient for all
normal needs, unless the summer happens to be unusually harsh.
There are traces of many old wells, though today only three or
four are in use.

As we approached the white fort and the fertile wadi below it, dotted with acacias and bedouin tents, we were interested only in spotting the other members of the expedition. Ian went off to the fort with Pat Gray, while I looked for a suitable camp site for us to stay for twenty-four hours. In the shade of the trees the ground was littered with camel droppings and an army of camel ticks and worse awaiting the unwary, so I chose a site on open ground. With the aid of HBL men the tents were laid out and then erected in a rough line. I wanted to see if they were all serviceable, the first opportunity I had had.

Ian returned, bringing with him Peter Whitehead, Don Stewart and Michael Woodford. It was the first time we had met. We stood uneasily in the sun, exchanging the sort of platitudes Englishmen usually exchange at such times, before someone suggested that we sit down. I organised some tea.

My first impression of the three new arrivals was of their height. All three were over six feet tall. Peter, I thought, looked extremely tough. His blue eyes were reddened by the unaccustomed glare, but they were friendly and he smiled readily. His hair had been appallingly cut in Nairobi, and instead of an even crew cut, was an unruly collection of tufts and spikes of different lengths. I wondered if the same person who had overhauled the gearbox had cut his hair.

Don, slimmer and younger, seemed very serious. Almost immediately he started searching for his plant presses and sorting out his equipment which he had last seen in Kenya. Michael was still looking very fresh from England. He had a cheerful manner and I took to him at once. Later I discovered that we had been to the same school, though not at the same time.

All morning we sorted out the kit. By now the staff had become distinct personalities. Musellim was proving to be the greatest find of the trip, a man of many parts. He was a bedouin from Thamud, a driver by trade. He was the hardest worker I have ever met among Arabs. Later his cheerfulness in the face of discomfort became proverbial. He would turn his hand to anything, showing a good eye for tracking, and a keen interest in the search for the elusive oryx.

A very different sort of chap was Saleh, the unsuccessful cook at the start of our expedition, but he had accepted the fall in status to bearer quite happily. He always looked as though he was about to burst into tears, but, if something amused him, his face became transfigured until he looked as cheerful as Musellim. He got on with his duties quietly, but conscientiously. Abdullah was the third bearer. He had only been taken on because Michael Crouch knew him, and felt sorry for him because he was out of work. He turned out to be idle and surly, and was the only complete failure among the staff. Finally we had to sack him.

The contractor had sent a stout party called Daruweesh to look after his interests, whatever they may have been, and also to carry the cash, which we needed to buy goats. We had viewed his portly figure and advancing· years with misgivings, but he became slimmer and seemingly younger as the trip progressed. Far from being a liability, he was most useful indeed.

Mohammet, the foreman and cook, was Michael's man. He was a delightful gnome, nearly always dressed in a grubby primrose shirt and long shorts, which were not long enough to hide the fact that he wore rugger shorts underneath. He was always smiling, and was never upset when we demanded food or drink at all hours. He was apparently supporting a large family of daughters somewhere in Wahidi. His cooking, based on a limited assortment of tins, was masterly, and he excelled at curries.

There was an assistant cook called Yeman. He was round, dark and unshaven, and he cooked for the staff, but was another man who would turn his hand to anything. Qassim, the Pick-Up driver, was a bit of a spiv and also a Yafa'i, which meant that he talked twice as loudly and twice as long as any other Arab— and Arabs in general are a people who are no laggards when it comes to conversation. He cared nothing for any man and despised us and the other Arabs equally.

Omar, Michael's orderly, was another type quite different from the local Arabs. He never worked overhard, remembering his status as an NCO in the Wahdi tribal guards, but he safeguarded Michael's kit jealously and looked after the guns. He had a mop of thick black hair and a surly face, which fortunately, was not a true mirror of his character.

The further we got from Mukalla the more we began to see the true worth of the really good team we had picked. Only Abdullah let us down, and after he had gone the others worked even better. I dread to think what might have happened if we had accepted the contractor's original choices.

The Piper aircraft with Michael Crouch and Mick Gracie aboard, was due at midday. They expected to take two hours over the trip from Riyan. We learned afterwards that Michael navigated not by maps but by memory which, judging by the inaccuracy of the maps, was a good thing. Just before they were due we motored to the air strip, a few miles from the fort and at the foot of the flat-topped hills and their attendant foothills.

At the airstrip, as we waited, it became very hot and some of us regretted not bringing shirts and hats. The canvas waterbag became very popular. Peter claimed that he was drinking water for the first time for twenty-five years. It didn't seem to do him any harm.

Mick picked up our position and circled us, peering out to examine the surface. Ian threw up a shovelful of sand to indicate the wind direction, but there was no wind. Most of it came down on his head and the occupants of the plane were none the wiser. When Mick was satisfied he brought the plane down (with the wind) and carried out the first of his many desert landings.

Michael Woodford's camera, the official one, whirred busily. The rest of us compared exposure meters, and found, as always happened, that none of them gave the same answer. Undeterred we 'snapped' the plane and then each other. The Fauna Preservation Society was going to get plenty of pictures of its expedition even if none were taken of oryx.

The Piper looked even smaller now with the empty desert behind it. We tethered it carefully to rocks, and left two HBL sentries to stand guard under the shade of the wings with a jerry can of water, which they were certainly going to need.

At last, after so many false alarms and so much bad luck, the expedition was complete . . .

Back in camp we had lunch and beers, and then a conference to decide duties. I was given the job of camp commander, as I had expected, and Peter was asked to assist me. Michael Crouch's Arabic was far more fluent than mine, and beside being the accountant, he was made the link between the guides and the HBL. This was a natural choice, as he knew most of the people, having dealt with them during the two years in the area. Don and the other Michael were put in charge of the ground arrangements for the plane, coping with the refuelling, and with the direction beacon. Mick was left with the hazardous job of flying the plane. The party was now officially organised, but, as usually happens, everyone helped everyone else, and we did the jobs as they came up. Later Michael Crouch took over much of the running of the staff, because Mohammet was his own man and understood him far better than he would ever understand me. We paired off to share tents, except for Michael who had his bed erected in solitary state in his own tent. In fact, we only used them for shade during the day, and all slept out at night.

Ian explained the future prospects. There were as yet no definite reports that oryx still existed, but on the other hand nobody was saying they didn't. From the moment we moved from al Abr we would be entering the country where the oryx had been plentiful only ten years earlier, but the Qatari raids had introduced a new factor. If there were still survivors, their normal pattern of behaviour might have been upset. It was even possible that they would not leave the sand.

We decided to push on the following day. The plane would follow us later, for there must always be someone on the ground when it landed. Our arrangements made, we carried on repacking, discarding what we could. In the afternoon Pat and Edith arrived to take us to see some rock drawings which we had heard about. Pat led the way, driving east along the track we would follow the next day, then branched off and followed a sandy wadi. We drove for forty minutes, the wadi gradually narrowing and the hills growing higher on either flank. There were pre-Islamic 'pillbox' graves on the hill tops, of an antiquity impossible to determine. They looked very like the wartime pillboxes scattered along the railways and by crossroads of wartime England. Some of them could have been fairly recent because the bedouin were inclined to bury their dead on the hill tops, presumably to ensure that floods did not disturb them.

The wadi became a shallow gorge with a sandy bottom. We were forced to stop for the cars could go no further. The guide led us nimbly over the rocks, down the gorge to where he started pointing out scribbles on the rocks. A hand was the most common sign, sometimes appearing in rows and rows. In many parts of the world a hand is painted on to the house to ward off the devil, and in other parts the hand is a menacing sign intended to instil fear. There was no one who could tell us why these hands had been drawn so often. There were no inscriptions, but numerous doodles in letters in the Himyaritic script. There were lots of drawings of animals, and of men fighting. Judging by the lightness of the rock and of the drawings on it, nothing that we found can have been very old, just pre-Islamic, I think.

We found drawings of oryx and ibex, camels and ostriches. There were men on horseback duelling with spears or lances, and there were others hunting the animals. If one of us had been an archaeologist we would have learned a great deal. As it was we could only marvel and pass on. I tried to find some sherds on the hills, which might date the drawings, but without success. It seemed that there had been no settlement in the valley, and we thought that the drawings had probably been done by people passing though, using the water holes and doodling while they camped or the animals were watered.

We got back to camp in time to give the Grays some tea. They were staying in the fort, and the fort boasted a bathroom. In the evening, just before dark, we drove across, clutching our pieces of soap and our towels. The bathroom consisted of a small dark room. There was a barrel of ice cold water standing in it, and a dipper. One bathed by pouring dippers of the water over one's head. It made us dance with shock.

Later Philip Allfree, the Assistant Adviser for the Northern

Deserts, and the only political officer (or for that matter European) north of the Hadhramaut, appeared. Al Abr is his headquarters. He took the invasion of his home by a mass of people very well.

In the middle of the night I frightened Mick Gracie by climbing out of my sleeping bag and crawling round the tent, dragging it behind me and muttering about hunting an oryx.

Michael Crouch acted as guide the following morning, and took us to the wells. The Saar women are famed for their beauty. They don't at all mind having their photographs taken, though they are apt to chide you for your impertinence—at the same time drawing back their veils to ensure that their handsome faces are not obscured. "Shame on you, Christians, shame on you," they shouted at us, uncovering their mouths and smiling. They were egged on by their husbands, who were proud of them. In almost any other tribe, the men would have come flying to protect their women's honour.

The Saar have been called "The Wolves of the Desert". Once raiding was part of their life. It is only in the last ten years that they have forsaken their old ways. The other tribes feared them for their bravery and their knowledge of the desert. They feared no man, called no man master, and, being on the frontier between the Protectorate, Saudi Arabia and the Yemen, were in a good position to play one state off against the other, and so avoid punishment. Only the Dahm matched them for ferocity and singleness of purpose, and al Abr was much fought over up to as late as 1948.

Since then there has been an uneasy truce between the Saar, the Dahm and the Karab. The Saar, who used to fight among themselves when nobody else was available, have been quiet. As a tribe they are as free as air and wander where they wish in that wild, isolated country.

We found these 'wolves' delightfully friendly. The men watering their camels at the wells greeted Michael like a long-lost brother, and included us in their welcome. A number of their women were waiting with the goatskin waterbags, while the men drew the water up from the well, and there was much laughter and a great deal of good-natured chaff.

One elderly man, in rather cleaner clothes than the others—he appeared to be wearing a white dinner jacket over his futah— turned out to be Mubarak al Kaher, a famous man and a fine guide. He still had three bullets in him, the results of raids, and he was apt to display these to strangers. He was impressive enough without these exhibitions, but he lacked dignity and his behaviour would have appalled the bedouin of the northern tribes. Most of the time he teased the women or wrestled with the men. It was he who insisted that the women pose for us. They had smooth round faces, light golden brown skins, large dark eyes, full of mischief, and excellent white teeth. One or two were very tall and very slender, the others were of average height. They were all dressed in black, with black veils, which seldom seemed to be covering their vivacious features. About their arms and ankles were silver ornaments. They wore no pantaloons as do the northern bedouin women, and their ankles were thin and shapely. When they walked, they moved with the utmost grace.

As the men emptied the water into the waiting goat skins, encouraged by al Kaher, they sang and shouted and splashed the waiting girls, getting good natured slaps in return. It was all very jolly, and quite unlike the jealous protectiveness of the bedouin and the cringing self-effacement of his women.

Their camels were of all shapes and sizes and all colours. They ranged through the shades between black and white. I wondered whether the black ones had come from the once sacred herd known as the Shuruf, which used to belong to the Mutair tribe until it was taken from them by King 'Abdul 'Aziz al Sa'ud after the 1930 rebellion. They were never ridden by the Mutair, but, in battle, led the tribe like four-legged shock troops. The Mutair were quite prepared to fight to the death to protect them, giving to them the same symbolism that Regiments used to give to their Colours in battle.

H. R. P. Dickson says that generally the white and light coloured camels come from the north, and the darker ones from the south. Here we must have been at the dividing line between the two. No tribe will admit that any but their own camels are the best in Arabia, but, on the whole the best riding camels come from the Oman and are known as the Umaniyah. The best general purpose animals come from the country of the Awazim in the north. There is as much difference between a thoroughbred riding camel and a pack animal as there is between a racehorse and a carthorse. Many tales of endurance are told about camels, and Lawrence rode over distances that impressed even the bedouin, but pride of achievement must surely go either to one of King Saud's messengers, who rode five hundred and thirty miles across the desert in five-and-a-half days to report the result of the battle of Shu'aiba in 1915, or the man of the 'Utaiba, who, Dickson says, escaped from the king's prison in Riyadh in 1925 and rode nearly eight hundred miles in eight days.

Among the Saar there does not seem to be the usual objection to riding the bull camel and there were many enormous bulls among the herd, as well as silken-nosed cows, calves and half-grown animals, still unweaned. In addition to the camels, flocks of goats were waiting their turn. They preserved a perfect discipline. At a call from their shepherdess, a section broke away from the main body and trotted down to the water without any of the pushing and biting of the camels. None of the others moved until it was their turn. There were no sheepdogs. This one girl controlled the flock like a sergeant-major. We watched them unbelievingly as each section arrived, drank and then moved away to another flock, as the next rank was called forward.

The goats were small but sturdy, and their coats were the same off-white colour as those of the rim and the oryx. White is not the best colour for camouflage, but it is certainly the best for reflecting the sun's rays, or so we decided later when we were discussing the coloration of desert animals.

We chattered to the tribesmen and their children, and wandered from group to group around each well. We saw one wrinkled and bent old blind woman. She guided herself with a stick in a straight, unerring line across the desert.

We left the Saar and after some more sightseeing in the area began loading the trucks. We were going to leave at lunch time,

View of the palace at Saiwun.

Main gate of Shibam.

but the trucks were to go off before us so that they wouldn't have to travel through the heat of the afternoon. Of all the places in the Northern Deserts, we had found al Abr the friendliest and the most interesting. The Saar may have had a reputation for treachery in the past, but this probably arose from the universal dislike which the surrounding tribes felt for them. The Saar never gave a hoot for anyone. Philby connects them with the Ausaretae mentioned by Pliny, so they are an old tribe.

Al Abr would repay a long visit from someone interested in the history of Southern Arabia. Today the bulk of the people passing through are the Hadhramis on the pilgrimage to Mecca. They come in truck loads. For them al Abr must be an unnecessary nuisance, a place for the showing of passports, and for customs inspections. Some of the travellers are not so innocent and a truck still stands in the fort compound, which was seized by the customs two years ago, when it was found to be smuggling arms into the Protectorate.

Al Abr is garrisoned by a company of the HBL, which has sections posted strategically at other wells in the area. It has changed little since the Wahabi soldiers came down to tax the Saar, and the fort, the wells and the scattered bedouin tents are much as they must have been in those days. Nothing represents the timelessness of the desert so truly as its wells.

Our camp bustled with activity. All the tents except one had been struck and the HBL were singing happily as they loaded our bits and pieces. Pat gave us one more Land-Rover to make up for the catching car, so, even with all our expedition present, we were not going to be too cramped. We never ceased to be grateful for the way Pat Gray came to our rescue and solved our problems. Another great gain was that at the fort Michael Crouch's Pick-Up, now promoted to catching car, had some supports welded on behind the cab, so those travelling in the back would have something to hang on to, when the car was actually catching.

CHAPTER 7

ACROSS THE NORTHERN DESERTS

"Commonly the Arabian desert is an extreme desolation
where the herb is not apparent for the sufficiency of any
creature."

Doughty

When all was ready we prepared to move, the trucks having
already gone on. We drove north-east up the wadi we had visited
the previous day, then climbed out of it over hills of black, unfriendly stone.

Peter had volunteered to travel with me in the open Land-
Rover, the one we were borrowing from the post at al Abr, and
which was being driven by a cheerful soldier called Nassir.
Michael Woodford and Don were both in the front of closed
Land-Rovers, where they were protected from the sun. Personally I would always choose an open car if possible, whatever
the temperature. Roof off and windscreen down is the way to
travel in the desert if you want to see everything there is to be
seen. The breeze and the good observation more than compensate for burnt skin and chapped lips. Ian had volunteered to travel
in Michael's old Pick-Up—the new catching car—so that he
could get used to its vagaries, not to mention those of its
driver.

We soon left the stony foothills and began to run over an open
plain where the going was very good indeed. We could have
made good time had not some of the vehicles started to overheat.
As soon as the temperature gauges showed 100 degrees the cars
were stopped, turned to face any breeze there might be and their
bonnets lifted. Nassir was the only one of the drivers who knew

82

that the quickest way to bring the temperature down was to leave the engine idling. The Pick-Ups showed themselves to be thirsty beasts and consumed a sizeable amount of our precious water at each halt. Fortunately the petrol systems behaved themselves and we were not troubled by evaporation, but the stoppages were frequent and very tiresome.

The HBL drivers were like sheep. When one vehicle stopped so did all the others. There was no convoy discipline, and the other drivers refused to leave the halted vehicle for the attention of the fitter who was travelling in the last Pick-Up. The stop was a chance to have a rest and they took it. My suggestion that only the fitter need stop and bring the vehicle on later, or that at least one car should go on to tell Pat Gray as convoy leader the reason for the halt, was greeted with derision. Later the HBL drivers complained to Pat's driver that I had tried to give them an order. It was a mistake none of us made again. They were a law unto themselves.

The plain over which we were travelling was bounded on the right by the range of hills, which marked the end of the Jol. It was broken in places by the mouths of wadis, draining northwards into the sand. The plain shimmered and danced in the heat. It was made up of a very fine gravel, though over large areas of it sparse shoots of grass had sprung up as the result of some recent rain or flood. This gave the ground a delightful green tinge, most refreshing after the rocks and stones of al Abr, but there were neither trees nor shrubs.

Once or twice we saw camels, and Peter and I played a game which I have often played in the desert: the game of guessing what each object was. In that heat the smallest stone became magnified, and every time we saw a dot, we tried to guess what it was. A man or a camel? A bush perhaps? More often than not it turned out to be a solitary black stone the size of a tennis ball. Sometimes the gravel reflected the blue of the sky and we saw great lakes, which raced away from us as we approached, then vanished altogether.

We passed Zamakh and later Manwakh, both somewhere

below the hills on our right. Each place had a well, which was guarded by an HBL section from the al Abr company.

We drove on in fits and starts. The rate at which our water was going down was alarming. The drivers and the other HBL soldiers seemed to have an unquenchable thirst. Our waterbags shrank, sagged and emptied. I had expected the Europeans in the party to require a considerable amount of water, because they were unused to the heat, but, in fact, they were little affected, and watched aghast as our water supplies diminished. Luckily at this stage there was no great shortage for there was water ahead of us, but it boded ill for the future, when there wouldn't be.

One of the most striking features of the country was the complete absence of birds. We were too late for the migration and there did not appear to be any residents.

We were aiming for a place called Khashm al Jebel—we were to meet the plane there—where the hills on our right and the sands on our left converged. All afternoon we watched the tops of the sand dunes through our binoculars, getting steadily nearer until we were able to see the massed ramparts of the Rub'al Khali —"the Empty Quarter". A name, incidentally, not used by the local bedouin, who refer to the areas as "Ar Riml"—"The Sand".

Our various halts had made us late, and we soon realised that it would be a race against time to get there in time to meet the plane. We lost the race, but only just. The hills and the sands appeared to join ahead of us, and there was a prominent hill, which gave its name to the place. The plane caught us up when we were still a mile or so from our intended camp site, but it landed quite safely without our help, though it had to taxi the best part of a mile to catch us up.

At Khashm al Jebel there was no water, no sign of a building or any form of life. We had expected to come up with the trucks, which had set off earlier, but there was no sign of them. Apparently they had sidetracked and stopped at one of the HBL posts to rest out the hottest part of the day. Our own convoy had stretched over several miles, because, as time grew short, those of us who could, had pressed on in an attempt to beat the plane. Somewhere behind us we had left the two Pick-Ups and one of the Land-Rovers. Pat went off into the gathering dusk to look for them. Ian was in one of the Pick-Ups. So, unfortunately, was the cook.

Our camp site had a clean beauty. The sand was pale, almost white, and there were no signs of old camps, though others must have chosen the same place to halt. We refuelled the plane. After dark the stragglers came in. The day had not been particularly tiring, but the frequent halts had been frustrating and it had been very hot. However, we had covered 114 miles, and I was pleased to see how fresh everyone was, particularly as they had not had time to get acclimatised. We were glad when supper arrived and we were all in bed before nine. It was during the night that the trucks arrived, and, after a couple of hours, they set off again to get across the sands while it was cool. I hardly noticed the noise, and slept well.

We were up at four, ready to move before first light. The plane took off at five, when it was just light enough to see the ground clearly, though Mick said that he could hardly see his instruments. Once again Michael Crouch was the passenger, and one of the guides went with them as well. The rest of us started as soon as the aircraft was out of sight, and, at once, our troubles began. Don Stewart's driver, a small bow-legged man with a perpetual yawn, had had no experience of driving over sand. He bogged his Land-Rover at once, and continued to bog it on every possible occasion that day—not to mention a few occasions I would have thought impossible as well. The fitter and the soldiers in the rear Pick-Up were forced to stop each time to push him out, and we all had to lend a hand at one time or another. Don took it philosophically. None of us was allowed to drive the HBL vehicles, and, as he was unable to speak the driver's language, there was nothing he could do about it. Even the guides said that they could drive better than this driver, of whom more later.

The route started by winding between minor dunes, only a few feet high, but quickly climbed until we were travelling on the sands themselves. Here the dunes were taller. Pat, in the lead, had an inferior guide with him, which didn't help. There was no track to follow. It was a case of keeping direction as best we could. We saw no signs of old tracks, not even the one left by our own trucks which had started before us during the night.

We had had no breakfast, hoping to get over the worst of the sand in good time before it got too hot before stopping to eat. This was not to be. The good drivers picked their way carefully where the texture of the sand indicated that it was hardest and they got through without mishap. But, on the top of every sand ridge, we all had to stop while Don's vehicle, with its attendant Pick-Up, caught up.

The sands were red and yellow, ribbed in places, and in others scaled like fishes. The wind had left strange and beautiful patterns, and over them we could see the tracks of animals and insects. They were as easy to spot in the sand as they would have been in snow. At first the dunes followed no particular formation, and they lay like whales stranded in the jumbled sea of sand. This route led over an offshoot of the great sands, and, in a way it was the more difficult to cross, because the dunes had no dependable pattern. We couldn't drive along the valleys between them, but had to drive east no matter what direction they were lying.

Slowly we battled on. As it got hotter other cars began to bog, though not with the monotonous frequency of Don's. Over-heating troubled us as well and the vehicles, and their drivers, consumed vast quantities of water at the many halts. However it wasn't all loss. Every time we stopped, Don and Michael Woodford searched for shrubs and plants for their collections. Ian and Peter examined the sand for tracks. One never knew, there just might have been an oryx that way. We found traces of rim, Dorcas gazelle, foxes, hares and jerboas. We found the ruts made by snakes' bodies and everywhere were the delicate handprints of lizards. Dung beetles had left their distinctive marks among the other spoor, but of oryx there was no sign. On the flanks of the dunes Tribulus, and a form of Tamarisk, grew, but very little else. In places the plants looked fresh and green, but in others, where no rain had fallen, the roots and branches were as brittle and blackened as though they had been in a fire. The dunes grew bigger as we progressed, and they stood out in sharp reds and whites against the sky, changing now from blue to the yellow tinge of heat.

It became very hot indeed. Pat got bogged. Edith put down one of a series of paperback books which she had been reading imperturbably all the way from Mukalla, got out and pushed. Everyone pushed. The sand was hot—far too hot for the Europeans to walk on in bare feet, though not too bad for the Arabs whose feet were as tough as leather anyway. My car got stuck, too—the first, and only time, that Nassir fell from grace. He had shown himself to be an outstanding driver. Indeed when we did stick, it was because we were trying to get close to Don's car to help him.

The only vehicle which did not get bogged at all was Ian's Pick-Up, though it was an awesome sight. Often airborne, it bounced and clattered its aged way over dunes and across the soft patches in between, sometimes tilting at an alarming angle, sometimes landing on three wheels, sometimes on two. The only way to drive it was flat out. Providing it kept up its momentum it could get through. Qassim knew this. He also knew that if he did stick, it would be no easy matter to get free again, because he had two-wheel drive only. Time and again he forged clattering past the rest of us, with Mohammet and the rest of the staff hanging on as best they could, steam and a smell of burning wafting across from the suffering machine. Ian said later that he and the seat met only at intervals. At least he didn't have to push.

By eleven we had reached the worst. We were still unshaven and still breakfastless. Pat decided to pump up the tyres, which till then had been at reduced pressure, when the guide indicated that we were at the end of the soft sand. The guide was dead wrong. As soon as we moved off again, almost every vehicle stuck. When we caught up with the trucks shortly afterwards, we saw that one had broken down. A bearing had gone and there was nothing that could be done. The soldiers had put up an awning and were resting in the shade. Pat investigated and came to the depressing conclusion that the truck would have to wait until another bearing had been brought out from far-off Mukalla. Ian suggested that our plane be sent back to fetch it, but a decision was deferred for the time being.

Pat sent a wireless message to Thamud, our destination, asking for a truck to be sent out to take over the load from the broken-down vehicle. We pressed on with the cars into better conditions. The sand dunes ran in the direction we wanted to go so we were able to run down the hard white valleys between them. Soon we ran out of the dune country altogether, into an area of low stony hills. It was uncomfortable going for each car left a long column of choking white dust behind it. These hills gave way to mounds of sand concealing the roots of dead or living plants. We ploughed round each hummock, following a wide wadi. There were signs of recent rains. The ground was cracked and thirsty fissures gaped at the sun. Where the rain had fallen, mud remained. There was a smell of dampness in the air. Nassir shouted and pointed. We saw a lake. A small muddy lake, it was true but this time not a mirage, though in a few days it would have disappeared again.

Pat made for a place called Hassa, where there might be water from a water pump over an old oil company bore-hole, but when we got there we found that the pump was not working, part of it having been taken away to be mended. We stopped anyway on a stony hill nearby where we could catch the slight breeze which had got up.

We were putting up the flysheet from a tent to give us some shade, when the breeze changed to a sudden gale, knocking everything over and tearing one corner of the sheet. The gale disappeared as quickly as it had come, but the damage was done. We shaved, and had our breakfast-lunch at one in the afternoon. It had been quite a morning.

Don and his driver were not on speaking terms. Not that that made much difference, because they had no means of communication anyway.

A wash and some food made us all feel better, and with great difficulty we persuaded the staff to get a move on with their own lunch. We managed to get them moving by three, though it was obvious they were used to a more leisurely régime than ours.

Soon after we had started we passed another lake, and, in the distance, we saw one or two camels, the first living things we had seen in twenty-four hours. The sun moved with relentless slowness overhead and Peter got very burnt, particularly on his knees, so he wore a headcloth like an old lady's shawl over his lap. Evening came eventually and found us running along a well-defined track across a wide plain. Ian saw two gazelle, and I spotted a bustard. Ian and Musellim between them caught a dthub, an edible lizard growing up to two feet or more in length. They live deep in holes and are quite difficult to catch, because they can run as fast as a trotting man and always make a bee-line for their burrows.

The dthub is lawful food, it is said, because the Prophet was once entertained by a very rich, but very mean man. This man was so miserly that he produced a cat instead of a fatted calf for the Prophet's supper. But the guest, from whom nothing was hidden, called the cat forth from the pot, and it came out alive. Then the Prophet prayed to God that the man should get his just deserts. God answered his prayer and the man was turned into a dthub, which was made lawful eating.

We became very fond of dthubs, although we never ate one. They often broke the monotony of a day's hunt, and on many days were the only living creatures which we saw at all. Often we surprised several at once as they sat nodding at the entrance to their holes. They lived in colonies. Each dthub had its own area and we never saw a case of poaching. They had very clean habits and reserved certain parts of their territory for their bodily functions. Most of the ones we saw were an off-white colour, getting darker as they grew older, but there were some with brilliant yellow heads and yellow bodies.

If we came across one far enough from its hole, it was always worth chasing. Some of the Arabs would eat them, though not all. It added a touch of light relief to see the reptile, head down, tail up, scuttling across the ground like an angry fighting vehicle, pursued by one or other of the party. It is said that the female lays between fifty and sixty eggs at a time, and then returns to eat them all except for three, just before they are due to hatch.

Shortly after the dthub had been caught Peter and I were woken from our doze of weariness by a vicious clanking in the engine. Nassir switched off quickly. The fitter came up and diagnosed a burnt-out bearing. We agreed. The noise was unmistakable. We were only sixteen miles from Thamud and it was bitter to break down so near to our destination. Don stopped to see what was wrong, then he and the fitter set off to catch Pat, but he was travelling fast on the last lap, and they didn't come up with him until they had arrived at Thamud.

An HBL Corporal was left behind with us. We unpacked two of the chairs and sat down. It was remarkably peaceful after the day's labours. Night was upon us before we noticed it, but we were quite content. Though we had no food, the Arabs had some. There was plenty of water, and when Nassir returned from a hunt for firewood, there was the cheerful glimmer of a fire. Nassir proceeded to make khubz the bedouin way. He mixed flour and water into a ball with much slapping and patting, then when he felt that he had pummelled it sufficiently, buried the whole lot in the embers to cook.

He 'brewed up' as well, and having made tea for Europeans before, we were saved from the usual bedouin brew in which at least one large tin of milk is poured into the kettle before the tea has come to the boil. Nassir's tea was delicious. We only had a mug and a glass between the four of us and there was much polite argument before Peter and I agreed to use them first. The Arabs were determined that we should be their guests and treated us with the courtesy that this means in Arabia. I had the glass—a mixed blessing because I had to drink the tea while it was still scalding so that I could pass the glass on.

While we were savouring this Nassir turned our supper over once or twice in the cinders, keeping them well stirred and glowing. When it was ready the khubz was retrieved from the ashes and divided into four parts. Even Peter, who had watched the culinary methods with considerable suspicion, took his share gladly. We found the khubz very satisfying. It is certainly a form of food which goes a long way. We were very grateful for it that night. The Corporal then made the coffee served hot with ginger. It tasted wonderful.

After the coffee Nassir put on more water for tea and we sat and talked of the oryx which the two Arabs had seen, and of other travellers and British officers whom they remembered. They were surprised to learn that we didn't know them as well. Nassir had been the driver when the two oryx had been caught the previous year, and he was a mine of useful information. He said that one of the oryx had been followed for sixty miles, a statement that gave us food for thought. Later we suggested to Pat that it would be very helpful if Nassir stayed with us, but Pat had other duties for him, and we were forced to take Don's driver.

About eight we saw lights in the distance, well to the north of the track. We turned on our own lights, and signalled with my torch, but the vehicles went by several miles away without seeing us. At nine, quite content with our lot, we got out our beds. The desert was clean and silent, and there was a lot to be said for avoiding the bustle of setting up camp. The stars looked kindly down on us and we went happily to bed.

CHAPTER 8

THAMUD

"The well lining of rude stones courses, without mortar, is
deeply scored (who may look upon the like without emotion)
by the soft cords of many nomad generations."

Doughty

We were waked at midnight. The recovery party we had seen
earlier had got lost and returned to Thamud before again setting
out to find us. I was quite unwilling to get out of bed, but
stumbled up and helped to pack up and transfer our kit to another
Land-Rover. We were away, still half asleep, within minutes,
leaving our old car to be towed in more slowly.

We reached our camp at Thamud three-quarters of an hour
later. Ian appeared to find out what had delayed us, and the inde-
fatigable Mohammet got up to make tea. By half-past one we
were sound asleep again.

Next morning I saw that the camp had been pitched on the
new air-strip, on a black gravel plain between two wadis about
three miles from the fort. Ian decided to send the Piper back to
Mukalla to fetch the bearing for the broken-down truck; the
rest of us were to remain at camp that day, and go on again on
the morrow. It was a pleasant change not to have an early start
and, after the plane with Mick and Michael had taken off, we had
the day to ourselves. There was a rumour that the Grays, who
were staying in the fort, had a refrigerator. During the morning
I motored over there, and Edith gave me an ice-cold drink and
allowed me to leave our ration of beer to cool.

Thamud fort, which is garrisoned by the HBL, is a square,
functional building, painted dazzling white. It has one gateway,

and towers at the four corners of the walls. A few outhouses nestle outside the wall, one of them containing a bathroom. The fort is quite well appointed and there is even electricity. When Michael Crouch had been here, he had installed an air conditioner, but when Edith tried it out, all the lights went off. It was never tried again.

The well stands outside the fort. Apart from a few inscriptions in different parts of the country, it is the only trace of the Thamud people. The well mouth was in the centre of a mound, which itself gave some indication of the well's great age. I looked down it. It was lined with stone, and had obviously been reconditioned at some time. The stones were deeply scored by ropes. I couldn't see the bottom, and there was no way of telling its age. As I leant down, I felt strange sympathy for a people I had never known who had disappeared from the face of the earth almost without trace.

There is a tradition that the prophet Hudd cursed the people of Thamud, and swore that they would be wiped out without trace. He was very nearly completely successful. Hudd was entombed in the Wadi Maseila, which is an extension of the Hadhramaut, and his tomb is the holiest place in South Arabia, the object of an annual pilgrimage. Hudd has been connected with the Eber of Genesis, but all we know is that he was a prophet of the Ad tribe who, like the Thamud, were supposed to be a race of giants. His tomb marks the place where, it is said, when the prophet was being pursued by enemies, the rocks opened to receive him. The story adds that they did not completely close behind him and the cleft can still be seen. His camel was not included in the sanctuary arrangements and was turned to stone outside.

A little way from the fort was the house of the man who was to become one of the most important members of the expedition. This was Tomatum, a famous guide and desert guard. He is a man with considerable influence in the area. He had been engaged as our principal guide. While Tomatum was with us one of his young sons fell into the fire and was quite badly burned.

His family kept the news from him, in case it should worry him and affect his tracking ability.

The day passed quickly. There were many small jobs to be done and some of us caught up with our letter writing. Ian disappeared into one of the wadis to shoot birds for his collection. Occasional shots marked his inroads into the scant bird population. We took the opportunity to buy two goats for it was by no means certain that we would be able to buy them at Sanau. They were small white animals and bleated pathetically to each other to give themselves confidence.

In the evening we drove to the fort, and had a shower under the contraption which Michael Crouch had rigged up. It produced a deluge of ice-cold water every time a chain was pulled. It was most refreshing. After that we sat with the Grays and drank our beers, still frosty from the refrigerator. They tasted like nectar. We had rationed ourself to two a day to make them last us until the end of the trip. Cold beer never tastes sweeter than when it is drunk as the sun goes down after a hot, wearing day in the desert, and each can was very precious to us.

Next morning we were up at five and packed up and ready by seven-thirty, when the trucks were sent off. The rest of us waited until eight-thirty when the plane arrived back. On the way back from Mukalla, via an overnight stop at al Abr, they had landed by the broken-down truck and had been able to give the fitter the part he needed.

Once again we set off before the plane, which was to catch us up at Sanau. No one was quite sure where it could land, because the main strip was at least ten miles from the Sanau fort, and we wanted somewhere much nearer than that.

We were on the move by nine, driving along a very pretty wadi full of acacia trees and other vegetation. It was also full of dthubs taking their early morning constitutionals and I managed to catch one before it got to its hole. I only just caught it in time. It didn't dodge, and I was able to pick it up one-handed on the run. As no one had told me whether they had teeth or not, I clutched it round the waist. The dthub was passed to Musellim to look after.

Later it was photographed and finally eaten by Nassir to whom I gave it in return for his excellent supper at our breakdown camp.

We hadn't seen so much vegetation since we had left the Wadi Do'an. It was a very pleasant change, and we were making good time, too, along a reasonable track.

We had just passed over a small rise, when we heard shots behind us. We ran back to the rest of the convoy, which had halted, and was disgorging HBL soldiers. An ambush, I wondered as we ran, and I was reminded of Doughty's grim description,

Two chiefly are the perils in Arabia, famine and the dreadful-faced harpy of their religion; a third is the rash weapon of every Ishmaelite robber.

But only about three shots were fired. Three bedouin appeared from among the bushes, one older man and two young ones. They came up to us.

"Any news of rain?" they asked.

I remarked to Peter that it was a good thing that the English didn't discharge firearms every time they wanted to discuss the weather.

The three did not even need water and stood back placidly when we drove on. As recently as 1948, there had been a battle around the Thamud well between twenty-five Rashid and Mahra, and some hundred and fifty Abida raiders. Five had been killed. It is still not a country in which one can treat shots lightly.

We followed the fertile wadi almost all day, until the afternoon when we found ourselves running across a wide plain. There were black mounds over it, one or two of which looked as though they might have been ancient settlements, but we did not have time to investigate. The hills on either side of the plain were low and the wadi was very green, so that it was a disappointment not to see any living thing other than the dthubs. It should have been an ideal place for gazelle and their absence was depressing.

The country, in fact, looked very similar to that which appears in most American western films. There were sandstone bluffs, a limitless plain ahead of us and enough vegetation to conceal the United States Cavalry. But of the oryx—not a sign.

The HBL convoy straggled over several miles with Pat well in the lead, Edith immersed in her book beside him. Now and then someone would chase one of the more vulnerable-looking dthubs, but no more were caught that day. Some of the vehicles were again having overheating troubles.

At last we saw a gazelle and everyone's spirits rose. At least something lived in this empty plain.

When we reached Sanau Pat led us away northwards along the track which led to the main airstrip. We passed a lone low hill and halted. The ground was so flat that it looked as though the Piper could land anywhere about here. We chose a suitable spot and motored up and down it several times to see if there were any bumps, and to give the fliers something that would be easy to spot. At each end we turned in great circles to mark the limits of the strip.

We decided to camp under the lee of the small hill, which would give us some shelter if the wind brought dust-storms down on us. We marked out a place for our tents, one for the cookhouse and another for the vehicles. A good camp site is a very necessary thing, particularly if there is a strong prevailing wind as there is at Sanau. It is most important that vehicles are prevented from turning and disturbing the ground above the camp, and this always requires strict supervision, because some driver will always attempt to do just that. We also chose a place where there was some cover for our primitive sanitary arrangements. The Arab is quite as modest as the Englishman in this respect, except on beaches which seem to be exempt from their rules.

We planned to make Sanau our base camp. We knew the only other water source in the area in which we were going to work was at Habarut one hundred and fifty miles away on the border with Dhofar. We planned to put up our forward camp somewhere between the two places, and thus be able to draw water from both. Any oryx we caught were going to be stabled

All the lines of Shibam are vertical as though the only space
left was in the sky.

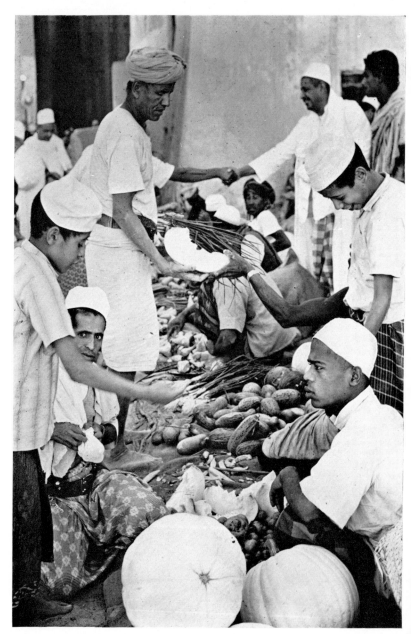

Shibam market.

at Sanau, where our carpenter would build stalls. The bulk of our stores would also be left at Sanau.

There was little that we could do that evening. We walked up the temporary air-strip we had chosen carrying shovels, and levelled off any small bumps. Then we waited for the plane to arrive. I sat on top of the hill with a smoke canister to indicate the position of the strip and the direction of the wind. Unfortunately when the plane arrived, the canister failed to ignite.

The plane circled. Ian threw shovelfuls of earth into the air—this time making sure that there was a wind. Mick saw the strip and was just going to land, when he saw Ian throwing this sand about, and thought that he meant he shouldn't land, so he sheered away and then came in at right angles to the strip. More shovel loads of sand were thrown up. By this time Mick was thoroughly puzzled, and the next time he decided to take no notice and landed parallel to the strip we had prepared. Luckily there were no obstructions, and he careered quite safely, though bumpily, almost up to the camp where he stopped.

Michael Crouch and Tomatum got out of the plane, looking rather relieved, and inquired the reason for Ian's antics. It was apparent that there was a certain lack of liaison between those on the ground and those in the air. We realised that landing was always going to be a problem in the desert, when the strip and the surrounding ground were indistinguishable, and when our smoke signals failed to work.

That night Michael Crouch went down with fever, probably a recurrence of the malaria which he had had earlier in the months. He retired to bed covered in blankets and a huge black sheepskin, and full of pills.

We sat in a tent and there was some alarm when two camel spiders, the size of saucers, came running around. However, we rallied and caught and bottled them. The other sport was dealing similarly with the enormous number of moths, attracted by the light of the pressure lamp.

That night, like most nights, we all slept out. Usually the wind dropped before evening, and none of us wanted to miss the satisfying feeling of sleeping under the desert sky in which, because of the lack of humidity, the stars are twice as bright as they are on the coast. Shooting stars spit and scatter like fireworks, and the moon, when it rises, casts a smooth white radiance over everything. These nights in the desert are experiences which no one should miss. They more than compensate for the hostility of the sun in the cloudless daytime sky.

It was cold that first night, cold enough for two blankets after midnight, and the men shivered under their inadequate covers. At dawn the sun and the flies raced together to wake us up. There was a great deal to be done before the sun really got up. All the rations were unloaded, and the boxes, sacks and cartons emptied on to the ground, so that we could see for the first time what we had been given by the contractor. It was not an encouraging sight. Mohammet shook his head, when he saw the limitations of the menu. Peter did more than shake his head. There were, I remember, 162 tins of tuna. There was also not nearly enough tinned fruit, and very little variety in anything. There were some luxuries like oyster soup (which later caused Ian acute discomfort), but there was also a huge pile of processed pork meat.

We planned to take fourteen days' supplies forward with us, and Mohammet began to separate what we wanted. The contractor's man complained that half a sack of rice was missing from their rations, and we suspected it must have gone the way of most of the expedition's rope, and have been extracted in error from the loads at Thamud or al Abr. Neither of these losses was serious. The most serious deficiency was the amount of lemonade powder (known as "jungle juice") which had been brought. We needed that to conceal the horrors of the local water. It came from a well which produced good clear water—but with one snag in it—it contained ten per cent Epsom Salts. A second well, which was used when the pump broke down, was said to contain eighteen per cent. As it turned out, none of us was seriously troubled by it, rather inconvenienced at one time or another. However, we were not in a part of the world where one could be snobbish about water. Peter told me that he had never seen Ian drink so much on any of their trips in Kenya, and he himself claimed to be drinking it for the first time for a quarter of a century.

Ian and Michael went up to the fort, where the storerooms, attached to the fort, were going to be turned into our stalls. They found that the mason, whom we were due to meet there, instead of waiting for us, had set off on a camel for Thamud, and someone would have to go to try to find him. It was at Sanau, too, that it was discovered that the carpenter was not the one who had practised putting the crates together in Mukalla, and Ian had to teach him again from scratch.

The HBL Mulazim (Lieutenant) proved difficult, and would not do anything to assist in the building of the stalls, refusing to remove his stores from one of the rooms, which did not belong to the HBL anyway. However, Pat talked to him over the wireless and ordered him to co-operate. We found few cases like that which marred the general spirit of co-operation, although the feeling in Sanau was definitely pro-Qatari. The Arabs could not see anything wrong in hunting the oryx to extinction. Later another Mulazim took over and things were much better.

Sanau fort was like Thamud in appearance, but if anything, more desolate. Apart from the fort, which was only the size of a six-bedroomed house, and its few outhouses, there was nothing but the wells, and half a dozen tattered bedouin tents, which were not really tents at all, but rude shelters, open on one side. They were squalid in the extreme. They might have been romantic out in the clean desert, but not among the filth which surrounds a well in constant use.

Sanau is backed by light grey hills against which the fort stands out like a lump of sugar. The hills are flat, desiccated and produce nothing but the blinding reflection of the sun.

We pitched two tents to act as storerooms, one for ourselves and one for the HBL, and slowly began to sort out our difficulties. The carpenter made up for his ignorance with his keenness. The mason was tracked down and persuaded to turn his camel round. We had ordered six lactating goats some weeks before, in case we found unweaned oryx calves, but the Mulazim hadn't brought them. An old woman who could supply them was tracked down some miles from the fort and an order placed with her. Somehow everything was done that day. The carpenter started work, the tents were filled with our stores, and the vehicles maintained and prepared for the next move.

We were, of course, shooting (or rather hunting) in the dark. There had been no reports for some time of sightings of the oryx, and we had no means of knowing if there were any left in the area.

CHAPTER 9

IN MAHRA COUNTRY

"Scholars believe that the Mahra are descended from the
ancient Habasha, who colonized Ethiopia as long ago as the
first millenium B.C."

Wilfrid Thesiger

Sanau is in the Mahra country, between the Qaʻiti state and the
Dhofar border, stretching north up to the Saudi Arabian frontier.
It is a land that has never been properly explored. The locust
control are the only people who have penetrated it to any great
extent. The Mahra have their own language, which is of Semitic
origin. Bertram Thomas compiled a vocabulary, but there is a
great field of research open to anyone interested. Its connections
with the other languages spoken in Dhofar, such as Shahari,
which I once attempted to learn, have not been fully understood.
It is the language which the Minaeans are said to have used before
the days of Islam.

The Mahra have peculiar customs. The women are not
allowed to milk camels or cows. In the old days men were cir-
cumcised the day before their wedding. Happily for modern
bridegrooms this seems to have been a custom which has not
been maintained, but an equally barbarous one was certainly in
existence when Thomas explored the Mahra country some years
ago. He describes some of the hair customs of the women.

Within a month after marriage has taken place, as a sign that
she is a maiden no longer, a long strip of skin about three-
eighths of an inch wide is removed with a razor, like a parting
through the centre of the head, so that the hair never grows

there again—a scalping operation extremely painful, and sometimes fatal.

Being married must have been a mixed blessing in the old days and one wonders how many partners survived the operation before and after the ceremony.

The experts had painted a gloomy picture of what might happen if the Piper were forced down in Mahra country. The oil prospectors have at least a company of soldiers as an escort. Soon, no doubt, the country will be opened up, and there will be forts and political officers in the Mahra, but, at the moment, it retains the exciting challenge of the unknown.

The Sultans of Socota are the recognised rulers of the Mahra state, but have never been able to bring much peace or prosperity to the country, preferring, probably wisely, to stay safely on their island. The present Sultan has only visited the country once. His visit was made only recently and was such an unprecedented act that all the sections of the tribe stopped their interminable bickering for at least a day. However, the new-found spirit of goodwill did not last very long.

Typical is the story of two important members of the tribe who went to Socotra to pledge allegiance to the Sultan. They were royally entertained by the ruler, but he happened to mention that an old Mahra woman had recently died on the island, leaving an inheritance. He asked the two men whether they knew the old lady's relations so that they could be paid the money, some four thousand shillings.

The two men instantly smelt profit, and said that, by a curious coincidence, they happened to be from the old lady's sub-section. They would see that the right people got the money. The Sultan was delighted to have solved the problem with so little trouble and paid the money over. One of the men, Sulaim bin Dameish, bought masses of rations with this money, and brought them with him on the same plane which was bringing the Sultan on the state visit mentioned above. At Thamud he had the rations unloaded for disposal to his own advantage later. When the party reached Sanau the other conspirator, Schlomat Ali (an interesting name with Hebrew connections) asked for his cut, and was told that he could sing for it—there being less honour among thieves in the Mahra than elsewhere. Schlomat complained to the Sultan, and told him what had happened. The Sultan was so angry that he hurled his coffee cup at the wall and impounded the rations. His face had been blackened and he was furious. All the Mahra thought it a great joke.

This same Sulaim was also responsible for another oft-told tale in the area. A locust control man had one day mentioned that he admired the way the Mahra smoked their tobacco—in old cartridge cases with a hole pierced at the end. Sulaim collected a mixture of camel dung and straw, filled his pipe and offered it to the man, who accepted. It nearly killed him.

The Mahra are generally called after their mothers, not their fathers. Our guide Tomatum who was of the Mahra, was an exception to the rule. He was called after tomatoes of which his father had been inordinately fond. He was only half Mahra anyway. Childbearing is a simple thing among the Mahra. The women work up to the day of the birth. They bear the child in the quadruped position, under a tree or in a cave, with sometimes the assistance of another woman to help them to stand up afterwards. This probably accounts for the high infant mortality rate but the women are back at work the next day.

On our first morning at Sanau we found hundreds of camels around the well, with more of the highly-disciplined goats we had first come across at Husn al Abr. The Mahra women we saw were veiled and it was impossible to see whether they matched the Saar for beauty. Later we learned there were two mad women at Sanau. One was a young girl of seventeen or so, who showed an alarming tendency to tear off her clothes at any moment, and the other, much older, thought she was a man— and an HBL soldier at that. Both were treated with the usual kindness which the Arab will always show for the mentally afflicted, providing he or she is not violent.

The Mahra drawing water at the well were a wild looking lot

with tousled thatches of hair, shining teeth, and thin muscular bodies. They were quite friendly, though reserved. Perhaps because there were many camels patiently waiting their turn, and they had no time to pass the time of day.

We left Sanau at six-thirty in the morning for the Wadi Mitan, eighty-five miles away, where we were going to set up an advance camp. We knew there was an airstrip there. Edith and Pat Gray were going with us on their way to Habarut, the last of the HBL posts which Pat wished to inspect. We took with us Michael's Pick-Up, an HBL Pick-Up, two Bedford Model R trucks and two Land-Rovers, one of which was fitted with a wireless.

It was necessary for us to rearrange our travelling positions, and still preferring to travel in the open, I elected to travel in the back of one of the trucks with two goats. Abu Darabis, the stout sergeant in charge of transport made repeated efforts to get me to travel in front in the stuffy cab. At each stop I had to explain that I preferred the rear of the truck, where I could lie on the baggage, and see all that there was to be be seen. He and most of the soldiers thought I was a little touched.

The track ran east over very bare stony ground with wide unbroken horizons. We saw the usual dthubs, and a baby gazelle, which ran parallel with the truck for a brief moment, giving me a good view of its gracefulness. All went well until the driver of my truck failed to see a bump and we went over it with such a jolt that the front spring was broken. Everything was thrown into disorder in the back, and the generator engine bounced on to one of the goat's feet. There was an agonised bleat from it, and a rush by the HBL and myself to release it.

It would take at least an hour to change the spring, and Pat was anxious to press on. We unloaded some of the tents, the only thing which the truck was carrying that we would need immediately for shade in our new camp, and reloaded them on to our one remaining truck. We left the broken truck and the fitter to follow on when the spring had been replaced.

Ian made room for me beside him in the cab of the Pick-Up. I enjoyed travelling with Ian or Peter. They both had an enormous

fund of amusing stories about big game hunting, or about the
Safaris which Peter had organised, and the sort of people who
went on them. Both of them had travelled in most parts of the
world, and both had been soldiers and sailors before working
together in the Game Department. Now they were on opposite
sides of the fence. Ian was conserving animals and issuing licences
for their shooting, while Peter was responsible for providing the
maximum amount of game for his clients. It did not stop them
from being great friends, or from going on trips together whenever they could. Both had happily given up their valuable leave
to come on what might be a wild-goose chase for oryx.

Qassim, the Pick-Up driver, had lost a good deal of his
spivishness, and he had shown himself to be a good, if over-
exuberant driver. But on this part of the journey he had an off
day and got well and truly stuck going through a wadi with a
soft sandy bed. The necessary spell of digging did nothing to
lessen his contempt for the other drivers, who were quite beneath
the notice of a Yafai'.

Yafai's are among the warlike races of the world. Their only
export has been fighting men, who have provided the mercenary
armies of Hyderabad as well as of Arab states. Occasionally they
have taken over the states which were employing them, and the
Qa'iti state itself was ruled by a Yafai' family. The trouble with
Qassim's driving was that he despised the bumps as much as he
despised the other drivers and potholes were beneath his notice.

Despite this mishap we reached the camp in the Wadi Mitan
earlier than we had expected. We pitched our camp on clear
ground on a slight rise, where we hoped to catch any breeze.

Pat and Edith, who was still cheerfully reading, departed towards Habarut. They took with them the wireless truck, which
meant that we would be out of touch with the world until they
returned. They expected to be away only a day and would leave
us the wireless on their return. They left behind a section of HBL
to keep an eye on us.

It was time for the plane to arrive. Ian and I walked about
looking for the strip, but were unable to find it. The ground was

completely flat in all directions and covered with tufts of yellow grass. Apart from one or two lumps where sand had built up around the roots of shrubs, and one or two dthub holes, there were no obstacles. The plane was on time. This time the smoke canister worked perfectly, but, unfortunately, the wind was far from constant. Every time Mick made his approach, the column of smoke billowed out in a new direction, at one stage obscuring altogether the place where we hoped he would land.

As usual Mick brought the plane in to a perfect landing without any assistance from the ground party.

The truck with the broken spring also turned up. After the driver had had a rest, we sent it on to Habarut to pick up water for we had had word that there were twenty-six empty drums there which we could borrow. They would solve our water problems, at least temporarily. It was now 1 May and we were on our own for the first time and ready to start.

PART 3

"The Oryx owes its continued existence in Arabia to its ability to live in places that are inaccessible to the bedouin on account of their waterless character."

Cheesman

CHAPTER 10

THE WADI MITAN

"Behold lightning in the far distance,
May its bounty fall in Umm al Hait,
Continuous and flowing rain
Flowing along between sand and stream course
Until it pass from Bu Warid onwards . . ."
Bait Kathiri song

We were camped on the steppe which divides the mountains of the Jol, north of the Wadi Hadhramaut, from the sands of "the Empty Quarter". We were confined in our area of search by the border to the east, and by the great sands in the north. To the south and west we had unlimited room to hunt. We knew, however, that no oryx would be likely to venture far from the sands towards the coast, which ran roughly east-west over two hundred miles to the south of us. There had been no favourable reports to encourage us to go westwards. It was in the steppe area between the sands which could no longer support the oryx, and the more populated edge of the mountains that we must search. Ian worked out that it gave us an area of six thousand square miles.

Each year as the weather gets hotter in the spring, the bedouin, who have been grazing their camels and their flocks in the sands move towards the water holes, either at Habarut, Sanau or Thamud, or even further towards the mountains. They cross the steppe and spend the summer along the fringe of the mountains because only there can they find the permanent water without which their animals and themselves could not exist. Behind them come the oryx and the rim, both searching not for water, but for fresh pasture, where there has been rain, and for shade.

It is said that rain falls on an average once every fourteen years in any one spot, sometimes in a few showers, sometimes in a sudden storm. Infrequently there are floods, when the monsoon strikes the mountains further north than usual, and a torrent washes down the wadi until it loses itself in the sand. Vegetation can exist on that water for years afterwards, and there had been one such flood two years earlier down the Wadi Mitan, from which we hoped to benefit.

We could only hope the Qatari murderers had left enough oryx for them to make the spring migration this year.

The steppes consist of wide grey plains which are covered in places by a sparse yellow grass. After rain and from a distance one has the impression of being on Salisbury Plain. There are low grey hills, patches of gypsum, rough rocky gullies and wide wadis, with either a gravel bottom or a sandy one. Both are treacherous for vehicles. They are filled with hummocks and tussocks where the plentiful scrub has taken root, and they form an obstacle to fast travel. There are variations, of course, and each of our hunts was over slightly different country, but the chief memory, which all of us retain, is of the yellow plains cut with bush-filled wadis, usually in just the place where we did not want to be impeded.

Navigating the Piper was going to be a problem even with the aids which we had brought, and I could understand why the first pilot had turned down the job. Mick Gracie, though not claiming to be expert in desert navigation, seemed quite unimpressed by the difficulties. Nevertheless he was not able to fly and navigate at the same time and we were going to be forced to rely on our directional beacon to a great extent. Events that day were to prove that relying on machines might entail many hazards. As we assembled our equipment to start work in earnest a whole series of disasters occurred.

We had already discovered at Sanau that the high frequency wireless ground station was out of action. It had been assembled in Kenya with ten-amp fuses, instead of the fifteen-amp it required, and as a result was useless. We hadn't worried too much about that because the plane would be able to talk to the HBL, who used sets on the same wavelengths as the aircraft. But when Ian and Mick, with Tomatum as navigator, set off to fly down as far as the sands, to get an idea of the country, and to look for oryx, Mick found that his high frequency set was not working any more. While they were up, the beacon was unpacked from its crate and its aerials rigged. The charging engine, which was to drive it was also prepared and filled with petrol. It was found to have a leak. Peter managed to solder this. The charging engine then worked well, but the beacon didn't. It pushed out far more power than it should, and looked as though it was about to explode. Sadly Don switched it off. None of us knew the first thing about beacons. That was that!

So far, out of the items which we had brought from Kenya, the catching car, the ground wireless, the air wireless and the beacon had all let us down. And we had not even begun to look for the oryx.

Ian's report when he got back was more encouraging. Where one of the wadis drained into the sands, the floods of two years ago had left a green fertile patch of ground, which Tomatum said would attract oryx if anything would. They had seen about eighteen rim which had fled in all directions at the noise of the aircraft.

Still we all felt rather depressed that morning with all the mechanical set-backs. It hadn't been a good start.

Ian, however, started carefully preparing the catching poles. These consisted of lengths of aluminium, which could be bolted together giving an optimum operating length of thirteen foot six. In the butts there were lead counterweights, and the poles were light, flexible and very strong. To each pole was attached a running noose by means of pieces of cotton and tape.

The catching team was to consist of four people. The driver of the Pick-Up would be Peter Whitehead, who could be relied upon to anticipate the animal's movements. He had had plenty of experience in catching animals in Africa, but he was going to find it rather different in a vehicle without the small turning circle and powerful acceleration of the catching car.

At al Abr Peter had done what he could to modify the Pick-Up. Supports had been welded on the back for the two men who would have to stand there, and to which the catching poles could be attached. But there was nothing that could be done to improve the vehicle's performance except to clean out the petrol system, so this was done.

The car was not the only machine which needed its petrol system overhauling. The Piper was found to have both water and dirt in its tanks and Mick had to drain these. It was lucky that the fault was spotted in time, because the plane could not now make a forced landing. It had no means of letting us know where it was, or what was wrong. I had a look at the wireless in it, but my knowledge was far too limited and I could not locate the fault. To take out the set for a more thorough examination would involve taking out a large part of the inside of the cockpit. We decided to leave it as it was.

Lunch was not a very cheerful meal and it wasn't improved when Mohammet reported that Abdulla was refusing to obey orders. He was the bearer Michael had engaged because he felt sorry for him, and there was now a first-class row between the two. It ended in Abdulla being sacked. He was no loss. He had already proved to be bone-idle and very argumentative.

The thought of being sacked infuriated him. "I might die on the road," he said. He got little sympathy. "I've got friends in Aden who will fix you if I do," he told Michael. We were not impressed. We gave him ten days' rations, and, with the advance of pay he had already got from the contractor, he was really doing very well out of us. Pat could take him back the next day, at least as far as al Abr.

It looked like the expedition's black day, but in the afternoon things began to improve. The Grays returned from Habarut and brought exciting news. They had found Mabkhaut bin Hassana, one of the best guides of the Eastern area, just going on leave and had stopped him. He had told Pat that his son had recently seen

The oryx settled down well, and were later transferred to the
Phoenix Zoo in Arizona.

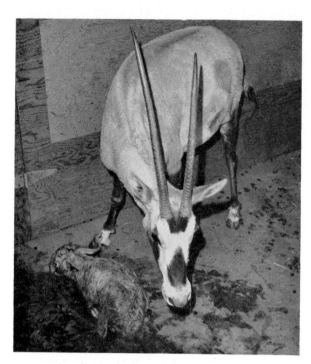

The birth of our first calf.

The success of the expedition can be judged by the health and happiness of the oryx family.

tracks of oryx which had been made after the last Qatari raid. The tracks had been of two animals. He had agreed to postpone his leave to act as a guide and was coming on with our water truck. He would be with us that night, or next day.

We now had the two best guides of all with us, and their knowledge of the different parts of the area would be complementary. The atmosphere in the camp brightened. We now knew that there were still oryx to be caught. It was up to us, and with Tomatum and Mabkhaut we had given ourselves the best possible chance of success. The disappointments of the morning were forgotten. Edith took photographs of some of the expedition, then she and Pat said goodbye and departed on the long road back to Mukalla, taking Abdulla with them. They took a lot of mail, and the first of Ian's reports for the Society.

We were really on our own. The HBL wireless was our only link with the outside world.

In the evening, when it was a little cooler, we set off with spades, hoping to dig up some desert mice for our collection. We tried several likely-looking holes, but without any luck. They were all deserted, except for an occasional baleful lizard, which strongly objected to being disturbed. We walked a long way before we gave up in disgust. Omar said that it was too dry and that all the animals had left to find a more fertile area. But there was plenty of grass and shrub about, and I think that there must have been some other reason. The holes were not easy to dig, because they branched into a network of tunnels and dead-ends, and it was difficult to uncover the whole system. Indeed, once or twice, the animals may have been laughing at us from some further tunnel which we had failed to unearth in the sandy soil.

Dusk came on quickly as we walked slowly back. The party working on the plane finished at the same time, and we walked back together towards the tents, where a pressure lamp gave out a bright welcoming light. We were able to wash and drain away the dirt and tiredness of the day. We allowed ourselves a pint or two of water for washing, and with care this went a long way. We gathered round the table and drank our ration of Allsopps,

FOTU 8

or our Sanau water liberally disguised with whisky. A pleasant ceremony.

While we were sitting there the truck from Habarut arrived. It brought not twenty-six drums, as we had expected, but nine. There had been a miscount at Habarut apparently, although it was difficult to see how anyone could count nine and make the answer seventeen more. So our water problems remained. We were able to work on the basis of three gallons a day per man—which may sound a lot, but wasn't in the heat in which we worked, and we had to allow for the thirsty vehicles. We could, of course, have managed with much less, and at times we thought that we would have to. One cannot take chances when the nearest supply is six hours away.

We were none too well supplied with petrol either, since we had not been able to bring much forward in the two trucks from Sanau. Ian decided to send a truck back there to fetch both petrol and water.

That night a space satellite passed overhead. The Arabs were quite excited by it but they got used to it on subsequent nights. Personally, I felt sad that the last unspoilt pleasure of the desert, the nights of solitude beneath the constellations seemingly so close above our heads, were solitary no longer, with the Americans or Russians trespassing among the stars.

The next day Peter and Don set off with Tomatum and Mabkhaut north-westwards to look for tracks. The rest of us continued to get everything ready. We had our first sick man. Michael's self-effacing garage-hand was suffering from acute dysentery. Michael Woodford was the nearest thing to a doctor that we had, and he had brought a large selection of pills out from England. He began his career of pill presenter, which later was to gain for him a great reputation at Sanau. Someone suggested that he might be struck off the vet's register for unbefitting conduct—treating humans—but he appeared to enjoy the change of having patients who could answer back.

Ian took his gun and set off up the wadi, looking for birds to add to his collection, and I went off to look for mammals. I spent a long time digging fruitlessly at what appeared to be fresh holes with fresh tracks going in and none coming out. In the sand around the clumps of vegetation in the small sandy wadis among the grey hills, I was able to distinguish the spoor of jerboa, mice, lizards and snakes. I left the snakes alone and hoped that they would offer me the same courtesy. There are twenty-nine species of snake in the Protectorates and nine of these are dangerous. Unfortunately I didn't know which they were.

I didn't seem to be having any luck, but occasional shots from the wadi indicated that Ian was hot on the trail of some luckless fly catcher, or of some other small bird. As the morning got hotter, so my enthusiasm waned. I sat for some time on one of the hills. Apart from Ian I could see nothing moving in any direction. I made my way back to camp.

Ian returned soon afterwards, bewailing the fact that he hadn't got his usual skinner with him. He began to skin the birds in the tent. A wind got up and blew feathers over us, and the heat dried the corpses more quickly than Ian could work on them. He plucked at the dessicated bodies, and curses, feathers and powder filled the air.

The sun was vicious and we found that water gave us little relief. The HBL did not differentiate between petrol and water drums, and the Habarut water was far from the delectable liquid which Michael Crouch had described in such glowing terms and to which we had all been looking forward. Instead we discovered that it had a high octane content, which only liberal application of lemonade powder could hide. The taste of petrol struck when the water was half-way down the throat, and it caused us to gulp like goldfish and then fill the tent with monumental belches. It would have been dangerous to have struck a match at that moment. We agreed that there was little to chose between Sanau salts and Habarut petrol.

One of the goats had been killed and Mohammet made an excellent curry out of it. Even the food tasted vaguely of petrol, but we rapidly became accustomed to it. We kept an ear cocked for the sound of our reconnaissance party returning. They had left equipped to spend the night out, but they had been told to return at once if they found anything. At a quarter-past two we heard the sounds of their engines, and soon they came into sight.

The news was very good. The tracks of two, or possibly three, animals had been found, and one was so recent that it looked as though it might only be a day old. It was only thirteen miles from our camp site. The party had motored on and found another track, about three weeks old, between thirteen and sixteen miles from the camp. Don and Peter had continued searching and further away had found droppings and tracks, which the guides said were ten days old. No oryx had been seen, but they had put up half a dozen rim.

This was what we had been waiting for. Quickly Ian decided that we should move our camp forward to a more central position. Tomatum suggested that we should move twenty-seven miles to a place where there was a prominent wadi junction, and where there was a place suitable for the Piper to land.

This was agreed. Everyone was gripped by a sense of urgency. We packed hurriedly. We couldn't take everything with us, because one of our two trucks was on its way to Sanau, so we decided to leave three of the soldiers as a guard with a tent and all the useless kit such as the beacon and the wirelesses. Most of the petrol would have to be left, as well, until it could be collected.

The little convoy was away by four-thirty, led by Ian and guided by Don and Peter. Mick, Tomatum and I were left to finish the stowing of the kit, and follow on in the Piper. At five we were just leaving when the first bedouin arrived. I was surprised that none had turned up before. He had no news and we had no idea what he was doing. He was alone and on foot. We left him sitting happily around the beginnings of a fire with the soldiers.

It was my first flight in the Piper. Since the wireless had broken down, we had been using Tomatum as our only navigational aid. He was the only one of the Arabs who was willing to entrust himself to the frail machine, and even he did so with reservations, relying on prayer to see him through. This meant that either Michael Crouch, or I had to fly as well, as we were the only Arabic speakers in the party and we alone could pass on Tomatum's directions to Mick.

There was very little room in the plane. It was so light that one man could lift the tail. The two passengers sat side by side behind the pilot secured by one safety strap. Tomatum and I climbed in. Luggage had to go on our laps. There was no room anywhere else. Mick saw that we were safely, if uncomfortably, installed, and climbed in himself. We could now see nothing in front except for Mick's back. By craning one's neck it was also possible to see the dials and some of the controls.

Taking off was always amusing because Mick couldn't see much forward until the tail came up, and any bumps, ridges and dthub holes had to be taken as they came. We took off into what wind there was and I exchanged a sickly grin with Tomatum. We headed north-west, the plane climbing slowly. Even with its small load, it was heavily laden. We cruised along between seventy and ninety miles an hour, the earth scarcely seeming to move beneath us, and I was able to see how bare the steppes were. It was going to be very easy country to get lost in. As we gained height, the sands came into view, away to the north, the dunes piled high, sharp and dark-shadowed in the setting sun. They looked like a very choppy sea.

We followed a wadi, which stretched out like a black finger across the grey steppes. It was a good landmark, and easily distinguishable from the air. We saw the line of trucks after we had been flying for twenty minutes. They moved slowly like raindrops down a windowpane, leaving behind them a smear of dust. For a long time we didn't seem to be gaining on them, but eventually we caught them up, and Tomatum began to look out for the camp site. Then he pointed down and said that we should land. I passed this on to Mike.

Communications in the plane were somewhat primitive, and consisted of a length of rubber tube, which was usually used for filling the oil tank. One end of this was placed by the speaker's mouth and the other end in the listener's ear. If one didn't mind a mixture of speech, petrol and oil in one's ear, it worked, though, as I discovered, not very efficiently.

Tomatum's signs might have been perfectly understood by a camel, but to me there did not appear to be any difference between his signs for left, right and straight on. I tried to pass on the directions. Mick's neck got redder, and he became rather cross, because every time he prepared to land on a particular piece of ground, Tomatum saw something he liked better. Finally, Mick gave up and picked his own spot. The ground was not nearly as flat as it looked, and there was a series of very pronounced ripples in it. We bounced on the crest of one, and landed sickeningly just short of the next. I found this most alarming, but Mick and Tomatum seemed to be used to it. Nevertheless, when we had finally stopped, Tomatum gave a broad grin and the thumbs-up sign. He wasn't the only one who was feeling relieved.

The trucks had caught us up while we had been looking for a place to land. I found that we had stopped where the wadi forked. This could be clearly seen from the air. It was already getting dark, and there was no time to do more than unpack the beds before night fell and the persistent satellite passed over our heads.

The actual hunting party was over twenty strong, including the seven Europeans. The Arabs were Mohammet and his assistant; Michael Crouch's crew of three; two HBL sergeants, one a bedu always grumbling, the other Abu Darabis, in charge of transport, a cheerful fat Negro as good as the other was bad; four soldiers, the HBL drivers and a signaller.

In addition, there were the two guides, so vital to our endeavour. We were to discover that they could not have been more different in character. Tomatum was the more sophisticated, with more experience of working with Europeans. Political officers liked to employ him. We rarely saw him depressed. He was cheerful in every situation. He had a strong personality and the other Arabs instinctively deferred to him although he had no tribal standing, being half Mahra. In his younger days he had been a conspicuous companion of *Bin Dualin*—The Cat—the most notorious raider of his time. Tomatum had also seen service with Bin Abdut, the last of the Kathiri robber barons in the Hadhramaut, who is now living in Singapore. Once Abdut had impulsively offered a prize for the taking of any life belonging to an enemy tribe he was fighting at that time. Tomatum had spent one night making his way stealthily through the date gardens round an enemy village. At considerable personal risk, he had got close enough to the enemy stronghold to shoot a donkey and a dog. He had then returned to claim his reward, which Abdut was forced to pay, no doubt bitterly regretting the looseness of phraseology he had used to make his challenge, for, of course, he had wanted human lives.

I have never met a tribesman of note, who wore less clothing than Tomatum. He was always bareheaded, and he seldom put on more than a futah, leaving his body uncovered. This was most unusual, but certainly gave him great freedom of movement. In the early morning he wrapped his green shawl about him, and sat hunched like an old Granny, waiting for the sun to bring him to life.

He was very knowledgeable about the sands and the animals which inhabited them, and he was able to give us a great deal of useful information about the oryx, all of which he had gained through his own experiences either hunting or when acting as a guide. He could tell the age of a spoor at a glance, could identify the animal, its age and its sex, and could usually say what it had been doing. He was quite tireless once a trail had been found, and was probably the key man of the expedition.

Mabkhaut, on the other hand, was a much simpler person, older and inclined to be crotchety. He wheezed and grunted whenever he had to climb in or out of the Land-Rover. He was often very tired, and inclined to lose interest. However, his reading of the tracks was as expert as Tomatum's, and when a fresh spoor was discovered, he shed his years and his fatigue, and trotted along the trail almost as nimbly as Tomatum.

Mabkhaut was of the Bait Imami section of the Ruashid

Kathir. He said his prayers almost every time we halted, crouching low over the ground, after some perfunctory ablutions with sand. He was always fully clothed as a good Moslem should be, and I never saw him without his head cloth and his gold agal. He carried a knife in his cartridge belt and an old rifle, which never appeared out of its cover, and which he eventually took to leaving behind. This was unusual. An Arab and his rifle are not usually so easily parted.

The combination of the two guides was as near perfect as one could wish, for the one complemented the other. Tomatum could have worked alone, but it would have been much harder for him. Mabkhaut needed the example and encouragement of a younger man to overcome his tiredness and Tomatum was there to provide that. Both knew different areas better than the other, and this, too, was a great help.

When we had our vehicles assembled we were as ready to hunt as it was possible to be.

CHAPTER II

THE SEARCH

"The Wothayhi falls only to the keenest hunter."
                                                          Doughty

Our first day of hunting was a long and exhausting day. We were up before four, a good hour before dawn. We found that Michael Crouch was suffering from migraine, and we were forced to leave him behind. This was the first of many early starts. They became so much part of the normal routine that we thought nothing of them. Up at four and to bed by nine became our routine. That first morning it was difficult to get up, particularly for the Arabs. The night had been unusually cold, and they had suffered from lack of blankets and had stayed up most of the night talking to keep themselves warm. I was cold in my down sleeping bag so I couldn't blame the Arabs for being sluggish with cold.

Some days later we discovered that Mabkhaut, with the typical improvidence of the bedouin and with a fine reliance on the Almighty, had brought nothing at all. We had to look round for something with which he could cover himself.

We had hoped to leave by four-thirty, but the Arabs were not ready until nearly five. The hour before dawn is not a kind hour, and they felt the lash of our tongues as we waited impatiently to start. By five it was completely light, and in another half-hour the sun would be up.

We were still finding our feet and Ian was tolerant of the delay, but it was vitally important that we should gain an early start. As was later proved, chasing animals after nine-thirty could have fatal results. The hours around dawn were precious, and we could not afford to waste them.

Peter Whitehead drove the Pick-Up, with Ian beside him. Don and Mick were in the back ready to unfasten the catching poles which were attached to either side of the vehicle. Michael Woodford and I travelled in the Land-Rover, with Tomatum and Mabkhaut, and we led the way. In the rear came the Model R, with the two travelling crates lashed to its sides, and a party of men perched on the crates, or on the cab. They were needed to lift and carry the crates, if we used them.

This was to be the pattern for all our hunts, though people changed vehicles on different days. Only Mick remained true to the back of the catching car, quite the most uncomfortable position. He became a much-loved figure of fun for the Arabs, and a morale booster for us, for, however depressed and weary we felt, he always looked in even worse condition as he hung grimly on with his moustache streaming behind him in the wind. Often he appeared to be airborne, when the truck hit a bump, but he refused to give up his chosen position and seemed to derive some strange pleasure from the discomfort.

We led the way out of the camp and drove east, picking our way across a branch of the wadi and then on to the steppe beyond. The country, which was to become so familiar, unfolded slowly. From the moment we left camp, the guides were on the look out for spoor, and that meant restricting our speed to ten miles an hour, or less.

We drove over a stony, undulating plain, with low wind-rounded hills light grey in colour but with scars of white gypsum —perfect camouflage for an oryx. Every white dot we saw had to be investigated with field glasses. The surface of the steppe was firm and provided no difficulties for the normal driver.

Unfortunately ours was far from normal. He was the one who had given us so much trouble coming across the sand, and he was quite the worst driver that I have ever come across. It soon became evident that he had bad eyesight, and as the days passed the guides were to become more and more exasperated. They would point out distant objects to which he should drive, and then a few seconds later that he would veer away, travelling at right angles to the way they had indicated. Besides being blind he was deaf, either naturally or by intent, and he would never respond to orders from the two guides or from Michael or myself. Simple words like halt had to be shouted two or three times before he would react, and by that time it was probably too late. This menace also seemed to have a perpetual and unattractive yawn, and an insatiable thirst. In addition his notions of the workings of a gearbox were rudimentary. He always accelerated when changing up; if when changing down, he engaged a gear cleanly, it was a matter of congratulation all round. Whenever we came to a soft patch we stuck owing to his inability to change down. He never improved and caused more bad temper among the members of the expedition than anything else, and I felt sorry for Tomatum and Mabkhaut, who always did their best. Tomatum once remarked, when the driver had done something particularly stupid, "I may be only a simple bedouin but at least I can drive a car." It was a great pity that so useless a person should have been sent with us.

The remainder of the HBL (except for the ever-moaning sergeant), the superb wireless operator and the Bedford Model R drivers who were both experts and nursed their vehicles and precious cargoes through all sorts of country without getting stuck, proved to be men their commander, Pat Gray, could be proud of. But on our first hunt, all this was in the future . . . both good and bad.

We felt the thrill of the chase as we moved slowly forward, the sun in our faces, giving the best possible conditions for seeing any spoor. We wound among some low, white-sided hills, about thirty feet high, and then out on to another grey gravel plain. Dthubs scampered for their holes, but we took no notice. We were after different game.

"Gusr", shouted Tomatum excitedly. It was his term for a spoor. We stopped. We all got out. Tomatum cast about at a fast trot, looking very important. Mabkhaut moved more slowly, but the excitement had gripped him as well.

Tomatum looked, Mabkhaut looked, we all looked. The HBL

chattered. Ian and Don Stewart strode among them like pur-
poseful Secretary birds. Michael Woodford photographed
everything and everyone, except himself. The tracks were plain
enough for everyone to see. It was an exciting moment for those
of us who had come so far.

Tomatum told me the news, which I passed on. The tracks
were old, about ten days, and were made by a solitary adult. We
decided to follow it, for it would give us an idea of where the
animals were heading. We turned south, and began to follow the
spoor with difficulty because the driver could not see it at all and
had to be directed constantly. The track led us across the steppe,
which was covered with small tufts of yellow grass giving the
impression of an English downland after a dry summer, towards
a low line of hills.

A fox was spotted, running away from us, its brush trailing on
the ground. It need not have worried. Nothing could divert us
from our quest. A mouse, which I would dearly loved to have
caught, disappeared into a hole. We could not stop. The spoor
showed up clearly in places, but, in others, it petered out. We
had to search sometimes on foot until the guides picked up the
track once more. The other trucks waited a little way behind.
There was no point in them following all the twists and turns, but
we had to, because the animal had been in no hurry and had
moved in anything but a straight line.

We reached the line of hills. Almost at once we came across
the track made by another oryx—this time only about four days
before. We followed that track, but again the beast did not seem
to have had any particular end in view and the spoor meandered
about, and us with it. The ground became very rocky and
broken. Michael Woodford and I and the guides were forced to
search the sandy beds of the gullies leading down from the ridges,
while the others remained patiently on the skyline.

There was great excitement when we put up two rim, which
went bounding away unmolested. The rim were to cause us a
lot of trouble later, because the adults were the same off-white as
the oryx, and each white speck had to be carefully examined, and

its identity resolved. Also we had to look at each patch of gypsum, at white stones, reflections, in fact anything that looked at all white. The rim was easy to distinguish in motion because it bounded like most gazelle. The oryx move in a far more dignified manner at a steady gallop.

To our chagrin, we appeared to be moving in a circle. We dropped into a wadi with a gravel surface the colour of slate. It was treacherous stuff and we got stuck several times. The only way to take it was at speed, and that we could not do while we were tracking. The Pick-Up also got bogged down.

There was an abundance of tracks in the wadi, and we tried to unravel them. Camels, passing by in the winter months, had left tracks, as fresh as if they had been made during the night. There were small piles of gazelle droppings, and some old ones left by oryx. These were a great help to the guides in determining the age of the spoor, as they rolled them knowingly between finger and thumb.

Tomatum claimed to be able to tell the sex of the oryx by its droppings. He said that the female defaecated as she walked, leaving a distinctive trail, while the male stopped and left his mark in a tidy pile. This proved to be generally accurate, but, in one case, was completely wrong. It proved to be a method we couldn't rely on.

At twelve we stopped. The early excitement had died away. We had followed several tracks, but none of them had been made recently and they had all petered out, or had been dismissed by the guides as not worthy of notice. Still we had established that there had been two lone adult oryx, and one with a calf in the area, and, though the tracks were not fresh, they had been made after the Qatari raids. We had seen for ourselves that our quarry still existed.

We had not brought a fly sheet with us and the sun was extremely hot. Tomatum and Mabkhaut took the Land-Rover on to look for tracks in the neighbourhood. The rest of us huddled uncomfortably under the Model R, where there was just sufficient shade for all of us. The Arabs produced tea. It tasted as though it had been made with petrol rather than with water, but it was most acceptable. We lay panting and regretting that we had come out so ill-equipped.

Someone produced some khubz, but it was old and leathery. None of us ate very much. I had told Mohammet to pack a lunch for us, and this turned out to be a tin of herrings and some tinned pineapple. The herrings went down well with most of us, but Peter, who was more used to the smoked salmon and other luxuries on the safaris he organised, shuddered, and contented himself with the fruit which swam warmly in its juice. The sand blew in gusts over our supine bodies.

The guides returned. They had drawn a blank. They joined us under the truck. The minutes dragged slowly as the sun crawled through the sky above us. Flies settled happily on those who had gone to sleep. The sand piled against the stationary tyres. Those of us who couldn't sleep lay soaking in sweat and self-pity. This was not quite the "Leucoryx lark" we had imagined.

The thermometer near the roof in the Land-Rover registered 120 degrees in the shade. There was nothing to be gained by going on while the sun was overhead. The spoor was almost impossible to see without the tell-tale shadow marking the trail, when the sun was at an angle. Tomatum did not want to start until two o'clock, but we felt that anything was better than languishing in our present position, and decided to move half an hour earlier. We had had more than enough of that particular piece of desert.

It was a fruitless afternoon. Disappointingly there were no more tracks. It was an anti-climax after the encouraging start. However, we did cover a rough square of country, making sure nothing had entered it recently, so at least we knew where the oryx weren't. We could cross off a slice of the six thousand square miles search area. When we got back to camp, we totted up that we had travelled just a hundred miles. Not a great deal perhaps, but quite enough at the pace at which we were able to travel. Certainly more than enough in that heat. We had learnt a lesson.

We had come to realise that it was much too hot to hunt during the heat of the day. We must start before first light, work until half-past nine or so, and then break, continuing in the late afternoon until dusk. We must also be prepared to spend the night out. Each hunt would have to be a two-day affair. Otherwise we would waste too much time moving to and from the camp. On the second day we would be able to start straight into the hunt at dawn.

At the camp we were pleased to learn that the truck had arrived from Sanau with water and fuel. The Pick-Up had left again to bring in the remnants of our old camp at the oil company site. We would leave some of the aviation fuel at this old camp—not even the Mahra were likely to be able to find any use for that—and bring it along later. That night Ind Coope's beer reached a new high in popularity as we removed the dust and dryness from our throats. The exhaustion slipped away from us as the sun set and the evening star looked brightly down on our small camp. The satellite passed over as usual, and we listened to the BBC news on the wireless. The world seemed very far from us.

At four we were up, except for the Arabs who had to be cajoled into wakefulness. This time we packed our beds, took rations for two days and made sure that there were sufficient tarpaulins to provide shade.

After trying to the east of the camp, Tomatum was anxious to try in the opposite direction so we headed west. This time Michael Crouch who was feeling much better travelled in the Land-Rover with me, as well as the other Michael.

We turned towards the sand, heading in the direction where Mabkhaut said he thought there had been rain. This meant that someone had probably seen lightning flickering on the horizon in the last few months. By eight we had stopped on a slight rise, and Mabkhaut, after digging a hole in the ground, and plunging his arm in up to the elbow, announced that we had indeed found the place where there had been rain. There was little trace of it for the uninitiated. The earth had a faint discolouration to back up his story, but there was no layer of grass or any other vegetation to attract the oryx, who, like all desert animals, follow the rain. After a storm rim, oryx and any camels that might be about would converge on the area. There were no signs that they had done so in this area.

Mabkhaut said that he had seen a storm here some weeks ago. He believed that it was the only place where rain had fallen this year, but, as it had fallen on a barren stony plain, the animals must have been as disappointed as we were by the lack of vegetation. At this he shook his head sadly. He obviously felt that he had been let down.

After we had drawn a blank we held a conference, and decided to drive westwards to the Wadi Shu'ait, looking for tracks made by any oryx entering, or leaving the sands. We snatched a cup of tea and a khubz, and then drove on north-westwards, where the peaks of the sand dunes already showed up as sharp yellow pyramids against the sky.

The going got softer. We climbed, and crossed a tongue of sand which stretched out across our path. We got safely across, picking our way between the dunes wherever there were patches of hard underlay. Once over this the Model R got a puncture and there was a long halt for the wheel to be changed. We were on flat hard sand, completely devoid of vegetation, and it got very hot as we waited. Then Tomatum suggested that the truck and the Pick-Up should go south to avoid the next range of dunes in our path which were going to be more difficult to cross. The Land-Rover, he said, could search the sands and meet the other vehicles at the mouth of the wadi, behind the dunes.

So when all was ready the two trucks swung away following the grain of the country, leaving us to pick our way gingerly between low dunes of clean white sand, trying wherever possible to keep to the strips of gravel between them. We saw no sign of life, except for a Saker falcon and a young hare, which I saw crouched under a bush as we went past. I tried to catch it, but it was away like the wind.

Michael Woodford told me I should have stuck a stick in the ground and hung my coat on it. The hare would then have watched the coat, while I crept round behind it and caught it. It appeared that this was an infallible method among Dorset poachers. I had neither stick nor coat, so the advice was not much use to me.

As soon as we entered the mouth of the Wadi Shu'ait, we came across a great deal of life. There were lizards, sitting in the tops of the bushes. They had vermilion tails, and a bright blue pouch under their chins. They remained stationary until the last possible moment before scuttling down the bush and on to the ground, where they bobbed their heads three or four times before making off. They lost their colour as they ran, so that, by the time they had run a few yards, they had changed to a pale brown colour. We identified them as Agamidae. Their bright colours are said to be assumed during the mating season. Later Ian kept one for a short while in a dark place and it turned nearly white.

They were amusing creatures and fun to pick up, an indignity which they didn't suffer lightly. They would try to bite, and chattered with rage. They became a common sight on our searches and we soon gave up molesting them. Ian's captive became quite tame and would settle palely, but quite happily, on his sleeve, where it watched us goggle-eyed but imperturbable. We eventually lost it after leaving it out to grass too long.

The bushes in the Wadi Shu'ait were studded with them. We also spotted an apple-green snake with black button eyes. It lay waving gently from a bush almost indistinguishable from its green background. Perhaps the snakes, too, are able to change their colour to suit the background. We crept up to the snake to try to catch it, but when it considered that we had got too close it shot away into the bush and that was the last we saw of it.

Michael Woodford kept stopping to collect plants, He was very pleased with some cucumber-like growths, which he was collecting for Kew. Tomatum said they were the sort of plant which oryx dug up for the moisture which they contained.

The wadi was alive with rim. In the space of a mile we saw eighteen. One presented too good a target to be missed. We had searched the wadi and there was no sign of oryx, so I felt that we might risk a shot. The dunes on either side would muffle the noise. Tomatum borrowed the driver's rifle. This was a major operation, because it had not been seen or cleaned since Mukalla, and was found at the bottom of the car behind the seats after an amazing amount of junk had been moved. The rim stood patiently waiting while Tomatum loaded, removed some of the filth which had accumulated on the sights and made aim. When he fired the rim shook its head sadly, as though at such bad markmanship, and looked reproachfully at Tomatum.

The rim was less than a hundred yards away, as Tomatum fired again, and missed. This was too much for the rim's dignity. It walked sedately away out of view. Tomatum had set his sights at three hundred which probably accounted for the bad shooting, and Mabkhaut teased him unmercifully about it, chiefly because he, like the rest of us, had been looking forward to fresh meat for dinner.

We followed the wadi, going through more dunes and then out into the open where we could see the other two vehicles waiting for us. We put up more rim, but there was no sign of oryx at all, despite the fact that the area was rich in plants which they liked. Rather sadly we prepared to call a halt. We had seen so much game and only our quarry was missing. It was getting too hot to continue. We found a suitable place to lie up in the middle of the wadi. There were plenty of bushes to give additional shade and firewood. Stony brown plains stretched away into the shimmering distance. The wadi bed itself was hard and yellow and reflected a fierce heat.

We parked the three cars side by side and stretched two tarpaulins between them. Michael Crouch produced a number of rugs and we were soon comfortably installed in the shade while Mohammet made us tea. After tea Michael Woodford went plant hunting up and down the wadi, and I wandered around looking at the lizards. I never tired of watching them changing colour as soon as they realised that they were being watched.

The sun crept slowly overhead. The Arabs lay with their faces covered, silent and still. Mick dozed behind his moustache. Peter, clad as usual in khaki shirt and blue rugger shorts, discoursed on the miseries of our existence, and came in for a lot of teasing about his luxury travels in Kenya. The rest of us read or talked. Fortunately everyone had come provided with plenty of books, and they lasted the whole trip. The water-bags passed round in a monotonous circuit. They contained vintage petrol as usual, and we were already running short of lemonade powder with which we were able to conceal the taste up to a point.

Once again Allsopp's came to our rescue. The party was now fairly divided between those who drank their daily ration of ale in the middle of the day, or at the first hot halt, and those who saved it up for the evening when the heat had gone out of the day. For either school of thought the beer session was one of the high spots of the day.

At two we moved again, and at once put up two more rim. The Pick-Up crew chased one for practice over the flat plain, which gave perfect catching conditions. They made a few passes, then let the animal go. Apart from this small excitement the afternoon passed uneventfully. We followed the wadi south for some miles until its sides changed from flat brown stony steppes to small grey cliffs, pockmarked with caves. Here the bed became soft and gravelly. There must have been a great deal of water down it at some time. We climbed out of this and turned east.

We began to search all the small patches of vegetation which might have attracted oryx. This was Mabkhaut's area. He led us surely from place to place, but there were no signs of tracks. We did see one enormous black dthub, at least three feet long, but at that time we were investigating an old spoor and had no time to try to catch it. This was a pity for it may well have been a new species. It was of a different colour and a foot longer than any of the others we had seen.

By evening we had reached an area of black stone steppes with a few patches of scant vegetation, and now and then a lonely acacia tree. The sun began to go down so we halted for the night. It was a simple camp. We put up our safari beds on whatever piece of desert took our fancy and unrolled our bed rolls.

Mabkhaut said that there were one or two more places we could try on the following day working in the general direction of our camp. In this way we would complete another square of our search area. Before we bedded down Ian said that we would leave as soon as it was light enough for the guides to pick up tracks.

So ended our second day's search. The west had even less to offer than the east it seemed. Still we now knew that no oryx had left, or entered, the sands in an area twenty miles or so west of our camp.

We went to sleep disappointed, but not discouraged.

We were up at four, which unhappily was becoming a familiar hour and were searching by five. Almost at once we came on a very recent spoor. "Gusr", Tomatum shouted. It was so recent that we could all see it. Both guides got very excited and transmitted this feeling to the rest of the party.

The spoor was difficult to follow, because we were crossing a region of grey and black stones, and sometimes we were forced to try to pick up the trail in better ground ahead. This we managed to do but it was a laborious business. The guides showed great pertinacity and patience. At times they rode in the Land-Rover, but the driver was so clueless that, for the most part, they preferred to trot ahead of us. When, however, it became obvious that the chase would be a long one, Mabkhaut returned to sit in the car, and Tomatum perched insecurely on the bonnet and directed the driver with hand signals.

The Pick-Up kept well away from us, moving from high ground to high ground. The Model R was well back out of the way. In the Land-Rover we circled, doubled back and cast around. The animal was not moving in a straight line. That meant that it was not aware of our presence. If it had been it would have made a bee-line for the sands.

We picked our way across a wide wadi, dotted with bushes, and up the hills on the far side. We halted while Tomatum tried to follow the spoor over the rocks. We saw that the Pick-Up was tearing away in the west. Suddenly it stopped, and we rushed after it. When we had caught up we discovered that through their binoculars Ian and Don had seen an oryx in the distance. Then it disappeared.

Mabkhaut made no secret of his disbelief. However, Ian and Don were convinced that what they had seen had been an oryx. We started to search the area where they thought the animal had been seen last, but there was no trace. We stopped to decide our future plans and to snatch a hasty breakfast.

The two guides were insistent that we should follow the spoor we had been tracking all morning. They said that there was no doubt that we would catch up with the animal, which had no idea we were after it. The wind was in our favour, and the animal would soon be looking for some shade to lie up in. They were strongly supported by Michael Crouch, and we all finally agreed that it seemed the most sensible plan. There was no sign of the animal that Ian and Don were sure they had seen, and it was important to take the guide's advice whenever possible, otherwise they would be discouraged, feeling we had lost faith in them.

We returned to the stony hill and Tomatum sought out the trail. The sun climbed over our heads, and we began to wonder whether we were going to be too late and have to give up because it was too hot for catching.

We came upon some fresh droppings. Tomatum felt them and said happily, "Made this morning". The track was very clear and even our driver was able to follow it, but in another hour the sun would be too high for us to see it. We pushed on as quickly as possible, keeping half an eye on our watches. Progress seemed very slow, but it was sure. Tomatum was as excited as a terrier. We crossed a wide plain—ideal catching country. Still the spoor led us on, first towards one shallow wadi, then on to another. "He's looking for shade", Tomatum claimed. The catching car kept pace with us, about half a mile away to our left.

"Go very slowly", Tomatum ordered. "Look under every

bush." We started to search a small flat wadi containing a few spare bushes. The Pick-Up crew switched off and waited for us to comb the area. Then they saw it.

The oryx got up two hundred yards away from them. They went into instant action. Peter switched on. The truck thundered forward, Peter's foot hard down. The oryx streaked away in a straight line. In the back Don and Mick struggled desperately to unfasten the poles. They had been tied to the sides of the truck by string, which had frayed and was very difficult to unknot. As the truck hit bumps, Mick tearing at the knots with both hands, bounced like a yo-yo.

In the Land-Rover we kept quite still in order not to disturb the hunt. All our eyes and our hopes were fixed on the magnificent sight of the oryx galloping steadily along, a hundred yards or so ahead of the Pick-Up.

The truck crashed through a wadi and on to good catching country beyond. For a moment we saw both hunters and hunted on the skyline. The oryx was going with head down, the truck lurching and bumping as it steadily closed the gap. Twice the pursuers appeared to catch the animal up, but each time the animal veered away. Then with a burst of acceleration, they shot up alongside the animal. Now they were in a position to take control of the hunt.

Ian had been given a catching pole by this time and was all set. Waiting until they had run into a suitable stretch of ground, he told Peter to close the distance between vehicle and oryx. Peter swung the wheel and as he loomed alongside the oryx, the beast turned its head and tried to hook at the car with its rapier-like horns. Peter was unsighted. Peter, mindful of its welfare, clamped on the brakes to avoid a collision but there was a bump as the oryx hit the Pick-Up broadside on, then bounced off, rolling over and over. It was up in a flash and galloped off again, apparently none the worse.

In the original catching car this would not have happened, because the driver would have been able to see the oryx. It was fortunate that no damage was done.

The engine stalled as Peter slid to a halt, but roared into life again at a touch and they were off after the animal. Remorselessly the distance was closed again and this time as the truck came alongside Ian made a pass at the animal with the noose. It fell over the horns, but the oryx shook it off and galloped on. Again the car caught up, and this time Ian was able to get the noose over the horns and one front leg. Peter eased the Pick-Up to a stop and Ian drew the animal towards him. Don jumped off and caught the infuriated animal by the tail, keeping out of the way of its vicious plunging rear hooves. Peter also leapt out and grabbed the horns, and then gently tipped it over on its side. Ian and Mick blindfolded it, and swiftly tied its legs.

One in the bag! It was the dreamed-of moment of triumph.

In the Land-Rover we drove up, the Model R behind us, its passengers singing and shouting. We stopped a few yards short, saw that everything was under control, and got on with untying the ropes to get the crates off the truck.

The oryx lay still, Peter and Ian were holding it down without difficulty. Michael Woodford gave it an injection of anti-shock solution of 3cc. of Betsolan (Glaxo). It didn't seem to mind this at all.

The din was fearful. The oryx was snorting heavily. Every Arab shouted at the top of his voice, Ian bellowed orders and Peter swore steadily. We edged a crate near to the animal. We put the box on its side with the doors at each end open, then slowly we lifted and pushed the animal into it.

The most difficult part followed. The blindfold and the ropes would have to be removed simultaneously.

We slid the doors as close-to as possible, while Ian lay grasping the animal's four feet, and Peter kept hold of the horns. At the same moment they unloosed the knots freeing the captive, let go, and the doors were slammed shut. There was a thundering noise as the animal struggled to get to its feet. One of the horns had got wedged in a crack between two of the planks. One door was opened sufficiently for helpers to reach in and assist the animal out of this position. It had to be done quickly for too much struggling by the oryx in that position could have broken the horn. Carefully we eased the crate right way up.

Then we stood back to admire our prize. It was blowing a bit, with disgust as much as exhaustion; otherwise it was none the worse for its experiences, except for its tongue which it had bitten at some time during the capture, and which was bleeding slightly. He was a fine bull oryx, estimated to weigh about two hundred pounds, and to be between two and three years old.

It took eight men to lift the crate into the back of the truck without tipping it. When it was up it was lashed with the head towards the front so that our oryx might get the benefit of any breeze there might be. With time now to think I looked at my watch. I was surprised to find that only thirty minutes had elapsed since the sighting. Driving as gently as though on eggshells we started the half-hour drive back to camp.

Our feelings can be imagined. Above all, I think, we all felt glad that we had in some measure justified the risk which the Fauna Preservation Society had taken, when it had allowed the expedition to continue after such discouraging reports. We had caught an oryx and proved that our methods were the right ones. Of course we had to keep him alive, and that might prove to be the most difficult job of all. Ian remarked that it was almost an embarrassment to have been successful so soon, because we knew that the preparations for the animal's reception at Sanau were nothing like complete.

All the way back to camp the Arabs improvised songs of triumph. At the camp the jubilation was tremendous and we had to stop the more excited from climbing all over the crate. Things quietened down after a while and Peter rigged up a tarpaulin over the crate to give the animal some shade. It was decided to leave the crate on the truck, which would head for Sanau with its precious load almost at once. Michael Woodford, as vet, and Don were to go with it and stay in Sanau to look after the oryx. Michael Crouch would also go to check the arrangements, and then bring the truck back to us.

Michael Woodford was most upset at this idea. He felt he

would miss the rest of the hunting, and produced several good reasons why he should remain. Ian was not to be moved. He rightly considered that Michael was the most likely person to be able to keep the animal alive. When the animal was doing well, he might then be relieved by one of the less qualified members.

The signaller got busy sending the good news to Pat Gray, and through him to the Society and the world's Press. It was a rather self-satisfied party which sat down to lunch of specially concocted curry to celebrate our first oryx—noted in our diaries "captured 10 o'clock May 6".

CHAPTER 12

THE SEARCH CONTINUES

"In days gone by, no doubt, the oryx antelope ranged the deserts bordering Moab and Edom, but they are now restricted to the inner deserts of Arabia."

Carruthers (1915)

After lunch the Model R left for Sanau with its precious burden. It would be a tiring trip, because, though Sanau was only eighty-odd miles away, over quite a good track, the party would have to stop for ten minutes in every hour, and for an hour periodically, so as not to tire the oryx too much. We wished them luck, but for a long time afterwards Ian and Peter fidgeted and went over everything that had been done. They were unhappy at seeing the oryx passing out of their care so soon. They needn't have worried. The animal couldn't have been in better hands.

In the evening we despatched Mabkhaut in the HBL Pick-Up to buy some goats. The big Arab feast—the 'id al Kabir—was approaching, and we felt that the men more than deserved a party, particularly as we were not going to be able to give them the holiday they would normally have had. Dureweish went to act as bodyguard to Mabkhaut and his bulging money belt, which we hoped would not be seen by any Mahra who might get ideas.

Ian decided that we could have a holiday from catching next day. It would give the drivers a chance to do some much needed maintenance.

Holiday or not most of us had a great deal to do. We had caught our first oryx, but it remained to be seen if we could repeat our success and found a breeding herd. We were cheered to hear at first light that the Model R had arrived safely at Sanau, and that the oryx had stood its journey well and seemed fit and docile. This was very good news for all of us, but especially for Ian, who, as leader, had had to make the decision to move the animal so soon after capture. There was no rest for him that day either. We had a constant supply problem which he had to resolve. Water and fuel needed constant replenishment, and great care had to be taken in deciding which day the truck should leave and what the breakdown of its cargo should be. Ian kept the supply problem in his own hands, and had the worries of possible shortages to add to those of bringing oryx back alive. However, he was always imperturbable. The only time we saw him ruffled, was when he was skinning birds in a high wind with sand blowing over everything and the sun drying the specimens before he had time to finish.

To cut down the number of mouths to feed, and, more difficult, to water, we had sent back four of the soldiers to Sanau. The six we kept were really too many. There was no likelihood of anyone interfering with us so we used them to help about the camp and for lifting crates. The sergeant who was a grumbler, went from bad to worse. He complained of overwork continually, though he was seldom off his bed. In the beginning he was always talking importantly about where he should put his Bren gun. It was as well that he didn't understand some of the suggestions from the European party. Whether he really had a Bren gun we never discovered. It never appeared. He and his men lounged happily in their tent all day, except for those who were accompanying the hunting party, and in the mornings they were usually last up. During the day, far from being overworked as the sergeant claimed, they lay around waiting for the next meal. More than once Abu Darabis, the transport sergeant, had to tell him not to be such a drip, or its Arabian equivalent.

I started my 'holiday' day by going on air reconnaissance with Mick, taking along Tomatum as navigator. Because of the lack of wireless communication we were to fly a pre-arranged box search in case of accidents. Ian told us to fly ten minutes east, then north to the sands, ten minutes west and down the wadi. So if we didn't return they would of course know where to come and look for us.

We took off bumpily over the ridges and climbed to the comparative coolness of the dawn sky. We flew over the country we had searched on the first day. It was most noticeable how patchy the vegetation was. There were no signs of recent rain.

We flew our first ten minutes without seeing a living thing, and then turned north. Tomatum looked out of the left-hand window, and I out of the right. Mick looked in all directions, except backwards which was not possible without breaking his neck. The Piper we were using had dual controls and it would have been easy for someone in the back seat to inadvertently touch the throttle, or brakes. This could be disastrous, and as we were very cramped I decided to keep an eye on Tomatum, especially when we came in to land.

We followed a minor wadi, stretching like a winding green shadow against the sombre grey background. Very soon the sands appeared in front of us—the real sands of the Empty Quarter. The peaks and pyramids of sand rose a good five hundred feet into the air from the tumbled dunes which lay like a barrier across our path. We swept over the outlying ones and turned west, following the line of the country towards the mouth of our own wadi.

For the first time we saw movement. Our passing overhead sent a herd of rim scattering in all directions. We left them running panic-stricken hither and thither as we gained height again, after taking a close look to see there were no oryx among them. We saw a solitary white dot browsing at the foot of one of the dunes and went down again to investigate. It was only a lone buck rim, totally unaffected by the general panic. It regarded us with distaste and went on grazing.

We flew back down the wadi towards the camp. The wadi basin was green and comparatively fertile after the floods two years earlier, but the wadi itself looked no more fertile than any

of the others. The search took us an hour. We made our usual
hazardous landing from ridge to ridge, and Tomatum gave his
usual thumbs-up sign when we had bumped to a halt.

The rest of the day passed fairly uneventfully. The goat-
fetching party was three hours late getting back and we were
starting to think of sending out a search party when they rolled
into camp. Mabkhaut had seized the opportunity to dally at his
home. Michael Crouch returned in the evening, having left the
oryx safely ensconced with Don and Michael Woodford at
Sanau. He told us that he had found a certain amount of chaos
there. The HBL officer had refused the mason permission to use
a truck to collect stones for his building operations, and the stalls
were not ready. Instead the HBL had not even moved out of one
of the residency storerooms which was going to be used by us.
We decided to ask Pat Gray to send a stern signal to Sanau about
all this.

On May 8 we were up as usual at four and on the move before
five. We again headed east. An hour out we began to search
seriously. I had taken Don's place in the back of the Pick-Up,
leaving Michael Crouch sitting in state in the back of the Land-
Rover with the two guides in front with the driver. We were all
rather jealous of his comfort as he lolled among the bedding,
except perhaps for Ian, who did not think much of comfort in any
form.

We scanned every patch of vegetation for tracks, but found
none more recent than those which we had come across on our
first search. We drifted slowly east, Tomatum and Mabkhaut
wracking their brains for new places to search. We veered south,
and at nine we in the Pick-Up spotted three white animals
several miles away up a broad wadi. They were so far away and
the ground was shimmering so much in the heat that it was
impossible to identify them. Ian led us round in a wide flanking
sweep behind some hills, but when we emerged from them into
the wadi there was no sign of the animals, and no sure way of
knowing exactly where they had been.

The two guides hadn't even seen the beasts and were both

inclined to disparage anything they hadn't seen for themselves. We sent them off up the wadi to search for spoor. They came back to report that they had found tracks only of rim. With that we had to be satisfied.

By this time it was hot enough to make us stop. We chose a suitable place in the wadi and put up the tarpaulins and had breakfast. I walked up the wadi to look at the rim's tracks. There were a few nodding lizards in the tops of the bushes. We bowed gravely at each other. Then they took fright and rustled away down stairs and into their cellars. The only birds I saw were a couple of bifasciated larks. These were probably the most common bird we spotted on our travels. In flight they were a gay sight in striking black and white plumage, but on the ground they reverted to a dull sandy colour. Occasionally they gave a high-pitched whistle, but I never heard them sing.

After this I joined the others lying supinely about waiting for the hours to pass, sleeping, reading and passing the high-octane water-bags to and fro. No matter how hot it was, the water kept beautifully cool in canvas water-bags, which were hung over the side of the vehicles to catch the breeze as we drove along. A goatskin contained our cans of beer and they, too, kept cool as long as we kept the bag filled with water. They were a perpetual temptation.

For breakfast we usually had several cups of tea and a khubz, or some homemade bread with jam. For lunch we invariably had cold meat, either tinned, or goat if we were lucky enough to have some, and after that tinned fruit. We took large pink salt tablets once or twice a day, and vitamin pills whenever we remembered. There was a certain monotony about our diet, but it was eatable and there was always enough. Peter sometimes drew unflattering comparisons between our commissariat and that of his own company, which, it appeared from his remarks, kept people alive on lobster, or when that ran out, on caviare and smoked salmon. When Peter grumbled he was unmercifully teased. He took it well. "How would your firm have served this?" we would ask, indicating a particularly revolting piece of fried spam. Peter would shudder. "Not even to the animals." To his surprise we all survived.

We started to hunt again at one-thirty. Later we were to realise we were mistaken to start so early in the full heat of the day. We drove slowly down the wadi examining the ground around the more succulent bushes. We drew blank and stopped to discuss the next move. While we were talking an excited hubbub broke out on the Model R. We looked round. It was a sight we had only dreamed of seeing. Three oryx were galloping away down the wadi about four hundred yards away, a fourth animal we couldn't see to identify running with them. We went after the oryx at full pelt. Mick and I were flung about in the back of the Pick-Up as we tore at the ropes binding the poles, Ian yelling at us to get a move on. Peter cursed a non-stop string of frightful oaths as the vehicle bucked over the bumps as he drove directly across country without regard for springs or passengers.

Steadily we gained on our quarry. They were a magnificent sight. They ran in a tight bunch, the sun gleaming on their white coats, streaking for the far side of the wadi. We tried to head them off, but couldn't quite make it. The three animals breasted the hill ahead of us, and then scattered. We went after one heading to the left.

Immediately we found ourselves in country that was a chaos of spurs, gullies, ravines, hard rock and soft sand, all inextricably mixed up the one on top of the other. It could not have been worse hunting country. The truck, engine screaming, bucked like a mad thing, sand and pebbles showering up from under the wheels. Somehow Peter kept going, his curses rising to a crescendo.

The oryx dashed in and out of the hills, doubling back and changing direction every few yards. We ploughed along behind it as though through some devilish maze. In the back we hung on to anything to hand, sometimes each other, sometimes the sides of the truck, to avoid being thrown out. Once or twice we were thrown together with a bone-shattering impact. One particularly vicious bump caught Ian unawares as he was bending down. I heard the crack of his ribs breaking and the gasp of tortured lungs as he hit the side of the cab. The Land-Rover and the Model R tried to keep up. Several times as the oryx doubled back they were across our path, Ian flinging orders at them to get out of the way.

The oryx tore round into a ravine and disappeared. We had lost it. There was nothing to do but stop and think things out. We weren't sorry to get a breather. Both Mick and I had grazed the insides of our arms, until they were quite raw on the catching ropes and the padded sides of the supports. Ian was in considerable pain.

We had only just slithered to a halt, when one of the Arabs shouted: "He's lying down," and pointed up a gully. At once we were off again, and so was the oryx. We were lurching across rocks now, but the end was in sight. The oryx was limping along, its tongue lolling out, obviously exhausted. On a flat piece of gravel it turned wearily at bay, and Ian noosed it easily as we ran alongside. It was too weak even to threaten us. I leapt out and grabbed its tail and Peter the horns. A few seconds later it was trussed and lying panting on the ground. Peter gave it a trickle of water and Ian the usual anti-shock injection. It had been breathing in great rasping gasps, but after the injection it began to calm down.

Oryx number two was in the bag. But there was one slight disappointment. Peter had followed this particular animal because he had thought that it was the only female among the three, but we found that we had caught another bull. At any rate it was a good capture and the Arabs had the crate off the truck in very quick time. We got the oryx in easily enough for it put up no resistance, and stood quite quietly inside as we lifted the crate back on to the truck.

The chase had taken a lot out of all of us. It had gone on for twenty minutes, far too long in that heat, and, in addition, we had the work of getting the crated animal on the truck and lashed down. By this time Ian was looking pale, and was in great pain, but he refused to rest and said we would have a go at one of the other animals still at liberty. Then he bound a head-scarf round his chest, got back in the Pick-Up and gave the order to get moving.

We told the Model R driver to follow us very slowly, and returned to the wadi to pick up the trail. We found it easily. There was no mistaking the deep impressions made by the hooves of the running oryx.

We tracked the spoor back up the side of the wadi to the place where the animals had scattered and then on into a patch of precipices and sharp rocks. There was a great shout from all of us as we saw a clear plume of yellow dust in the late afternoon sun. It was an oryx on the run, heading away from us.

Peter's curses during the first chase were nothing to those on the second. For a long time it seemed that we would never make up any of the ground between us and our quarry. Once we stuck, but managed to reverse our way out of trouble. Ian sat tight and Mick and I hung on as we jolted over jagged black rocks which threatened to tear our tyres, or wreck the sump. Several times we were near to sticking but Peter somehow got a little more boost from the labouring engine, though there were ominous splutters from the petrol system. We could only hold our breath and hope for the best.

We struggled out of the area of gorges and devilish rocks, and then mercifully we were running on a flat stony plain. The oryx had been as impeded by the rough country as ourselves, but now it put on speed.

Our troubles weren't over, for the pursuit lay across sandy patches full of bumpy ridges piled up by the wind. It was like going over a piece of gigantic corrugated iron. I thought that the car would vibrate to pieces. Eventually our luck improved. We ran on to perfect flat catching country. After the clouting it had taken the truck wasn't pulling as it should, but despite this we started to overhaul the oryx. We still weren't out of the woods though, because in the back of the Pick-Up there was total confusion. The two poles and their ropes had got tangled together as a result of the frantic chase. As the vehicle steadily gained on the oryx we managed to free them just in time. Ian took up his position. He missed with the first attempt and the pole touched the ground and bent. His second try was successful and oryx number three was safely caught.

Almost before we had stopped Peter and I were out of the car and hanging on to our respective ends of the oryx. The animal was gently lowered to the ground, trussed and blindfolded. Ian gave the anti-shock injection and Peter poured water gently into its mouth from a chagul. The animal did not seem at all blown and lay quite quietly without panting. Occasionally it whoofed at us. We propped it up in a sitting position and waited for the Land-Rover to arrive.

It was a moment of tremendous triumph for this oryx was a beautiful cow. Our ambition to begin a herd was now a distinct possibility.

When Michael arrived there was much camera clicking, and everyone tried to get in the picture. Peter had already fallen in love with the oryx, which seemed to enjoy being stroked.

The Model R which had fallen behind, as the driver had nursed it with great care over the appalling country, now arrived. Quickly the crate was untied and the oryx lifted inside. It stood blowing at us through the cracks in the planks and shaking its head, as we lashed the crate down in the truck.

At that moment our sense of jubilation was shattered. Someone called to Peter that he thought the bull had died. It was true. Sadly we lifted the body out of the crate on to the ground. Peter and one of the Arabs gutted it, and its insides were placed in a box for future examination. The liver was ruptured and that was probably the cause of death, though we would have to wait for Don's autopsy before we could be sure. In fact, subsequently, the cause of death was found to be overchasing.

It was now more important than ever to keep the female alive. We felt hopeful because it hadn't been chased in the full heat of the worst part of the day. Also it was in far better condition than the bull. Still we all felt sad—Tomatum perhaps the saddest of all—as we drove slowly back to camp in the dark, each man wrapped in his own thoughts. The fact that the bull oryx would almost certainly have met its death in the next year was no comfort. We were there to preserve, not to kill.

Thinking back, I don't see that we were at fault, except perhaps in starting too soon after lunch. We had had no indication that there were oryx in that particular area. If we had been following a trail we would certainly have waited until later in the day. Still, having seen them we had to chase and, if the country had been kinder, the hunt would have been shorter and all might have been well.

Later, when Michael Woodford and Don carried out their examination of the corpse, they discovered a .303 bullet lodged in one of the hind legs. This accounted for the odd splay-footed gait we had noticed during the chase. Tomatum said that it must be the oryx which a bedouin had fired at, and wounded, two months earlier, but it could also have been a survivor from the Qatari massacres.

It was a slow and careful drive back to camp. Ian was in pain, but the female oryx appeared fit.

Ian decided to go on into Sanau so that he could be bandaged up by Michael Woodford and take the oryx with him. He also wanted to see how everything was progressing there. He refused to take the easy way out and fly. Instead he had his bedding laid out in the back of the truck near the crates, and with plenty of codeine and whisky inside him, said he felt ready for anything. We had supper and put the cow oryx on the truck for the trip to Sanau. It had been an eventful day. We had seen three oryx running together, and might well be the last Europeans who would get that opportunity on the Arabian Oryx native ground. We were still puzzled by the identity of the fourth animal which had broken cover with the oryx. Some of the Arabs said that it was a baby oryx, and some that it was a rim. The young of both animals are fawn coloured and no one had had a close enough look to be absolutely sure. It was obvious that we must find out, and Peter and I volunteered to go back and check the next morning. Tomatum said that he doubted very much that it was a baby oryx, but that, if it was, the mother must be the third of the animals we had chased, and that she would return in a day or so to look for her youngster.

The Pick-Up had not stood up to the merciless punishment of the chase and needed a new half-shaft pin and a new hub. It was thought that these might be obtainable at Thamud, and we arranged that Michael, Tomatum and Mick would fly there at first light to find out. This left Peter and I alone for a day or more. Mabkhaut had asked several times for leave, and we thought that this might be a good opportunity for him to have a couple of days off. I told him he could go home after we had checked on the mysterious fourth animal.

Ian set off that night for Sanau, and I am afraid we were all too tired to stay up and see him off. In the morning the plane took off and Peter and I left immediately afterwards in the Land-Rover, with the wireless vehicle as a second car in case we broke down. We did not take the catching poles, but Peter took a length of rope, claiming he could lassoo anything with it.

We drove straight to the wadi where we had surprised the oryx. A strong wind was blowing, but we found the spoor easily enough, and followed it back to the place where they had been lying up, when we had startled them.

They had picked the spot very cleverly. There was a small white knoll which commanded an excellent view in all directions. The white stone matched the coats of the animals perfectly, and they had dug themselves small sandy beds against the rock on both sides of the knoll, so that they could move with the progress of the sun, keeping in the shade. No wonder that we hadn't spotted them until they moved.

We searched the ground thoroughly, but there was no sign of baby oryx. The spoor of the three adults showed up most clearly in the gravel of the wadi bed. We also found the tracks of a rim. Mabkhaut declared that he was satisfied that there had been no other oryx about and we made tea and had breakfast. Then we drove back to camp by a devious route, hoping to shoot gazelle for the pot. We spotted some, but all our shots missed. Mabkhaut looked disgusted.

Mabkhaut left to go home as soon as we returned to camp. After he had gone the camp seemed strangely empty. A few soldiers lay like corpses in their tent. The Sanau water had begun to take its toll, and Peter began to suffer from an upset stomach so he went to bed. This stomach trouble was to continue to plague him.

At lunch time we received the welcome signal that the truck had arrived at Sanau and the cow oryx was in good shape. The bull was also doing well. We heard later that the mason and the carpenter had still not completed the second stall. The cow oryx had to wait in her travelling crate for two-and-a-half hours before she could be moved into a new stall, and this did her no good, though neither of the captives seemed to be too upset by the noise of hammering. After this she was put in her stall, adjacent to that occupied by the bull. Further contact was not thought to be desirable at this stage.

Later Michael Woodford described to me the care taken to look after the captured oryx. The first, which he and Don had brought in from camp, had travelled for ten hours in its crate, and had developed a sore on its rump, caused by rubbing against the crate. Otherwise it arrived in good shape. The crate had been placed against the door of the stall and the sliding door opened. The oryx, which had stood up throughout the journey, had been in no hurry to move, and it was two hours before it walked into its stall. The door was then shut behind it, and the crate removed for further use. Later a smaller travelling crate was put against the door, so that the oryx could get used to it before it set out on its further travels. It refused to eat for two days, but this was natural and not particularly worrying. Michael had filled in time by opening his clinic for the bedouin who came flocking to see him with real or imagined complaints.

When the female arrived she had been in her crate for eighteen hours and had travelled lying down. She continued to lie down in her stall for the next four days, and she also refused to eat.

A thousand pounds of grass and lucerne had been ordered from the Hadhramaut and this was being gradually brought up in HBL trucks. It was far too rich to be given to the oryx at once, but it was important that we should start them on this new diet before they left for Kenya where there would be none of their usual foods. In the meantime the HBL Pick-Up was left at Sanau to be used for daily foraging trips.

Michael slept on the roof of one of the stalls, where he could keep an eye on the animals, and on the inquisitive Arabs. Don slept in the tower of the fort on the roof above the room which we had been allowed to take over. For the first day or two both men had their work cut out to stop the soldiers and the bedouin from bothering the oryx.

Michael thoroughly enjoyed his clinic for humans which he had set up. At first he found that he had to deal mainly with eye diseases, the scourge of the desert, and later with limbs that had not been mended properly after broken bones. One day he had just finished treating three bedouin children for trachoma, when an older bedouin turned up with the same complaint. When Michael had treated him, the man asked whether he had used Chloromycetin or Aureomycin! They were the only two English words which he knew, and he pronounced them perfectly. Several Arabs brought gifts of camel's milk as a sign of appreciation for treatment. This was very nice for Michael as bedouins say camel's milk is the best of all milk—and I agree. It is delicious.

But best of all the oryx were not only staying alive, they were slowly recovering from the initial shock of capture.

On May 10 the party began to reassemble in the forward camp. Peter and I were glad to see them. Inactivity suited neither of us. Next came the plane with the spares after night-stopping at Sanau and, bringing up the rear, Ian and Don appeared with the Model R and more water. Ian was wearing a handsome white strapping around his chest, which became known as 'the leader's bra'. He claimed to be feeling much better, but none of us believed him. Turning, particularly in bed, was obviously a painful effort for him.

We made plans for a hunt on the next day. Don would take Ian's place in the catching team, Ian travelling in the back of the Land-Rover. Don designed a sort of life jacket, made from a blanket, which he could tie around his body and so avoid suffering the same fate as Ian.

We were up even earlier than usual, at three-thirty, and away, heading once more to the east. We were driving over familiar ground. Our chief hope was that something might have entered the area since our last search.

We were driving along when Michael and I simultaneously shouted "Halt!". We had passed two hedgehogs going fussily along across the desert. We jumped out and collected them. It seemed churlish not to offer them a lift. We expected them to act like normal hedgehogs, that is, curl up at once like all the others we had known and stay that way giving no trouble. We were mistaken. One of them, a female, behaved as she should have done. Not so the male, who immediately carried out a tour of inspection. He sniffed importantly at the spare wheel and then at Tomatum, who almost jumped out of the car. He seemed to think that it was possessed by a Jinn.

'Herbert' or 'HH', as he was to become known, made a circular tour of the party, pausing by each hand or foot to sniff disdainfully. His small, pointed, energetic nose was everywhere. His beady black eyes took in everything, while his large ears took in the slightest sound. Nothing would induce him to curl up. It was obvious that he wasn't going to miss a thing.

Bertram Thomas says that the bedouin believe that hedgehogs will attack snakes, "but go in craven fear of the vulture, on whose approach they will weakly unbend and, abandoning their natural protection, become ready victims". It is hard to imagine Herbert being so easily fooled.

Herbert was later identified as one of the Arabian race of Ethiopian hedgehog with the proud name of *Paraechinus aethiopicus dorsalis*. He and his mate were the only animals we caught that day.

It was one of the hottest days we had had, completely windless and very oppressive. Nobody was sorry when Tomatum said that there was no point in going any further, or in staying out for the night. We had searched further east than ever before and had found no tracks at all. At least, we knew that no new animals had entered the area. We also failed to find any trace of the third of the three oryx. It must have headed north into the sands.

Back in camp everyone was sent out looking for beetles for the two hedgehogs, whom we popped into a large cardboard carton. That night Herbert went to sleep spread-eagled in a saucer of tuna and milk. He had to spend most of the next day washing himself.

The next day was a holiday. Not without regret Herbert's mate was added to our collection of dead preserved animals. We had to do it, for hedgehogs were among the animals we had been particularly asked to find. We couldn't stomach the idea of killing Herbert. Nobody could kill an animal with such a personality. Indeed, he became the expedition mascot.

The following day, May 13, was the first day of the 'id, but we carried out another search to the south-east. We saw no tracks, and indeed no living creatures other than an Auger buzzard and some dthubs. We had managed to get some goats, so the Arabs were able to celebrate their feast. Some of them were almost unrecognisable in smart clean clothes, which they had kept specially for the occasion. They came one by one to our tent to give us their good wishes and to receive ours. In the afternoon the goats were killed and there was quite a party.

During the day we had a great piece of news from Michael Woodford in Sanau. Through wireless messages we had been keeping in touch with the progress of the two captured oryx. We knew that the female oryx had been refusing to stand up and that Michael had introduced a small white goat into its stall for company. The two had regarded one another apprehensively, then the goat had proceeded to eat all the oryx's food, and had had to be withdrawn. The lucerne had arrived, but Michael had decided against introducing it until the animals were eating their accustomed food properly.

We knew also that Michael had had an exciting experience with the bull oryx. One night there had been grunts and the sounds of the oryx pawing something in his crate, which was propped against the door of the stall. Michael had opened the far end of the crate and discovered that the animal had amused himself by dragging his water bowl into his stall. It had to be got back so the animal could be watered and Michael had crawled in to retrieve it, but when the bull blew hard and advanced his horns to the ready position, he had crawled backwards very fast indeed, getting out just in time. The Arabs had thought this a great joke. Another bowl had been placed in the crate, secured by a rope to the door.

Now on the day of the feast Michael sent a message that at last the cow oryx had perked up and had started to eat a little. Even better she had started to stand in preference to lying down.

We fell asleep with great contentment to the noise of the feasting Arabs. We were delighted about the cow oryx's progress. Also we were on the eve of an exciting day.

We had decided to enter the sands.

CHAPTER 13

THE SANDS

"They speak of the city of Ad,
Ibn Kin'ad—Obar!"

Philby

On the fourteenth we were out of camp by half-past four. Naturally we were all excited to be penetrating the sands for the first time. As the oryx refused to come out from their hideout in this wilderness, we were going to go inside after them.

We drove down our wadi until, just short of the sands, we came up to a ridge of hills. Against the hills the winds had piled up the sand into great dunes.

It was here that we picked up a twenty-four-hour-old oryx track leading north into the hills. Our spirits rose. The spoor was fresh for all to see. We were forced to bypass the ridge of hills but we picked up the trail again on the far side. Hours of the most frustrating tracking followed. The animal had walked in innumerable circles round and over the little hills which dot this area. We crossed our own tracks several times. Then, to add to our troubles, the tracks of the oryx started mingling with the tracks of yet another animal. Still we forged on until a strong wind rose, which blew sand into the spoor as we watched, and soon made it impossible to tell the age of the tracks. At last Tomatum had to admit he was beaten. We decided to halt.

We camped on top of one of the rounded grey hills, trying to avoid some of the dust which the wind was blowing over everything. Even so, it still swirled through the vehicles until we managed to blot it out a little with our bedding and the tarpau-

154

lins. We had breakfast. We were all disappointed, Tomatum more than anyone. The day had started more favourably than any other. If only the wind hadn't got up we would surely have found the oryx.

During the long morning of furnace heat we either slept or lay and gazed at the pointed heads of the huge dunes along the horizon, behind which, mysterious and exciting, lay the southern edge of "the Empty Quarter". This great inland ocean of sand was first crossed by Bertram Thomas in 1931, then a year later by Philby and lastly, and more recently, by Wilfrid Thesiger, whose book of his journey is the story of an epic.

Since then the oil companies have prospected and drilled all over the interior of the sands. On the plains round the dunes the desert is criss-crossed with the tracks of the motorised hunting parties. We had passed places that morning where the Bin Thani raider's tracks spread in all directions as the battle fleet, on their balloon tyres, had coursed up and down several cars abreast, the hunters shooting down anything that crossed their path.

We had even seen the place where one such killing had taken place. It did not need Tomatum's knowledge to point out the horrible story written so clearly on the ground. We could see how several cars had converged at speed to where the ground had been disturbed by the animal's death-throes.

Even so, the sands of the inner core of the quarter remained unviolated. No car could cross them.

By midday the dunes, which further north climbed to five or six hundred feet, had merged into a shapeless, yellowness under the sun. They were impressive sentinels to bar our path beyond them. Firstly, because they were in Saudi Arabia, and secondly, because we could have crossed them only on camels, and camels could not make the journey at that time of year, when there was no vegetation to sustain them.

After a luncheon of the inevitable cold meat and warm tinned fruit, Tomatum pointed towards the sands and we prepared to follow him.

Almost at once we picked up the trail of the oryx we had been following in the morning. This time it led us straight towards a gap in the dunes to the west. There were some difficulties where the wind had covered the trail with fresh sand, but we managed to pick up the spoor again on each occasion. Fortunately, the animal was now heading due north, and had stopped its meandering, so noticeable in the morning.

Slowly we drew near to the first line of dunes. The track led close to the right-hand side of the gap. Then we lost it. Tomatum and Mabkhaut darted about searching but the wind had filled in the footprints. We followed Tomatum round the back of the dune. Five rim got up from the shade of some stunted tamarisks at the foot of the dune. They fanned out, three heading across the absolutely flat plain which lay between our position and the next line of dunes. We took no notice of them, and continued to look for the spoor.

The catching car, which was some distance behind us, must have mistaken the rim for something more interesting for they rushed past us flat out in hot pursuit of the three white specks already almost over the horizon. There was nothing we could do to stop them, and they disappeared with the Model R steaming along behind. We sat and waited for them to return.

The trucks returned with their crews somewhat crestfallen, and we quartered the plain until we again picked up the spoor. This time it led us off the flat plain towards a more broken area, heavily rutted and covered in black stones.

"The road to Ubar", Tomatum cried, pointing at the ruts. I felt a surge of excitement. I knew that very few Englishmen had ever seen this legendary road. Both Philby and Thomas had seen part of it, and Thomas deserves quoting for his feelings were very akin to mine:

"Look sahib," they cried. "There is the road to Ubar!"
"It was a great city, our father have told us, that existed of old, a city rich in treasure, with date gardens and a fort of red silver [gold?]. It now lies beneath the sands in Ramlat Shu'ait, some days to the north."

Philby, too, was told: They speak of the city of Ad ibn Kin
'Ad—Obar.

Wabar, or Ubar, was the city of the lost tribe of Ad. Its
whereabouts is now a matter of theory. The people of Ad, like
those of Thamud, were destroyed. The legends say, by divine
vengeance. In the Koran we find: "And to Ad we sent their
brother Houd [Hud?]." They were warned that although they
were of unusual stature they should still remember God and not
worship idols, but the people replied:

"Art thou come to us in order that we may worship one God alone,
and leave what our fathers have worshipped? Then bring that upon
us which thou threatenest us, if thou be a man of truth."

He was and he did. And to Thamud likewise was sent one
Saleh, but the tribe hamstrung the camel of God and rebelled
his command saying,

"Oh Saleh let thy menaces be accomplished upon us if thou be
one of the sent ones."

And he was as well and an earthquake surprised them and in the
morning they were found dead on their faces in their dwellings.

The Koran goes on to say that Lot and Shaib and other tribes
were punished, "And we rained a rain upon them, and see what
was the end of the wicked." It was certainly no fun being found
out in those days.

In AD 1117, Nashwan bin Sa'id, an archaeologist, is quoted by
Thomas as having said that:

Wabar is the name of the land which belonged to Ad in the
Eastern part of Yemen. Today it is an untrodden desert owing to
the drying up of its water. There are to be found in it great buildings
which the wind has smothered in sand.

Despite our obsession with the oryx, we stared at the deep
camel-worn grooves heading straight into the sands, and wished
we could spare the time to follow them.

We crossed the road several times looking for the spoor among
the black stones, but without success. We moved further west,

still searching. We had started so optimistically again, but, once more, all the tracks petered out. The sun was setting as we drove down sandbanks, and between small fingers of sand already stretching out to cause new dunes. We searched the basins among the larger dunes, where the vegetation grew more profusely. Everywhere we found tracks where Bin Thani gangs had been before us, but we found no oryx.

We came across one strikingly green basin, clumps of yellow flowers nodding in the breeze. Tomatum pointed at the flower. "Zahar," he said, and then, "this is what oryx like best." We searched among the plants, but found no tracks of oryx.

We halted for the night on a flat piece of gravel beneath a towering razor-backed dune. Tomatum said that we should show no lights, and make no noise after dark. We were in the centre of the oryx country, and close to the verdant wadi bowl through which they might be expected to pass on their way out of, or into, the sands.

We lay exhausted on Michael's camel rugs, drinking our beers and waiting for supper. The breeze, which had been pluming the sand of the peaks like whiffs of smoke, died away, and the great silence of the sands fell upon us. It deadened all noise and quietened the usually noisy Arabs.

The silence was one which uplifted rather than depressed, and no one felt willing to disturb it. After supper I lay on my bed and looked at the stars. They seemed to be so close that they formed a ceiling above me. I listened to the silence and imagined I could hear the steady "pad-pad" of the unending caravans making their way through the cool of the night towards the strange "Red-silver city" of Wubar, now waiting patiently for discovery below the sand hills which towered above us.

In the first light of dawn the sands were a ghostly white. On Tomatum's advice we started later than usual so that the sun was up and there was no chance of any spoor being missed, or of any animal seeing us before we saw it.

We motored west, breakfasting on a windswept hill, then continued south-west looking for tracks. For a while, more out of desperation than anything else, we followed a four- or five-day-old track. Tomatum was taking our lack of success as a personal affront, and he and Mabkhaut worked harder than ever among the clumps of vegetation. We searched all the wadis one after the other, but drew a blank each time.

Finally we drove back to camp, subdued and disappointed. I was particularly depressed at our ill fortune for Ian had decided that it was time for one of the party to go back to Aden to arrange the evacuation of the oryx, and it was to be me because I lived there. Mick would fly me via Sanau to Ghuraf in the Wadi Hadhramaut the following day and then on to Aden, returning to camp afterwards. Peter would go to Sanau in the truck to relieve Michael Woodford, Michael going with him as far a Sanau. Ian would stay and try two more searches. He would have just enough petrol for this without having to use the plane's 87 octane fuel, which we had thought once or twice we might have to use to keep the vehicles on the road. We had several times run dangerously low because of hold-ups in the supply line.

The next morning the truck with Peter and Michael had left when Mick, Tomatum and I climbed into the Piper and took off.

We arrived at Sanau before the reception committee was ready for us. We circled the fort and saw men piling hurriedly into the Pick-Up. The air-strip was littered with camels and Mick was forced to make several passes at them before they condescended to move. When they did so it was disdainfully, and in their own time.

The truck with Michael Woodford on board arrived as we were taxiing to a halt. He was very pleased to see the first members of the party to visit him for some days. He looked fit and was better dressed than usual. He had even mended the hole in his bathing shorts. We complimented him on his more decent appearance.

We drove the familiar mile to the fort and had a look at the oryx. They both looked in fine condition and were eating well. The lucerne was piled against the wall of the fort and someone had to keep an eye on the bedouin's goats which would have disposed of all the forage in a very short time if they had been allowed to.

Peter and Michael Crouch arrived in the truck after a record six-hour run, and Peter vanished at once to view his charges.

After lunch, which was washed down with liberal supplies of camel's milk and beer, we returned to the plane and settled ourselves in for what was bound to be a bumpy flight to Ghuraf in the middle of the afternoon. Michael Crouch came along as navigator.

I will now jump a few days and describe events which I learned later from Ian and others.

The Piper arrived back at the camp and flew a short air reconnaissance up to the borders of the sands. They went into the sands up to the tenth of the lines of dunes, but found nothing and returned after an hour and ten minutes in the air.

Everyone had breakfast, and then the ground party set off. Ian was driving the Pick-Up, with Don in the catcher's seat, Mick as usual hanging on for grim life in the back. Michael Crouch, who had returned to camp with the Piper, travelled in the Land-Rover.

By ten-thirty the party had reached the edge of the sands and had seen nothing. They stopped for the midday halt. While Don was resting a small bird—a spotted flycatcher—walked across his mattress to drink from some drops of water which he had spilt. It was desperate for water and it was most unlikely that it would survive the crossing of the sands on its migration. Don left it some beer in a can under a plant to encourage it. It was to be a last routine check because by now everyone was beginning to think that there were no more oryx in the area.

At two-thirty they set off again. Half an hour later Tomatum shouted "Gusr". There were fresh oryx tracks among green vegetation at the foot of one of the dunes. They were about twenty-four hours old. Once again there was a wind which might spoil the chase, but Mabkhaut and Tomatum were determined not to be beaten this time. Despite the sun they followed the track on foot, walking or trotting for over two hours.

The animal had been making its way south, away from the sands. Tomatum said that it must be looking for shade. The Pick-Up got badly bogged, and when it had been unstuck Tomatum suggested a halt for the night. It would be disastrous if the oryx were seen just before dark. The spoor was getting fresher all the time, and the guides had every confidence that they could catch up with the animal the next day. The wind was also in a favourable direction and everything seemed set fair.

The usual precautions were taken to avoid showing lights, or making a noise and the party went swiftly and silently to bed, everybody fully conscious of the need for quiet in the desert where noise travels for miles. It was a night with a brilliant full moon, and the camp was electric with excitement at this last chance.

Everyone was up and ready for off at the earliest possible moment the next morning, but had to contain themselves with some impatience until it was light enough to see the spoor properly. Then Tomatum led off at a run.

The spoor led over a gravelly plain. At one point the oryx had broken into a gallop for some eight miles heading back towards the sands. Tomatum said that that was when the animal had heard the plane on the previous morning. The animal had then walked for a bit. After this rest it had broken into another gallop, this time in another direction. Tomatum said that it must have heard the vehicles at some time during the day. Each time the oryx turned north the party's hearts sank. If it turned into the sands it was lost. Hopes rose again when there were signs that the animal had lain down in the shade of a bush. It was obviously not alarmed. Even more exciting was Tomatum's belief that it was a cow, a bonus for a breeding herd.

Just short of the sands, the tracks veered south again. There was a hubbub of wonder from the Arabs. Everyone felt a new surge of optimism. Tomatum and Mabkhaut pressed on indefatigably, and the spoor was steadily becoming easier and easier for everyone to follow. By quarter-to-ten the oryx had been tracked back to within five miles of the camp site and the party was moving through a wide flat wadi bordered by a low but steep cliff. The Land-Rover continued along the wadi, the Pick-Up remaining on the high ground.

Eventually the spoor led across the wadi and the Pick-Up followed the Land-Rover across the wadi towards similar low cliffs on the far side. The Land-Rover was close to the far cliff and everyone was examining the bushes in the bed of the wadi, when suddenly an oryx rose out of a sort of cave in the cliff only fifteen yards away.

The Pick-Up was facing in the wrong direction, but Don looked round and saw the oryx which, after a brief look at the Land-Rover, had bounded on to the skyline. There it stood for an instant—a thrilling sight of great beauty before bounding away. The catching car turned with difficulty and set off in pursuit, the oryx leading by about two hundred yards. The car thundered across the wadi with a fine disregard for the clumps of vegetation, Mick hanging on desperately in the back, untying the catching poles. Such was the velocity of the truck that it managed to struggle up the twenty-five foot cliff without stalling on to the plain beyond.

The oryx was cantering away in a straight line yard by yard. The Pick-Up overhauled it, came alongside and Don roped it perfectly with his first pass. Ian jammed on the brakes and the oryx was pulled over. Immediately it began to rise but Mick jumped to the ground, grabbed its tail and worked his way along to its horns. He was lucky not to get stabbed in the process. A few moments later the pinioned animal was safely in the bag. It made no resistance when it was being crated, apart from a few disgusted snorts. It was in splendid condition, not at all blown after the short chase.

There was only one slight disappointment. The animal was a bull after all.

In half an hour the party was back in camp and the same day the oryx was sent back to Sanau in the Model R, arriving in very good shape. It was moved straight into its stall by Peter.

By this time the other two oryx were eating well, though their coats had lost their early healthy sheen. This was only to be expected, but it was rather worrying that they still refused to eat the lucerne. As I have said there would be none of their local food for them in Kenya, and we were relying on lucerne to bridge the gap.

The next day there was the last hunt. The Pick-Up had given up the ghost, and one of the two Land-Rovers was roughly fitted out as a catching car, but there was no trace of oryx and the hunters returned to camp at ten-thirty. It was a very hot day and no one was sorry to start packing up to move out for good. The wadi's attractions, nebulous at the best, had begun to pall. The Arabs had had more than enough and deserved a rest.

At Sanau the oryx appeared fit, so the expedition sat down to wait for me to produce an aeroplane to take them out.

CHAPTER 14

INTERLUDE—THE HADHRAMAUT

"And Joktan begat Almodad, and Sheleph,
And Hazarmaveth."

Genesis x. 26

Our trip in the Piper from Sanau to Ghuraf was without incident. We were heading for the Nazarmaveth of Genesis—a word, which some say, means death! We had some difficulty in plotting the course, because Sanau appeared twice on the maps several miles apart. However Michael was confident that he would pick up the right land marks, and that we could not miss crossing the great cleft of the Hadhramaut—the wadi for which Ghuraf served as airfield. We had a following wind which was a welcome asset; for the plane only had fuel for four hour's flying and we had expected the journey to take two hours and twenty minutes. In fact it took nearly half an hour less thanks to the wind.

It was the first time I had flown over the Jol, and I was impressed again by the extraordinary flatness of the country. We flew either over flat table-land or over precipitous gorges. There were no half-measures. There was nothing gentle about the country. It was unimaginably harsh, although the wadis glowed green and fertile against the drab brown of the ground above. It was a cruel land, empty and sinister and certainly no place for a forced landing.

Our course was a correct one and Michael was able to point out the few features which appeared on the map. It was reassuring to know that he knew where we were, although the trip was not a particularly difficult one, because we were bound to hit the Hadhramaut somewhere and it was only a question of knowing whether to turn left or right when we did.

In fact, we reached the wadi only a few miles west of Ghuraf and in sight of the white house which marked the airfield. Michael pointed it out to Mick and we turned towards it. As we lost height and speed it began to get a little more bumpy, particularly as we flew over the gorges. Trees and house took shape. There was no haze and Michael was able to point out the towns of Terim and Qatn, two of the principal centres of population in the wadi. The white house on the airfield turned out to be not one, but two buildings, one of which had two storeys. We circled the strip which was well laid out and looked luxurious after what we were used to. There was no way of telling which way the wind was blowing if there was a wind at all, but Mick must have guessed right, because we made a perfect landing.

We taxied towards the airfield buildings. Two soldiers came out, putting on their uniforms. They turned out to be customs men. They wore blue and white headdresses, which seemed a most attractive change after the red and white ones we had become used to, which were used by the Jordan army and the Trucial Oman Scouts as well as by the HBL. They shook hands with us and helped us to look for rocks with which we could tether the plane. They had not been expecting us. "If we had," the corporal said, "we would have got out the wind sock." They were most apologetic. "Are you from Saudi Arabia?" they asked. Our plane was painted green and white, the Saudi Arabian colours, and we put their questions down to that, but we learnt later that forty sightseers were expected that weekend from ARAMCO, the American oil company in that country.

There was no vehicle to meet us, but we were early and accepted the offer of the corporal to have some refreshment. We expected a car from Saiwun at four if our wireless message had got through. In the meantime Michael scribbled out a note in case it hadn't, and one of the customs men hailed a passing Land-Rover and asked the driver to deliver it to Saiwun.

We were taken upstairs. "Not in there," they said. "We'll use the ladies'." They led us into the ladies' waiting-room. "It's cooler in here", they explained. The two men fetched a carpet

and laid it on the floor. We took off our shoes and lolled grate-
fully on it, stretching out limbs cramped from the flight. One
man brought water, while the tea was being made. They were
perfect hosts—an example more customs men could copy—and
they never once asked if we had anything to declare.

Our Land-Rover turned up while we were drinking tea, but
we were in no hurry and drank the excellent brew slowly, chat-
ting to our hosts who were still professing regret at our reception.
They promised to keep an eye on the plane for us, and, after
saying goodbye, we set off.

Ghuraf was the airfield Peter, Michael Woodford and Don had
come to after Riyan had been flooded. They, too, had spent the
night in Saiwun, but there had been no one to show them around,
and they had not discovered the resthouse's excellent bathroom.
I had particularly wanted to see the Hadhramaut, and it was a
stroke of luck that I was now going to have that wish fulfilled.

The first Britishers to visit the Hadhramaut were the Bents in
1893, and they followed closely in the footsteps of an Austrian
explorer, Leo Hirsch, who visited Saiwun, Shibam and Terim.
The British had signed a protection treaty with the ruler of the
Qua'iti state in 1888—the Treaty of Shihr—but, apart from the
Bents, no Britons visited the valley until a Captain Lee Warner
and a Mr Little in 1918 (thirty years after the treaty, not forty, as
Philby alleges), and theirs was the first official visit. Shibam was
one of the towns represented in the Qua'iti flag, and lay further
down the wadi in which we were now running.

The term Hadhramaut used to cover not only the valley, but
also the coastal areas of Mukalla and Shihr and the Jol which lies
between. Now the Hadhramaut was more closely defined as the
valley itself with its tributaries, while the whole country was
known prosaically as the Eastern Aden Protectorate. The Protectorate consisted of the three states of Kathiri, Qua'iti and
Mahra. The Kathiri state was surrounded by the Qua'iti, but has
known greatness in its own right, and included the towns of
Saiwun and Terim in the wadi.

The Hadhramaut has a fascinating history. The people

believed that they were the sons of Joctan—this was supported by the Bible—and that they replaced the unhappy tribe of Ad. The name meant 'Death is present', which was not very cheerful. These tribes were defeated by the tribe of Kinda and became bedouin until the time of Islam. In AD 1489 the Kathiri dynasty became powerful under its leader Badr bu Tuweirak. The Yemenis, who had ruled the country for three centuries, were defeated and the wadi came under Kathiri domination.

The Yemenis had not been the first invaders. There had been Christian kings such as Imru Queis and there had been Abyssinian invaders as well in AD 844, while, long before that, the valley had been part of the Minaean empire of the Jawf al Yaman.

In the ninth century Ahmed bin Isa al Mohajir settled in the valley. He was a descendant of the Prophet and the ancestor of all the Seyids, the religious sect, which has now spread over a large part of South Arabia. Its followers never bear arms and are respected for their piety and learning. Their powers of arbitration have always been much in demand and the impartial justice of their decisions when settling tribal squabbles, was universally recognised. They had been the real rulers of the wadi for years, but, with all their spiritual powers, they were still unable to stop the wars, blood feuds and murders which bedevilled the country until the coming of Ingrams' peace.

In 1830 the Qua'iti state came to its present dominant position when Umar bin Awadh al Qua'iti, one of the Sultans of Hyderabad's soldiers, sent his sons back to the valley to their home in Qatn not far from Ghuraf, one of the principal towns in the wadi.

At this time the Kathiri ruler of Shibam was in dire financial straits, and there followed an only too typical slice of South Arabian history. The Kathiri Sultan, Mansur, sold half of Shibam to the Qua'itis of Qatn, but when many of their party were away visiting Qatn, he killed the remainder in a bloody massacre. There followed a period of continual fighting, and it was at this moment that Awadh sent home his sons. They, with their soldiers, spent the next sixteen years besieging Shibam—a moderately long siege by Arabian standards—and the inhabitants found themselves forced to eat leather.

The Seyids were called in to arbitrate, and declared that Shibam should be half Kathiri and half Qua'iti. This of course failed to satisfy the crafty Mansur, and, in 1858 he invited all the Qua'iti section to dinner, first having ensured that there was plenty of gunpowder to hand. The Qua'itis were more than used to this sort of treatment and accepted the invitation. However, they went in small groups, so that, although they all got a free dinner, there were never enough of them in the room at any one time and the fuse remained unlit.

Mansur, who should have known better, accepted an invitation to go to the Qua'itis for a return meal. They cheerfully cut his throat, and then butchered all the Kathiris in town. This was an unanswerable argument and Shibam has remained Qua'iti ever since.

The Hadhramaut like the other valleys in the area has always been noted for the high proportion of its inhabitants who have emigrated to Singapore, to what used to be called Java, to Malaya, India and the east coast of Africa. Everywhere they went they seemed to make money and quantities of it. At one time quite recently there were six or seven sterling millionaires living in the Hadhramaut. But however long the Hadhrami stayed away making his fortune, he nearly always returned to his birthplace in his old age. When the young men emigrated they often left behind their newly married wives, who languished in the top rooms of their high houses without the solace of their husbands' company. Travellers speak very highly of the hospitality which these grass-widows afford, and the HBL soldiers always looked forward to visits to the wadi. Today the valley shows many traces of the generous way in which the ex-patriate Hadhramis have spent their money.

In the 1930's the Qua'itis, Kathiris and the Seyids were all unable to keep peace in the area. The British had a responsibility for the area, which they only seemed to honour tardily, and then very slowly. Things changed when Sir Bernard Reilly became governor of Aden and it was high time that they did.

In the 1888 treaty: "In response to the request of the hereunder signing Abdullah ibn Umar al Qua'iti representing himself and his brother Awadh ibn Omar al Qua'iti, the British government undertakes to establish the protection of Her Majesty the Queen Empress's government over Mukalla and Shihr and their dependencies which are under their domination and within their frontiers."

For forty years this promise was not fulfilled and there was no protection for anyone walking along the coast or across the Jol or down the wadis. Protection was a word as empty as the Jol. In 1918 the Kathiris and the Qua'itis were induced to come to an agreement. The preamble to their treaty is so splendid that it merits repetition.

> In the name of God the Merciful, the Forgiving, and thereafter God Almighty said in his glorious book—Ye are a goodly race that went forth among the peoples commanding that which is approved and denouncing that which is forbidden, and ye believe in God, and the Almighty said . . .

In part five of the treaty the Abdulla Sultans (the Kathiri rulers) acknowledged that they accepted the 1888 treaty as binding on them—as if they themselves had made it. There was no getting away from the fact that the British were responsible, but it wasn't until Sir Bernard Reilly sent Ingrams to the area that our country accepted the challenge.

Ingrams found a ready ally in the wadi in the person of Seyid Bubakr bin Sheikh al Kaf, who had already spent a large part of his considerable fortune on the betterment of the valley and its people, and who had managed to win the trust of the bedouin from the surrounding Jol, whose friendship was essential to the prosperity of the wadi deep in their land.

The Seyid could not bring peace to the area by himself, but Ingrams could, because he had the force of the British government behind him, a force which was occasionally manifested in the form of the Royal Air Force. The two men were complementary to one another. Al Kaf produced the money—he was said to have spent 180,000 dollars on the east road alone—and Ingrams produced the impartiality and the power of the distant government, whose representative he was.

Most of the tribes were persuaded to agree to a three-year truce, while those who broke it were punished, though not very hard. Al Kaf built his roads while Ingrams ensured that they remained safe for travellers.

Unhappily famine struck the whole country during the Second World War at the very time that the position needed a long period of peace and prosperity. The sources of income in the East dried up and submarines prevented supplies reaching the Protectorate.

The people blamed al Kaf unfairly, but not unnaturally, for their hardships. He was living in complete poverty having spent all his money on the wadi and the people believed that he was pretending poverty, when in fact he was dependent on charity for a square meal.

Ingrams was powerless and could not help on a sufficient scale. Half the world seemed to be starving, the coasts were blockaded, and the British were being blamed, because it was a result of their war with the Japanese that the Hadhramis were divorced from their sources of money.

Just in time Sir Bernard Reilly flew in, saw how serious the position was and took action. Supplies were dropped by plane and the disaster averted.

Since those days an increase in the Colonial Office staff has enabled the Resident Adviser in Mukalla to station one of his assistants permanently in Saiwun, and he, himself, has an alternative house there. The administration is on a sound footing. There is peace everywhere and most, if not all, of al Kaf's dreams have come true.

We bumped along one of his roads, which had been built during the war to provide work for the starving inhabitants of the valley. Since then it had deteriorated and was now rippled with corrugations and pot-holed in places. Nevertheless, it was indubitably a road. The walls of the wadi reared up vertically red and brown to the sharp-edged table-land above. Secondary wadis entered the main one and down them we could see where landslips had brought down great chunks of rock on to the wadi bed, where they lay as big or bigger than the huddled houses which clung to the lower fringes of the cliffs out of the way of floods and other evils, but in a highly dangerous position from falling rock.

The houses were built of the same substance as the cliffs and matched them so well that they were difficult to pick out, and quite impossible to photograph from a distance. Castles stood on top of the ridges, which ran up to the cliffs, and walls, turreted and fortified but already falling into disrepair, encompassed the forts and sometimes the villages as well. They were no longer needed for defence and the day when people were marooned in their houses for fifteen years had passed.

The road ran round and sometimes through the fertile date gardens in the wadi bed. In the old days the trees had been killed off, burnt in the fields by whoever happened to be the enemy of the moment with kerosene imported from the coast. The villagers had been able to work in their fields only at night, and only then by keeping to the trenches. People who had seen the valley in those days compared parts of it to Flanders, so intricate were the networks of defensive trenches.

We reached Saiwun after forty minutes' drive. Saiwun is a scattered town. The Hadhrami likes space and privacy and villas have been built behind high walls, surrounded by date gardens, on all the flat ground around the town. In the centre the palace stands disdainfully looking down—a gleaming white sugar-loaf of many storeys. It looked not unlike the bridge of some large ship. Each storey was built slightly in from the last and the edges were decorated with lattice-work balconies, while at the corners, small white pinnacles broke up the horizontal outlines.

The sheer wall of the cliff provided a sombre backcloth to the rather Ruritanian appearance of the palace.

Saiwun is built at one of the junctions between the main and a subsidiary wadi, and the town is scattered, having outgrown in times of peace the confines of the town wall and its protecting watchtowers.

The Qua'iti Sultan has a palace in Saiwun as well. It was a good deal smaller than the Kathiri one of course, and the al Kaf family had not one but several. Most travellers have bewailed the onset of western architecture in the wadi, crying out that it spoils the unity and the character of the original. One heard the same when every blitzed town in England was being rebuilt.

It seemed to me, as we drove around the town, that the new fitted in very well with the old, and that extremely good taste had been shown. There were, it was true, some unlovely bungalows and one or two bleak and unexciting houses, but these have been built for the small European population. The Hadhramis have gone in for what I have called the 'Riviera' style of villa with perhaps a dash of English south-coast hotel thrown in. The houses retain the simplicity of the older ones and the results were generally pleasing. Philby called Saiwun the beauty spot of the Hadhramaut and that seemed a fair description.

In the days when Freya Stark was making her way up and down the Hadhramaut (with difficulty because of the variety and frequency of her illnesses) she had found that there were already eighty cars in the valley. All these had been brought in on the backs of camels, because it was before the day when Ingrams was able to be the first person to drive the whole way from the coast. On her second visit she noticed one particular one called a Crosby, which was a car long out of production even then. The Hadhramaut might prove a veteran car owner's delight. One of the Arabs suggested that as she was looking for antiquities, it might be included. All this showed the advanced state of the Hadhramaut in comparison with the rest of South Arabia in those days.

Philby was the first European to drive from Najrah to the Hadhramaut. He came, as I have already related, via Husn al Abr where his car caused a sensation. When he reached the valley, he found that far from being the first car there, there was already a traffic problem.

We called first on the Resident Adviser, Arthur Watts, who

was spending the five days of the 'id in Saiwun. Everyone who lives in the valley lives upstairs, as they do in Mukalla. We climbed up the outside staircase and announced ourselves.

Arthur Watts is often spoken of as the finest Arabist in Southern Arabia. He is also a first-class musician, and he has the happy knack, perhaps due to his musical ear, of being able to talk to each Arab in his own dialect: so that, if he was talking to a bedouin—it was as though two bedouin were talking—and if he was talking to a Seyid—he, too, sounded like one.

Arthur appeared very pleased to see us. He gave us tea in a room full of nesting sparrows, and asked us to dinner. He was giving the Kathiri Sultan a meal, which he said would be informal, as he looked at our travel-stained appearance. We accepted with alacrity, and, after exchanging news, excused ourselves.

We were invited to stay at the house of the Junior Assistant Adviser, Richard Etridge, and we learnt that Philip Allfree was also staying there. This would be the fourth time that I had met him in different parts of Arabia, and we were becoming quite used to it.

The Junior Assistant Adviser lived in a traditional Hadhrami villa, a pleasant house surrounded by date palms, paw paws and the sound of running water. Downstairs were the servants' quarters, and, best of all, the bathroom. This, like the baths in the other houses, was really a small swimming bath, large enough for one to swim a few strokes in any direction. The water was changed every other day.

As soon as we had met our host, and could decently withdraw, we stripped and plunged in. The water was ice-cold and the unaccustomed chill pierced our foreheads like a sharp knife. We rose spluttering and gasping and then allowed the real luxury of our situation to seep over us.

We swam, we wallowed, we sang and we shouted. We pointed out goose pimples to each other. It was our first bath for a month or more. No one was so unsociable as to wash in the bath. This was done standing on the edge with a dipper, while the dirty water drained away across the floor and out into the garden through a small outlet. Nevertheless the water looked a lot greyer when we had finished. It was an effort to finish. An ice-cold bath after a long period in the heat and dirt of the desert is one of the greatest luxuries on earth and we made full use of it.

We were loath to leave but we could not be late for Arthur Watts' dinner. We dried ourselves, shaved and sorted out the least revolting of our garments. Even so we looked a fairly unprepossessing lot when we had finished, and the dinner would be informal indeed.

Saiwun was 'dry'. The plane had not yet come in with people's supplies, and we became very popular when we produced a bottle of Vat 69, and were able to repay our hospitality a little.

It is fortunate that Arab meals are not the long-drawn-out affairs of their European counterparts. In Arabia one often waits three hours while the dinner is found, caught, killed and then cooked. During that time the host will ply his guests with tea, coffee, fruit and other snacks. If he has pressing business he may suggest that you would like to rest and will bring in carpets and cushions, and then leave you to sleep for a bit.

But, once the meal has been served, it is a question of 'Devil take the hindmost' and afterwards there is a cup of coffee and that is that. Food, the Arabs believe, is for eating not for making speeches over, and those who have sat through interminable speeches, while trying to remember their own spontaneous (though well prepared) jokes, may envy the Arab his directness.

The Resident Adviser was holding court on the flat roof over the ground floor of his house. Around the white parapet cushions and rugs had been laid. Several Europeans including two women had also been invited. There were general introductions, and then we sat down in an awkward square. One or two elderly Arabs, who looked like respectable merchants or perhaps government servants arrived, and, last of all, the Kathiri Sultan with his retinue.

The Sultan was a short man with an alert triangular face and very shrewd eyes. He looked younger than I had expected, but there was no mistaking his air of command. Small glasses of tea were served. In the corner a servant squatted keeping a charcoal fire alight and the tea hot. Conversation languished except in the 'high corner' where the Sultan and his host were engaged in animated chat some of which sounded suspiciously like shop. There were one or two polite inquiries about the oryx; but, on the whole, we found Arabs singularly uninterested in our attempts to save one of their own birthrights. The Press had not missed the opportunity to accuse us of imperialistic machinations, designed at destroying the Arab heritage. Perhaps they had read *Punch*, which had described us as 'hawk-eyed secret servicemen speaking little-known dialects'. But the general opinion was that we were something to do with oil.

Arthur Watts and the Sultan rose together and we followed them down the stairs. At the foot of the stairs dinner had been laid out on the floor, and plates of many sizes were stacked high with delicacies. We found places around the feast and sat down cross-legged or with our feet tucked uncomfortably under us, depending on the suppleness of our muscles. There was no need to be invited. One of the ruler's companions was already several mouthfuls ahead of us, and his claw-like hand systematically accumulated the contents of all the plates within reach.

There was little polite passing of tidbits to and fro such as one finds further north in Arabia. It was everyone for himself, and Arthur Watts alone remained courteous and attentive and divorced from the mêlée, and he cannot have had an opportunity to eat very much himself.

It was a very good dinner. There were dishes of rice which proved to be piping hot, which is not always the case at that sort of meal and the mutton or kid was delightfully tender. There were plates of liver and kidney swimming in rich gravies, and there were bowls of curry sauce. Alas there was no time for us to sample all the delicacies. The Sultan was on his feet, and regretfully the three hungry members of the expedition had to rise as well; for we could cheerfully have dallied considerably longer. We queued up to have a jug of water poured over our greasy hands—a much needed attention, because we had eaten with our fingers—and then we followed our host upstairs, where, after a cup or two of coffee, the guests of honour said goodbye. After they had gone we were offered something stronger to drink, but we crept away. It had been a very long day.

Richard offered us a choice of a variety of beds on the balconies of his house, and we sorted ourselves out and were quickly asleep. In the morning I discovered that Richard had slept on a mattress on the floor. This was hospitality indeed.

For all the electricity, telephones and swimming bath, the sanitary arrangements were still backward in the extreme. The lavatory was known as a Hadhrami longdrop. It consisted of a hole of minute circumference in the floor. One storey down was a stone floor, and periodically someone would come to remove the night soil and transfer it to the garden. In some villages no one could be found to carry out this menial task and the results were unattractive in the extreme. It was only the sun's heat which prevented the system from becoming unbearable.

I woke early, at our usual hunting hour. The bird song seemed to be deafening after the silence of the desert dawns. Bulbuls, weaver birds and warblers fought out a battle of song in the trees around the house, while sparrows chirruped from above our heads where they were nesting in the ventilation holes. Doves added a soft placatory note from the nearby palm, but it was quite impossible to sleep in the face of such music.

We bathed again, still revelling in the luxury of water about our bodies and then had a leisurely breakfast. Michael took us on a tour of the town. He wanted to buy some small items to take back in the plane—jungle juice and tinned fruit—but we went first to the administrative offices. These we found were in about the most dilapidated building in Saiwun. Here Richard and his Arab superior worked. I didn't envy them their background of squalor. There was an unhappy air of decay, but there was something new in Richard's office, I forget what. A shining new locker or table perhaps. Two or three soldiers stood sloppily around the door. They looked ashamed at having to guard so sad a building and they eyed us morosely. Inside a signaller was tapping out messages at a great speed to Mukalla. We gave him some more to pass.

No one should visit the Hadramaut without having a look at Shibam; for this strange city of Arabian skyscrapers has fired the imagination of all who have visited it, until they have discovered the filth which lies within.

We drove out to Shibam in a Land-Rover which Richard had lent us. It was a curious vehicle with a gearbox which possessed a will of its own quite unconnected to the gear-stick. The journey took us three-quarters of an hour over a slow track, which wandered through date gardens. Watercourses crossed it at intervals, so that the surface became a series of hump backs. In the fields and among the trees the women and girls worked and worked hard. We heard no laughter, and sometimes they didn't even bother to look up at the noise of our passing. When they did we were struck by the grave beauty of their faces, many of which showed the Javanese influence.

We gave a lift to a family who were trudging down the track. The woman had great difficulty in climbing over the side of the Land-Rover with modesty—lest she expose an inch of her face to our admittedly curious gaze. She had a babe in arms, which eyed us incuriously with large eyes. It wore nothing but an amulet. When they had gone we gave a lift to an old man, who insisted on shouting at us through his few remaining yellow teeth. He fingered his scraggy beard and asked us at the top of his voice whether we were Israelis.

Later we stopped for a minute to photograph Shibam from a distance, and we heard a small boy trying to repeat the homework which he had been given at school. "Long live Gamal Abdul Nasser and the United . . . Long live Gamal Abdul Nasser . . . Long live . . ." He never got to the end of it, and I felt sorry that he should have been given such a dreary rhyme to learn.

Shibam is picturesque from a distance. The town stands like a pile of druid's stones on an island. All the lines are vertical as though the only space left was in the sky. And so in fact it was— so closely packed were the houses. We drove through the town gate and stopped in the square just inside. It was impossible to drive further had we wanted to. Small boys shouted rude things at us, and small unveiled girls giggled and twittered from the archways.

Philby correctly remarked that "Sanitation does not interest the inhabitants." This was an understatement. The longdrops of Shibam expelled their ordure from several storeys up, down gutters and into a drain, which ran like an open sore down the centre of each tortuous alley into which the sun never crept. Walking and photography were hazardous operations and we didn't linger.

The town was filthy, but I dare say that above the filth several storeys up—most of the houses are six storeys high—a different life may be led. Freya Stark lay here suffering from one or another of her ailments and survived.

We were glad to leave the smells and the cries of the small boys behind.

Saiwun is a graceful, clean town in comparison. We took some pictures and then returned to Richard's house for yet another bath. After lunch we drove back to Ghuraf. Arthur Watts was leaving on the same plane and Richard came to see him off. We also gave a lift to one of the Saiwun football team, which was playing away at Terim later in the afternoon.

The Aden Airways plane was due at Ghuraf at two-thirty-five, and we were there on time. This time we sat in the men's waiting-room. From the ladies' came the shrill chatter of Arab women, veiled but far from silent.

There was a large crowd standing round the Piper. It must have been the smallest plane that they had ever seen. The arrival of the Aden Airways aircraft is an important event in the valley's life, and a large number of people had turned up just for the fun of watching the arrivals and departures.

By three o'clock conversation was flagging and by four it had petered out completely. Michael, Mick and I went for a walk over the flat earth runway towards a small wadi. We talked quietly of the expedition. Michael had planned to fly to al Abr that evening, but it was already too late, and they didn't want to leave without the mail which the plane was known to be bringing.

We walked back. We had given up hope. The plane wouldn't come today. But it did, landing at half-past four, two hours late. "I bet it's late because of a cargo of Qat", Michael exclaimed. Qat is the drug which Aden Airways fly into Aden every day to satisfy the craving of the colony Arabs, who do not seem to be able to do without it. They chew it endlessly, spitting an unpleasant green cud on to the ground at your feet.

"What delayed you?" we asked the pilot. "Oh, the Qat", he replied. Qat is a far more valuable cargo that the carriage of a few passengers even if one of them happens to be the Resident Adviser. We said goodbye and I climbed on board. It was sad to find that drugs were given a higher priority than people. Out of the window I could see Mick and Michael reading their mail, and then we were off. The Dakota seemed vast after the Piper and a steward dispensed barley sugar.

We kept low over the Jol, flying as quickly as we could for Riyan. The air was still warm and the plane dropped sharply once or twice in the turbulence over deep valleys. A veiled Arab woman in the next seat, lifted her veil and was sick with perfect decorum into the receptacle provided for such matters. The steward circulated with tea, squash and beer. We lost our race against the clock. When we got to Riyan the flare path had been lit, and this would add considerably to the cost of the landing fees. We stayed at Riyan for the minimum possible time and then were airborne again for Aden.

Already I seemed to have travelled a long way from the wadi east of Sanau and I was heading into a different world. The next few days would be hectic ones, while I tried to arrange for the movement of the oryx and the expedition to Kenya. I thought without joy of the interviews I was going to have, and the appeals to charity which I might have to make. But, in fact, all was to work out very well.

CHAPTER 15

FLIGHT OF THE UNICORNS

"A three days' journey in a moment done;
And always, at the rising of the sun,
About the wilds they hunt with spear and horn,
On spleenful unicorn."

Keats, from Endymion

Back in Aden I was trying to make transport arrangements for shifting the expedition and valuable live cargo. Group-Captain J. F. Davies, Commanding Officer at RAF Khormaksar, was most co-operative. He put me in touch with his Air Transport Wing, and told me that the Air Ministry offer of any assistance, without cost to public funds, still stood. I gave Squadron-Leader Perry of the transport wing an idea of our requirements, and he seemed hopeful that he could help.

I asked the Colony Veterinary Officer for a certificate stating that the Eastern Aden Protectorate was not a foot-and-mouth disease area. As there were no animals in the area he was quite prepared to sign the necessary papers, which would enable us to get the oryx into Kenya without a period of quarantine.

My luck continued to hold good. I heard from Squadron-Leader Perry, and his immediate superior, Wing-Commander E. W. Talbot, that an RAF Beverley was leaving for Riyan on the twenty-sixth of May to pick up the HBL stores, and then go on with them to Thamud and Sanau. The crew would night-stop at Sanau, and, as they would only be returning empty anyway, they would carry the expedition back to Aden.

Ian had told me to stress the importance of the animals not spending any time in Aden, where the humidity, not to mention

180

the glare of publicity, would not do them any good. The RAF had an answer for this. The Beverley was in fact flying to Kenya; it was a Kenya-based plane and there would be no need for the animals to be unloaded. If everything went well, the plane would only be on the ground in Aden long enough to refuel. Even if it should break down, Wing-Commander E. W. Talbot had a plan to cope with that. The routine Britannia from Aden to Kenya, would be held back a few hours to act as a reserve. This was the sort of thoughtfulness with which the RAF tackled our problem.

This was all a great gain to the Fauna Preservation Society, because this plan saved them twelve hundred pounds, the cost of chartering a plane to fly the oryx from Sanau to Nairobi.

I met the pilot and navigator of the RAF Beverley and was able to give them some details of the Sanau strip. As far as was known it was the first time that a Beverley had landed there. The RAF crew seemed to be looking forward to a trip that was a little out of the ordinary.

We took off before seven on the morning of the twenty-fourth. I never discovered how many RAF men were on board, but there were quite a number. They kept appearing from different parts of the plane all day. The first leg of the trip to Riyan was simple, and we followed the route I had travelled five weeks earlier with my beer and the pilgrims. I sat in the crew compartment and watched the huge array of dials which no doubt meant something to the crew, but which were quite incomprehensible to me. There was a constant supply of cold drinks, coffee and buns from the moment we took off. The RAF seemed to do very well for themselves.

Ian and Michael Crouch were on the strip at Riyan to meet us, having flown there in the Piper the day before. Mick and Sergeant Cracknell were trying to do something to the Piper's brakes, which had been giving more and more trouble each day. It had been decided that Mick should fly it solo to Khormaksar that day. Nobody envied him the role of arriving in the busy circuit at Aden and trying to land without wireless or other aids, while the air was full of Boeing 707's and screaming Hunters. I had once landed there in an Auster, and knew just how vulnerable one felt in a small plane in as busy an air traffic circuit as Aden's.

When we had loaded the Beverley we took off for Thamud. We flew low over the Jol, then the Jol merged with the steppes. Still we flew on. Ian and I looked at each other and at our watches. The plane did one or two turns. Still we flew on. One of the crew came back and asked if we could go forward. We weren't lost, but we didn't seem to be able to find Thamud either.

Twenty minutes later after a box search we found the fort, but we were not out of trouble, because we couldn't find the strip. There were two, one of which we had camped on on our way through, but it was the other one we were looking for. We flew along the bearing indicated in a previous report, but found nothing. We turned round and flew back. Then someone saw a column of smoke, and there was the strip—quite a long way from where we had expected to find it.

We flew over it while the pilot had a good look at it. It seemed to be in perfect condition and we turned in to land. At that moment an HBL Land-Rover drove nonchalantly across the strip and we were forced to go into a steep climb to avoid it. After the curses had settled we came in again and landed.

Tomatum was on the strip to greet us, and he was delighted to find that we had brought some sacks of rice and sugar for him. I showed him some photographs of the expedition. Oddly he had to be shown which way up to hold some of them. He recognised himself, which is more than do some Arabs, who refuse to accept responsibility for the truth.

The rations were unloaded at enormous speed by a crowd of singing soldiers. The air was dry and like nectar after the humidity of the coast. It was good to be back. We were off again on time for Sanau.

Thamud had been hard to find, but we expected Sanau to be much worse. Aircraft seldom landed there and reports of its position were very vague. Our greatest aid to navigation was a map drawn on the back of an envelope for us by Tomatum. Ian and I sat in the crew's compartment, keeping a lookout for land-marks. We need not have worried. At exactly the right time we spotted something white. It was the skeleton of a crashed RAF Valetta which was known to decorate the airfield. It was now thought to be acting as a minor palace for a bedouin who had got bored with goathair tents. We landed without incident.

A cheerful looking Don was there to greet us with his jungle hat pulled firmly over his ears. The RAF looked with disfavour at the bare surroundings, and began to unload their beds. A Land-Rover was waiting for us. We climbed in. The RAF officers sat in the back with me. There were no cushions and their faces registered disbelief, horror, anguish—and finally pain—as we were driven unexpertly from bump to bump the ten miles to the fort. My bottom had become immune to such shocks but the RAF were not so fortunate. They expected to be airborne only in aeroplanes. They perked up when we pointed out a brace of dthub which they could photograph, but it was still a very relieved party which staggered out of the car at the fort. The airmen had followed us in the Pick-Up, and we led them inside to enjoy the fruits of Ind Coope's generosity.

The same bedouin seemed to be watering the same camels at the well. They looked without interest at this sudden invasion of Europeans, most of whom carried cameras. The same goats were queuing in well-disciplined groups a little way from the well, and a few less well-behaved ones were browsing among the expensive forage which we had got for the oryx, but which we would not now be able to use. Peter was inside the stalls with Michael Woodford crating the animals. Peter had invented an excellent way of getting the animals into their crates. These were smaller than the catching crates, because we had discovered that the Arabian Oryx was smaller than its Kenyan cousin, and the crates were only five-and-a-half feet high and six feet long.

A wooden partition was pushed into the stall forcing the oryx into a more confined space. The crating team was able to stand out of the way of the animals' horns on the other side of the partition, which was gradually pushed towards the wall of the stall until the oryx had no alternative but to walk forward into his crate. If he loitered Peter was not above giving him a healthy slap on its haunch. This usually surprised the oryx so much that he moved very hurriedly and the sliding door of the crate was shut by someone standing on top of the crate. All three oryx were safely and easily crated in this way. Then came the business of getting the crates on to the truck. Each one weighed about five hundred pounds.

With shouts, orders, counter-orders, chanting and general chaos each crate was lifted carefully on to the Model R. It was very difficult to persuade the men not to tilt the crates, but the HBL Mulazim was very helpful and worked as hard as anyone until each crate was safely stowed.

The HBL seemed to enjoy loading the truck although it was hard work. Perhaps they welcomed the disturbance after the tedium of their day-to-day existence in the fort, or perhaps they were pleased to see the last of us. The RAF had already tired of the delights of Sanau and had returned to the familiar world in and around their plane, but it was dark before we had finished the final loading.

There followed what seemed like an interminable drive to the airfield. The driver could only drive at about ten miles an hour, because of his precious cargo, and it took us an hour instead of the usual twenty minutes to get there.

We reached the plane at last. The RAF were sitting around a number of small fires a few yards from the plane, which was home to them. We backed the truck up to the doors, and Mabkhaut distinguished himself by falling down the slit in the ramps. He wasn't hurt and joined in the general laughter. It took us some time to manhandle all the crates and to lash them down in the plane, but at last it was done and we were able to return to the fort for our last supper.

Mohammet had distinguished himself for supper. A goat had been killed and we ate it on the roof under the stars. I had brought some champagne back with me and it had remained cool in its container. It was a memorable meal and we sat and toasted a long life and a successful journey to the oryx. It was a fitting way to end our sojourn in the desert. . . .

After supper came the goodbyes. Mabkhaut was given a pair of binoculars, in addition to a fat tip. He then demanded a tent. We explained that they didn't belong to us, but he was not convinced. We also gave him a rubber hose which would be useful for getting water out of his water drum. It was a blue one and he said that he wanted a green one. That was too much, and I left Mohammet to sort out the details of the colour scheme with him.

All bedouin are avaricious, but they are also the most generous of people, and will readily kill their last animal to feed you. At times their grasping nature can become a real nuisance, but one had always to remember how much better off we must have seemed to them. Mabkhaut certainly believed that there was no harm in asking.

Herbert the hedgehog had been living in the smelly bathhouse. He had completely recovered from his heat exhaustion in the wadi and was making considerable inroads into the Sanau beetle population. He was helped into a small travelling crate which the carpenter had made specially for him. Irritable scratching noises from within indicated that Herbert did not approve of his change of quarters. It just wasn't what he was used to at all.

We picked up the last of our belongings, took a final look round and said our goodbyes. The staff were full of smiles. They had been promised a good tip when they got to Mukalla, but I think they were genuinely sorry to see us go. Mabkhaut appeared to be quite upset that the goose which laid the golden eggs was going. He had been satisfied with a bright green hose, and he promised to let us know if there were any reports of oryx in the area in the future. We were leaving the catching crates and poles at Sanau in case anyone came after us.

We drove back to the plane in the Land-Rover. We were all glad to be on the move, but it was sad to be taking one's last drive across the Northern Deserts, and I think that we would all have been prepared to return, preferably in the winter.

Most of the RAF were asleep when we arrived and their fires had burnt low. We unloaded our gear and laid out our beds for the last time. Peter had a last look at the oryx and we shared a beer. There was a frightful noise coming from the area of the crates, but it turned out to be Herbert, although it sounded like an oryx. He was gradually demolishing his crate with his sharp claws and keeping people awake with the noise. Eventually I could stand it no longer, and removed Herbert to a place in the desert where he could make as much noise as he liked. I left him scratching irritably.

The night was a disturbed one. The RAF weren't sleeping well in their novel surroundings and one or two of them walked round the plane cursing oryx, deserts and life generally. They were up again at three making tea.

We got up as the first tinge of dawn was showing in the sky over the hills in the East. I stamped out to bring Herbert in, but, alas, his crate was empty. Somehow he had lifted the sliding door of the crate and escaped. I searched the ground, but it was covered with stones all the size and colour of a hedgehog, and it was still too dark to see very far.

Disconsolately I returned and broke the news to the others. Herbert had had the last laugh, but none of us begrudged him his final triumph. He had shown far more character than a hedgehog should possess. From the beginning he had treated us as inferiors, taking the minimum amount of notice of us and not bothering to curl up. Now he would be able to get back to his normal routine, and we knew that there were plenty of others about. He wouldn't be lonely for long.

We packed up quickly. The great doors closed. Machinery hummed. We climbed up into the boom and settled ourselves for the three-hour flight. There were a few seconds of doubt, when one of the engines refused to fire, but soon all four were roaring healthily. One of the airmen came to check that we were strapped in and the plane lumbered forward, passing no doubt, Herbert, who probably had his tongue out. There was no wind and we took off before the sun had lifted itself over the horizon.

At once it became very cold. Those of us who possessed sweaters donned them hurriedly. The rest of us shivered and tried to stop our teeth from chattering.

We flew over the familiar steppes, heading for the Hadhramaut. The flat grey steppe country changed to the broken brown table-land of the Jol, broken for a few miles of intense cultivation as we went over the great valley of the Hadhramaut. We passed what I thought was the mouth of the Wadi Do'an, and after this the country became flat and sandy. I was able to pick up a well-known landmark, the Federal Regular Army camp at Ataq, just in the Western Aden Protectorate. I felt that it was ironical that the camp contained the officer who had caught the previous two oryx which had died after capture. Now three were passing over his head.

Immediately we had left Ataq behind the character of the country changed completely. An 8,000-ft. plateau formed the horizon on our right. Huge, thrusting crags, jagged and inimical reached out towards us. These mountains are among the wildest in the world. In places on the tops of sheer peaks and ridges small patches of cultivation showed the hard life which the local hill men lived.

We flew past Lodar and I was able to point out the incredible road which has been built into the wall of the plateau which towered above us, connecting the villages on the top with those below.

We droned over the Yafai' country, which was the home of Qassim, Michael's driver. It looked even wilder than the rest. For the first time we stopped shivering, the sea appeared on our left and we fastened our safety belts. The Beverley landed, the props were reversed with an angry roar and we stopped. The doors were opened and we started to sweat. We were back in Aden.

There was a crowd of RAF men to meet the plane. Many of them had helped us in some way and they were able to get their reward—a sight of one of the rarest animals in the world. The oryx were standing or lying placidly in their crates, apparently unaffected either by the flight or by the change in climate. A reporter and a photographer made some of the members of the expedition stand sheepishly with the crew at the foot of the ladder. Fortunately we never saw the results and we hoped that the public didn't either. Mr Wilson, from the Secretariat drove some of us away to breakfast, while the rest tried to keep the crowds away from the oryx.

Mick had arrived the previous evening and he had landed without incident. His plane was now in an RAF hangar where the wing was about to be removed. Unfortunately there was no room for it in the Beverley and it would have to wait. Mick agreed to stay on guard, while I drove Peter into town to do some shopping. We had only half an hour, but when we returned, however, we found that we had no need to hurry. The crates were being unloaded—the Beverley had broken down.

The foresight of the RAF saved us. The Britannia was standing by and the kit was being trans-shipped to it at once. We had plenty of time and I was able to take Peter home for a leisurely breakfast. The Britannia would not take off before eleven, but it would still be in Nairobi before the time when the Beverley would have arrived, so, apart from having to subject the oryx to another move, the breakdown was not unwelcome.

At take-off I said farewell to the oryx, for, of course, I was staying in Aden. The door closed and I was no longer a member of the expedition. By evening the whole operation would be over. Ian, Peter, Don and Mick were returning to their own homes in Kenya. Michael Woodford was going to travel with them to see the animals safely installed before flying home to England.

When the plane took off I knew that quite a high proportion of the surviving Arabian Oryx had left their native country.

We estimated that there were nine left from tracks we had seen. But for all we knew they might already have fallen to some bedouin's gun. We knew that some existed in Dhofar, if reports from the Sultan's army officers were correct, but no one could say whether any would be left in a year's time. If the wholesale slaughter by the Qataris can be prevented, there should be an opportunity for another expedition to rescue some more, for more are needed to start a breeding herd. I hope that there is another expedition, but it had better come soon.

The tail end of the expedition had its troubles in Kenya. On arrival they found that a particularly virulent form of foot-and-mouth disease had broken out at the farm adjoining the compound where the oryx were going to live, at Isiolo.

It was decided that the oryx must remain in Nairobi even though the climate was most unsuitable. Two professional animal catchers and exporters, Mr John Seago and Mr Tony Parkinson, agreed to keep the oryx until they could be moved to Isiolo after the outbreak was over and some stalls were lined with grass for them. The climate proved to be even more unfriendly than had been expected and the oryx stood shivering unhappily in their stalls. In the desert they were used to temperatures below freezing in the winter, but that was a dry cold, and they would not survive the wet cold of Nairobi for long unless something was done.

A conference was held. As a result, infra-red lamps, of the sort used in chicken brooders, were put into converted elephant and giraffe crates, and the oryx were shut in these at night.

The animals quickly grew accustomed to the local grass, and later began to feed on lucerne hay. By the tenth of June they had filled out, and were showing a definite improvement. The female and one of the bulls were put together in one stall, but the bull became aggressive rather than romantic and had to be removed before he injured the cow.

As the months go by the oryx appear to have settled down well. In July they were transferred to Isiolo. The Press had made quite a story out of the expedition. The Duke of Edinburgh was kind enough to congratulate Ian on our achievement, but the public's memory is short. Animals like the Arabian Oryx must be saved and this can only be done with the support of you—the public.

EPILOGUE

It is pleasant to be able to record an improvement in the oryx situation both in and out of captivity. The publicity given to the oryx at the time of the expedition and later has resulted in a great deal of useful co-operation from a great number of organisations and individuals.

It was thought in 1962 that the world population of oryx in the wild state was something less than a hundred. However, as a result of reports by members of the Sultan of Muscat and Oman's forces and by men of the Desert Locust Survey as well as from representatives of the various oil companies who are working in Arabia, the original estimate appears, happily, to have been pessimistic.

The numbers still roaming their last strongholds in Arabia are probably at least two hundred and perhaps more. Parties of a dozen have been seen during the last two years. These proud remnants of a once great population have withdrawn to two areas. The majority have retreated to the Jiddat al Harrasis, which is an area of gravel plains in the south-west part of Oman. There is a smaller group in Dhofar, east of the area in which the expedition searched in the Protectorate. There are reports of others, as well, in the Jauf area of the Yemen, and in other parts of Oman, but it is not likely that they exist and reports are invariably conflicting.

The chances of survival of these two groups are not good. The Sultan of Muscat and Oman has forbidden the shooting of oryx throughout his territory, but there is no reason to suppose that the bedouin in the Jiddat al Harrasis pay too much attention to this, and, indeed, there is no reason why they should voluntarily give up a traditional source of meat. The Sultan's edict will certainly make it difficult for so-called sportsmen to continue their mass slaughter, and the oil companies will respect the Sultan's wishes.

Nevertheless, the search for oil goes on, and the disturbance to the oryx by vehicles and men may be sufficient to drive the animals away from their last refuges, and to certain extinction.

The situation in Arabia is gloomy. There is encouraging news of the oryx in captivity. As a result of the generous assistance of Mr Maurice A. Machris, president of the American Shikar-Safari club, there is now a flourishing herd of oryx in the Phoenix Zoo, Arizona.

The club financed the move of the animals to the Zoo, as well as providing the money necessary for the provision of special enclosures and buildings. This has meant that the oryx are living in conditions and climate very similar to that of their natural habitat, and they are doing well.

The three animals captured by the expedition have been joined by a female from the London Zoo, which has just calved. H.E. Sheikh Jabir Abdullah al Sabah of Kuwait donated a female, and King Saud of Saudi Arabia, two males and two females. A male calf was born to the expedition female, and the total number at Phoenix has risen to ten. The females are showing every sign of increasing the population regularly, and, providing the herd remains free from disease, there is no reason why it shouldn't continue to flourish.

The only other oryx known to be in captivity are a further six males and three females in King Saud's zoo at Riyadh, an apparently barren male in the London Zoo, and two of unknown sex in the zoo at Taiz in the Yemen.

So, in July 1964, there is certainly hope that the Arabian oryx will survive. The best chances remain with the herd in captivity. It is difficult to tell how long the oryx remaining in Arabia can stand out against the inexorable march of civilisation into their last refuges. Judging by the rapidity with which their numbers have decreased in the last ten years, and even with the Sultan's protection, it is unlikely that they will survive another ten. Perhaps the best chance of all would be for a further expedition to capture another nucleus of a second herd, which could be bred somewhere other than in the Phoenix Zoo, as an insurance against any possible disaster.   Later the two herds could be crossbred, which would certainly strengthen the strain and prevent in-breeding. If there is another expedition it will be fortunate indeed if it finds so many good friends and supporters as did ours.

NOTES ON BIRDS OF SOUTH ARABIA

by Major I. R. Grimwood

(*Note:* The nomenclature used by Col. R. Meinertzhagen in his *Birds of Arabia* [1954] is followed throughout.)

The advance party arrived in Mukalla on 29th March, by when few paleartic migrants were in evidence.

Small parties of Kentish plover (*Charadrius alexandrinus*) were however quite common along the sandy beaches to the west of the town and remained so until the expedition moved inland on the 23rd April. Greenshanks (*Tringa nebularia*) were also present in some numbers until the latter date and one pair of redshanks (*T. totanus*) of unidentified race was seen on the 7th April. Several parties of curlew, numbering from five to ten individuals each, were seen near Ahwar, midway between Aden and Mukalla, on 17th April.

Duck were also to be found on most of the small coastal creeks and a pair of widgeon (*Anas penelope*), three male and seven female pintail (*Anas acuta*), one male pochard (*Aythya ferina*) and one male ferruginous duck (*Aythya nyroca*) were identified in a mixed party observed at close range on 6th April, some six miles west of Mukalla. This appears, in the case of the ferruginous duck, to be a considerable extension of the winter range as described by Col. Meinertzhagen in his *Birds of Arabia* (1954).

A party of grey geese, too distant for positive identification of the species to be made, was seen on the sea near Ahwar on the 17th April. Recent correspondence in *The Field* has indicated that despite the lack of records at the time of publication of Meinertzhagen's book, geese not infrequently visit Aden. The writer was informed that they also visit Mukalla regularly in small numbers. One individual was shot during the winter of 1960-61 by Lt.-Col. J. W. G. Gray, then Commandant of the Hadhrami Bedouin Legion, which was identified by him as a greylag goose (*Anser anser*).

No passerine migrants were seen at Mukalla other than a few European swallows (*Hirundo rustica*), and solitary individuals of the pallid harrier (*Circus macrorus*) and European kestrel (*Falco tinnunculus*), seen on the 4th and 7th April respectively, were the only examples noted of other land forms on passage.

The number of resident species seen in and around the town of Mukalla itself was also rather limited.

Hemprich's gulls (*Larus hemprichii*) scavenged along the shore in large numbers and swift terns (*Sterna bergii*) were also plentiful. The white eyed gull (*L. leucophthalmus*) was however only noted at Ahwar, some 200 miles further west, though conditions in both areas appeared to be equally suitable.

Large numbers of cormorants were seen flying across the bay in a westerly direction on several evenings, but they were too distant to allow of proper identification. Only once were these birds seen on the water and that was near Irga (approx. 130 miles W. of Mukalla) on the 16th April, when several hundreds of them were seen actively fishing in shallow water off a sandy beach. On that occasion soft going made it impossible to stop the car for closer observation.

Reef herons (*Egretta gularia*) were plentiful on the beaches immediately west of the town and in this area the white and slate phases appeared to be present in equal numbers. A solitary little green heron (*Butoroides striatus*) was seen fishing in a rocky pool. (While swimming at Aden one of these herons had been watched at a range of 6 ft. attempting to dispose of a crab it had caught on a shark net. The crab was perhaps an inch across the carapace and the bird's method, either by accident or design, was to rub all its legs off against the post it was perched on, before swallowing the body whole.)

Fan tailed ravens (*Corvus rhipidurus*) were ubiquitous in Mukalla, where they performed the function of principal scavenger, kites (*Milvus migrans*) being much less in evidence. The Indian house crow (*Corvus splendens*) and the house sparrow (*Passer domesticus*) which are so plentiful in Aden, were not noted at all.

Several pairs of blackstarts (*Cercomela melanura*) were seen in the Residency garden and on roof tops in the town and two pairs of Tristam's grackle (*Onycognathus tristami*) appeared to be nesting in the cliffs on its eastern outskirts.

A pair of mourning chats (*Oenanthe lugens*), presumably of the race *boscaweni*, were feeding a single fully fledged youngster in the same area (22nd April).

The drive inland in convoy gave little opportunity for careful observation but birds of all species appeared remarkably scarce throughout the climb up the coastal escarpment and on the rocky plateau to which it gave place to the north.

Blackstarts were the most frequently seen species during the ascent and pairs or single individuals were observed at all altitudes up to the highest point of the road at 6,000 ft., above Maula Mattar. None were however noted on the open plateau itself. During a halt at Nuwaima, perhaps 2,000 feet above sea level, where the presence of springs allows date palms, pawpaws and bananas to be cultivated, a large colony of Tristam's grackle occupied the overhanging cliffs. Nile valley sunbirds (*Nectarinia metallica*) and Palestine sunbirds (*Cinnyris osca*) were also seen among some flowering bushes, the former being noted again shortly after leaving Maula Mattar (5,500 feet).

Black crowned finch larks (*Evemopterix nigriceps*) were fairly plentiful in parties of ten to thirty throughout the plateau and a solitary black shouldered kite (*Elanus caeruleus*) was also seen.

After leaving Jahi the road followed by the expedition dropped steeply down into the Wadi Duan, following its course northwards to its junction with the western end of the Wadi Hadhramaut. Surface water, with consequent cultivation at frequent intervals, accounted for a marked increase in the number and variety of birds. Here the little green bee-eater (*Merops orientalis*) and African bulbul (*Pycnonotus capensis*) were seen for the first time and great grey shrikes (*Lanius excubitor*) were extraordinarily common, one or two individuals seeming to be perched on almost every bush. Fan tailed ravens and house sparrows were also abundant, particularly in the vicinity of villages, and at Hajarain a lanner falcon (*Falco Biarmicus*) was seen to swoop unsuccessfully on a flock of rock pigeons (*Columba livia*).

From the junction of the Duan and Hadhramaut wadis the road ran first through dunes and then across wide sandy plains where no bird life was seen until arriving at Al Abr on the 25th. There the wadi containing the well of that name is bordered for half a mile of so with a single row of thorn trees and it was there that the first signs of active migration were observed; barred warblers (*Sylvia nisoria*) being gathered in the trees and bushes in some numbers, together with lesser numbers of other warblers, one of which on collection proved to be an olivaceous warbler (*Hippolais pallida*). A fully fledged immature blackstart was also collected and desert larks (*Ammomanes deserti*) were seen for the first time.

The next 180 miles, which took the convoy across open sandy plains to Khashm al Jebel and then on a 70-mile hook through the sand sea to reach the plains to the east, produced no birds other than small scattered flocks of desert larks and a solitary raven.

After emerging from the dunes and on the way to Thamud, however, vegetation became less sparse and cream coloured coursers (*Cursorius cursor*), Macqueen's bustard (*Chlamydotis undulata*), and see-see (*Ammoperdix heyi*) were seen, as well as a pair of sandgrouse too distant to identify but which appeared big enough to be *Pterocles orientalis*.

Great grey shrikes once again became plentiful and a nest of this species containing two eggs was found 6 ft. up in a bush. A third egg had been added by next morning (28th April). Desert larks were abundant and bifasciated larks (*Certhilauda alaudipes*), whose flight and appearance is so much better described by the name of hoopoe lark rejected by Meinertzhagen, were seen for the first time.

From Thamud onwards the expedition entered the type of country in which it was to operate for the following month, based on a main camp some 190 miles further east, midway between Sanau and Habarut. This consisted of gently undulating "jol", i.e. sandy plains, usually with a light gravel mantle at an average altitude of some 1,500 to 2,000 ft., extending northwards to the edge of the Rub'al Khali sand sea, which in that region at least, starts in an abrupt line of red dunes several hundred feet high. The jol is intersected at intervals of 30 to 50 miles by broad wadis, the beds of which may be over a mile wide, running northwards into the dunes. The intervening country is covered by a network of shallow depressions and drainage lines and low hills of gypsum and calcareous rock occur at intervals. The main wadi beds are filled with scattered clumps of shrubby herbs 18 in. to 2 ft. high, with very occasional bushes, while sparse grass is to be found in most of the depressions where rain has fallen in the past two or three years. Elsewhere the ground is devoid of vegetation. No surface water exists.

Such surroundings, coupled with the extremes of temperature which occur, present a harsh environment to which few species of birds appear able to adapt themselves. The following is an exhaustive list of those noted during the month spent in the area:

Brown-necked raven (Corvus corax ruficollis)
Solitary birds or pairs occasionally seen amongst dunes or hills. Not observed on the Jol proper.
Bifasciated lark (Certhilauda alaudipes)
Found in pairs throughout the area including the depressions between dunes. Showed no apparent preference between the shrub vegetation of the wadis and grassy drainage lines. The remarkable difference in size between sexes gives the first impression that two species are present.

Bar tailed desert lark (Ammomanes phoenicuva arenicolo)

Difficult always to distinguish from the desert lark (*A. deserti*) in the field but those collected were from small flocks of from fifteen to twenty birds feeding in grassy depressions. This is an extension of range as recorded by Meinertzhagen.

Desert lark (Ammomanes deserti)

The commonest bird of the area frequenting both wadis and grassy depressions alike. Usually in small numbers up to five or six but, despite Meinertzhagen's remarks about flocking, a congregation of well over one hundred birds was seen on one occasion, very active amongst low weeds in a wadi bed. Neither an obvious abundance of seeds nor the presence of insects was noted to account for this assembly.

Unidentified lark one pair seen in rocky gorge. Possibly *Ammomanes dunni*, but identification uncertain.

Crag martin (Hirundo rupestris)

Seen only near rocky hills and gorges to the south and east of area.

Unidentified buzzard—single specimens seen on three occasions. Most prominent feature unbarred chestnut tails. Upper parts dark. Under parts almost white, streaked with dark colour in two instances and more uniformly dark in the third.

Unidentified sandgrouse—probably Lichtenstein's sandgrouse (*Pterocles indicus*) seen flying in pairs in the evening in the direction of water at Sanau.

Macqueen's Bustard (Chlamydotis undulata)

Not plentiful, but seen occasionally in areas of freshest grass.

See-see (Ammoperdix heyi)

Seen once only—a covey of four on rocky hillside.

An owl was heard once, apparently calling from the ground and one casting of a large raptorial bird was found.

In addition to the foregoing, individual stragglers left behind by the northern migration were often in evidence, a motor car apparently having the same magnetic influence on most of them as a ship at sea, causing them to home on it at sight and often follow it for miles (in the case of one swallow 23 miles) diving inside to take advantage of shade whenever a halt gave an opportunity. Of these the commonest were European swallows (*Hirundo rustica*), sandmartins (*Riparia riparia*) and spotted flycatchers (*Muscicapa striate*). One warbler, identified as a willow warbler (*Phylloscopus trochilus*) was however seen and one Upcher's warbler (*Hippolais languida*) collected.

APPENDIX 2/A

THE VEGETATION AND PLANTS EATEN
BY THE ORYX
by
D. R. M. Stewart and M. H. Woodford

The plant life of Central and Eastern Arabia has been described by Vesey-Fitzgerald (in the *Journal of Ecology*, 1957) and that of Southern Arabia by Popov (*Vegetation of Arabia South of the Tropic of Cancer*, 1958). Guichard has compiled a comprehensive plant list for Southern Arabia (1952) and Gilliland has described the vegetation of the south-west Rub'al Khali (1952). We were particularly concerned with making a collection of the plants growing within the habitat of the oryx, and learning what we could about those which the oryx prefers. A list of the plants collected is given at the end of this Appendix.

Within that part of the present habitat of the oryx explored by the expedition the vegetation is largely restricted to the wadi beds and the drainage lines leading into them from the surrounding Jol; however, the sand dunes bear a certain amount of permanent plant life, and after rain a flush of annual herbs and grasses may appear on the sands and Jol. Another place where we frequently found patches of vegetation was at the edge of the Jol where the latter meets the steep slopes of the dunes of "the Empty Quarter". Possibly a certain amount of moisture accumulates in such places after rain and sustains more plant life there than is possible elsewhere on the Jol.

The most typical plant of the wadi beds is *Heliotropium luteum* (Arabic rimram), whose dark rounded bushes two to three feet high indicate the line of a wadi from afar. Smaller bushes of various species of *Salsola* (rishi, tahyin, kakabit, hamala, arad),

Fagonia parviflora (darma), *Kanahia laniflora, Dipterygium glaucum* (ailgi, alqa) and *Zygophyllum coccineum* (lekawa) are also common. Other herbs appearing fairly frequently are *Iphiona scabra, Crotalaria aegyptiaca, Aerva javanica, Arnebia hispidissima* and a small species of *Convolvulus.* Very near the sands, especially in the "ramlat" where a wadi ends amongst the dunes, and on the Jol along the edge of the sands the yellow-flowered *Tribulus pterocarpus* and *T. alatus* (zahra) and a sedge, *Cyperus conglomeratus,* are common. Large bushes, which occasionally almost merit being called small trees, of *Leptadenia pyrotechnica* (marakh) occur here and there in the wadi beds, and are almost the only source of shade there apart from that provided by the occasional rocky outcrop.

The vegetation in the shallow drainage lines running off the Jol into the wadis is mostly composed of grasses of which, however, there are very few species. By far the commonest is *Aristida plumosa* (meluh, nussi, sabat); we also found occasional specimens of *Lasiurus hirsutus* and *Panicum turgidum.* The sand dunes carry a surprising amount of vegetation although the plants are widely spaced; most of the species are also found in the wadi beds or on the Jol, but one plant we saw only on the dunes was a species of *Ephedra* (ablab), a dark green bush growing to about eight feet.

In all these areas the abundance of the vegetation depends largely on how recently rain fell or, in the case of a wadi, when flood water caused by storms elsewhere last came down. After an area received moisture in one of these ways the vegetation may remain green for several years. Conversely, an area may receive no moisture other than dew for many years, and plant growth ceases or is very slight.

Our information on the plants preferred by the oryx comes from four sources, the literature, examination of the stomach contents of one animal which died during the expedition, analysis of oryx droppings and the deductions which can be made from the behaviour of the animals we tracked.

Carruthers (*Arabian Adventure to the Great Nafud in Quest of the Oryx*, 1935) states that the oryx feeds chiefly "on a tall yellow grass called nussi (*Aristida sp.*) . . . and also to some degree on the ghada bush, nibbling its tender young shoots". He also says that alqa (*Dipterygium glaucum*) is a favourite food, but that "the most succulent grasses such as nussi and sabat (*Aristida*) are doubtless their principal food" although "the young shoots of Tamarisk and other shrubs are sought for in spring. Even more desired are those peculiar juicy parasites that grow on the roots of the desert shrubs . . . There are two sorts, the red Tarthuth, *Cynomorium coccineum*, and the yellow *Phelipaea lutea*. These long spadices may be as much as eighteen to twenty-four inches long, and are full of liquid especially the major portion below the sand. The oryx dig for these so as to get at the best and most succulent end."

Talbot (*A Look at Threatened Species*, 1960) records that "according to the bedouin the favourite oryx food is zahar (*Tribulus*), and they are also fond of a sweet grass, nussi". Tomatum bin Harbi, the expedition's principal guide, said that the oryx always prefers fresh grasses, but that it also eats a number of herbs, including roots and the fruits of members of the marrow family, *Cucurbitaceae*. In captivity our oryx ate several of the gourd-like fruits of *Citrullus colocynthis*, a plant belonging to this family.

The stomach of the oryx which died during the expedition contained mostly unidentifiable grass together with a lot of the sedge, *Cyperus conglomeratus*. The oryx droppings collected during the expedition and later analysed microscopically all contained a very high proportion of the commonest grass in the area, *Aristida plumosa*. A small amount of another grass, *Lasiurus hirsutus*, was found in three samples. Herbaceous plants were only present in small quantities, the commonest being *Trephrosia apollinea*, *Tribulus pterocarpus* and *T. elatus*, *Cassia senna* and *Erodium byroniaefolium* also appeared in one or two samples.

Most of the oryx tracks which we followed kept to the drainage lines running off the Jol into the wadis, and the patches of vegetation at the base of dunes, rather than to the wadis themselves. This suggests that the plants found in these two areas are preferred to those in the wadis. In the drainage lines grasses are most common, and this tends to confirm the evidence from other sources that grasses form the major part of the oryx's diet, whilst it also feeds upon herbs to some extent, including the roots, fruits and spadices of certain species.

APPENDIX 2/B

Plants collected from the habitat of the oryx during the 1962 expedition.

Family	Name	Principal habitat
Amaranthaceae	Aerva javanica (Burm. f.) Spreng	Wadi beds
Asclepiadaceae	Kanahia laniflora (Forsk.) R.Br.	,, ,,
	Leptadenia pyrotechnica (Forsk.) Decne.	,, ,,
Boraginaceae	Arnebia hispidissima DC.	,, ,,
	Heliotropium luteum Poir	,, ,,
Caesalpiniaceae	Cassia senna L. var senna	,, ,,
Capparidaceae	Dipterygium glaucum Decne.	,, ,,
Chenopodiaceae	Salsola sp. aff. Subaphylla C.A.M.?	,, ,,
Compositae	Iphiona scabra Decne.	,, ,,
	Pulicaria crispa (Forsk.) Benth. et Hook.	,, ,,
Convolvulaceae	Convolvulus sp.	,, ,,
Cucurbitaceae	Citrullus colocynthis (L.) Schrad.	,, ,,
Cyperaceae	Cyperus conglomeratus	Jol at base of dunes
Euphorbiaceae	Euphorbia granulata Forsk.	Jol at base of dunes
Geraniaceae	Erodium byroniaefolium Boiss	Jol at base of dunes
Gnetaceae	Ephedra sp.	Sand dunes
Gramineae	Aristida plumosa L.	Drainage lines on Jol

Family	Name	Principal habitat
Gramineae	Lasiurus hirsutus (Forsk.) Boiss	Jol
	Panicum turgidum Forsk.	,,
Papilionaceae	Astragalus sp.	Wadi beds
	Crotalaria aegyptiaca Benth.	,, ,,
	Indigofera intricata Boiss	,, ,,
	I. semitrijuga Forsk.	Jol
	Tephrosia apollinea Link.	Wadi beds
Polygalaceae	Polygala erioptera DC.	,, ,,
Rhamnaceae	Rhamnus sp.	,, ,,
	R. sp. aff. leucodermis Baker	,, ,,
Zygophyllaceae	Fagonia cf. bruguieri DC. vel. parviflora Boiss	Sand dunes
	F. parviflora Boiss	Wadi beds
	Tribulus alatus Del.	,, ,,
	T. pterocarpus Ehrenb.	,, ,,
	Zygophyllum coccineum L.	,, ,,

APPENDIX 3

ACKNOWLEDGEMENTS

The expedition would like to thank the following organisations, firms and individuals for their assistance and co-operation without which we could not have been successful.

The Royal Air Force for their assistance in transportation.

The Resident Adviser and British Agent at Mukalla, Mr A. F. Watts, O.B.E., for his continuous support and his efforts on our behalf with the rulers of the Qua'iti, Kathiri and Mahra states.

Qaid J. W. G. Gray, Commandant of the HBL, for his assistance in administration and transportation.

East African Wild Life Society for the loan of its Piper Cruiser.

Aden Airways for assistance with the Piper and for free transportation of vital stores.

Electronic Aids E.A. Ltd. for building a portable radio beacon and for installing wirelesses.

Ker and Downey Safaris Ltd. for workshop facilities for building the catching car.

The Kenya Government for the services of Mr D. R. M. Stewart.

Mr John Seago and Mr Tony Parkinson for the loan of equipment, and for their expert care when the oryx reached Nairobi.

Messrs Ind Coope Ltd. for their generous gift of beer.

Bridport Industries Ltd. for nets and rope.

Burroughs Wellcome Ltd., Pfizer Ltd., Glaxo Laboratories Ltd., May and Baker Ltd., Parke, Davis and Co., John Wyeth & Brother, all of whom provided drugs.

F. A. H. Wilson, D.S.O.T.D., and others of the Secretariat, Aden for many kindnesses.

G. W. H. Dawson for his efforts with the catching car at Mukalla.

All those at Aden, Mukalla and Saiwun who entertained and helped the members of the expedition.

The quotations on pages 53 and 63 are from *The Southern Gates of Arabia* by Freya Stark and are included by kind permission of John Murray (Publishers), Ltd.

BIBLIOGRAPHY

Shebas Daughters	by	St John Philby
The Empty Quarter	by	St John Philby
Arabia Felix	by	Bertram Thomas
Alarms and Excursions in Arabia	by	Bertram Thomas
Arabian Sands	by	Wilfrid Thesiger
In Unknown Arabia	by	Major R. E. Cheesman
Arabia and the Isles	by	Harold Ingrams
Arabia Deserta	by	Charles M. Doughty
Arabian Adventure	by	Douglas Carruthers
Aden to the Hadhramaut	by	D. Van Der Meulen
The Southern Gates of Arabia	by	Freya Stark
The Coast of Incense	by	Freya Stark
The Persian Gulf States	by	Sir Rupert Hay
Northern Najd	by	Guarmani
A Narrative of a year's journey Through Central and Eastern Arabia	by	W. G. Palgrave
A Look at Threatened Species	by	Lee Talbot
Files of the Expedition		

Date: 6/24/20

SP J MCDONALD
McDonald, Kirsten
La sorpresa verde

Carlos & Carmen

La sorpresa verde

Por Kirsten McDonald
Ilustrado por Erika Meza

Calico Kid

An Imprint of Magic Wagon
abdopublishing.com

*For my two sisters—who always make room for me in their tents —**KKM***

*To my two Carlos, and specially both of my parents; who taught me to value changes, movings, carnes asadas, mischiefs, surprises and the beautiful moments you can only live with your family. Gracias: ¡los quiero! —**EM***

*A mis dos hermanas: que siempre me han guardado sitio en sus tiendas de campaña —**KKM***

*A mis dos Carlos y, en especial, a mis padres; quienes me enseñaron a valorar los cambios, las mudanzas, las carnes asadas, las travesuras, las sorpresas y los maravillosos momentos que solo se pueden vivir en familia. Gracias: ¡los quiero! —**EM***

abdopublishing.com

Published by Magic Wagon, a division of ABDO, PO Box 398166, Minneapolis, Minnesota 55439.
Copyright © 2017 by Abdo Consulting Group, Inc. International copyrights reserved in all countries.
No part of this book may be reproduced in any form without written permission from the publisher.
Calico Kid™ is a trademark and logo of Magic Wagon.

Printed in the United States of America, North Mankato, Minnesota.
112016
012017

THIS BOOK CONTAINS
RECYCLED MATERIALS

Written by Kirsten McDonald
Illustrated by Erika Meza
Edited by Heidi M.D. Elston, Megan M. Gunderson & Bridget O'Brien
Art Direction by Candice Keimig

Publisher's Cataloging in Publication Data

Names: McDonald, Kirsten, author. | Meza, Erika, illustrator.
Title: La sorpresa verde / by Kirsten McDonald ; illustrated by Erika Meza.
Other titles: The green surprise. Spanish
Description: Minneapolis, MN : Magic Wagon, 2017. | Series: Carlos & Carmen
Summary: For twins Carlos and Carmen, Uncle Alex's big green surprise turns
    into the best backyard camping experience ever.
Identifiers: LCCN 2016955309 | ISBN 9781614796176 (lib. bdg.) |
    ISBN 9781614796374 (ebook)
Subjects: LCSH: Backyard camping–Juvenile fiction. | Hispanic American
    families–Juvenile fiction. | Uncles–Juvenile fiction. | Twins–Juvenile
    fiction. | Brothers and sisters–Juvenile fiction. | Spanish language materials–
    Juvenile fiction.
Classification: DDC [E]–dc23
LC record available at http://lccn.loc.gov/2016955309

Índice

Capítulo 1
¡Hurras!

El sábado por la tarde, los García estaban en el jardín. Carlos y Carmen jugaban al fútbol.

Mommy estaba acariciando a su gata Spooky. Papá estaba preparando la parrilla.

Papá llamó a los gemelos:

—Su Tío favorito, Uncle Alex, viene hoy.

Carlos y Carmen dejaron de dar patadas a la pelota y corrieron hacia el porche.

—¿Viene Uncle Alex? —preguntó Carmen.

—¿Viene hoy? —añadió Carlos.

—Sí a los dos —se rio Papá.

Entonces Carlos y Carmen gritaron, dando saltos de alegría:

—¡Hurra!

Papá añadió con un guiño:

—Va a traer una sorpresa divertida. Una gran sorpresa verde.

—¿Una sorpresa? —preguntó Carlos.

—¡Dos hurras! —gritó Carmen.

—Y, also—dijo Mamá sonriendo—, pasará aquí la noche.

Carlos and Carmen se quedaron paralizados. Los ojos como platos. Y sus sonrisas se hicieron aún más grandes.

—¡Tres hurras si va a pasar aquí la noche! —gritó Carlos.

—¡No! —se rio Carmen, negando con la cabeza—, que Uncle Alex se quede a dormir merece, por lo menos, cuatro hurras.

9

Capítulo 2
La abultada sorpresa verde

Una hora más tarde, Uncle Alex llegó en su coche azul.

—¡Uncle Alex! ¡Uncle Alex! — gritaron los gemelos, corriendo a recibirle.

Los gemelos se apoyaron en la ventanilla de su coche. Miraron por todas partes dentro del coche.

—¿Dónde está? —preguntó Carmen.

—¿Dónde está la sorpresa? —dijo Carlos.

Uncle Alex sonrió.

—¡That's enough, ustedes dos! Déjenme salir del coche.

Los gemelos siguieron a Uncle Alex hacia la parte trasera de su coche.

Dentro del maletero, había una gran bolsa verde.

—No parece una sorpresa muy divertida —dijo Carmen entristecida.

—¿Ah, no? —se rio Uncle Alex—, espera y verás.

Uncle Alex cargó con la gran bolsa verde hasta el jardín. La abrió y la vació por completo.

Carlos y Carmen vieron unos largos palos plateados. Vieron unas estacas cortas y amarillas.

Y vieron un gran toldo verde.

—Vengan a ayudarme —dijo Uncle Alex.

Los gemelos ayudaron a desplegar el gran toldo verde. Ayudaron a pasar las estacas amarillas por las anillas que había por todo el borde del toldo. Ayudaron a clavar las estacas en el suelo.

Empezaba a ser emocionante. Empezaba a parecer una sorpresa.

Mamá ayudó al Uncle Alex a juntar los palos. Entonces, como por arte de magia, el gran toldo verde se convirtió en ¡una gran tienda de campaña verde!

—¿Nos podemos meter? —preguntó Carmen.

—¿Qué les parece si hacemos una acampada? —les preguntó Uncle Alex.

—¿Una acampada? —preguntó Carlos.

—¿Aquí, en nuestro jardín? —añadió Carmen.

—Sí, una acampada aquí, en su jardín —dijo Mamá riéndose.

—¿En la gran tienda verde? —preguntó Carlos.

—Sí, en la gran tienda verde —añadió Uncle Alex.

—¡Esta es la mejor sorpresa del mundo! —gritó Carmen mientras saltaba a los brazos de Uncle Alex.

—¡Creo que esto ya es una sorpresa de cinco hurras! —añadió Carlos, saltando a la espalda de Uncle Alex.

Entonces, con los gemelos abrazándole con fuerza, Uncle Alex empezó a dar vueltas y vueltas y vueltas.

Capítulo 3
Preparados

Los García prepararon su cena de picnic. Carmen trajo un bol con ensalada. Carlos trajo una cesta con totopos de maíz.

Mamá trajo unos cuencos de salsa verde y de salsa roja. Y Uncle Alex trajo un plato con rebanadas de sandía.

Papá terminó de asar la carne y anunció:

—La grilled meat y las tortillas ya están listas, ¡a comer!

Comieron rollitos de tortillas rellenos de carne asada. Comieron ensalada, totopos y salsas. Comieron jugosas rebanadas de sandía.

—¿Podemos ir ya a por nuestros sacos de dormir? —preguntó Carmen.

—Goodness gracious! Ustedes dos no saben estarse quietos —dijo Papá.

—Está oscureciendo —dijo Uncle Alex—. Tengo dos pequeñas surprises más para ustedes.

Sacó dos linternitas de su bolsillo trasero y entregó una a cada gemelo.

—¡Gracias! —gritaron los gemelos.

Capítulo 4
Acampada

Carlos y Carmen se metieron en sus sacos de dormir. Hicieron espirales de luz en las paredes de la tienda con sus nuevas linternas.

Contaron historias divertidas y cantaron canciones graciosas.

—¿Estás dormida? —preguntó Carlos.

—Casi —contestó Carmen bostezando.

Los gemelos se quedaron en silencio. Oyeron la música suave que venía de la casa. Oyeron a los grillos cantando en la hierba.

Oyeron algo que rozaba la puerta
de la tienda.

—What is it? —preguntó Carmen.

—¿Crees que es un monstruo? —
preguntó Carlos.

Justo entonces los gemelos oyeron un suave ronroneo.

Carmen se rio.

—Conozco a este monstruo.

Abrió la cremallera de la tienda y dejó entrar a la gata Spooky.

Los gemelos se volvieron a acomodar en sus sacos de dormir con Spooky acurrucada entre ambos.

Siguieron oyendo la música.
Siguieron oyendo los grillos. Pero
ahora oyeron unos pasos acercarse
más y más.

—¿Crees que es un monstruo? —
susurró Carlos.

Antes de que Carmen pudiera
responder, la cremallera de la puerta
empezó a abrirse. Uncle Alex metió la
cabeza dentro.

—¿Hay sitio para one more? —
preguntó.

Carlos y Carmen se rieron. Y Carlos le hizo un sitio a Uncle Alex.

Los cuatro se tendieron en la tienda.

Oyeron la música, oyeron los grillos y, también, oyeron un sonido de pasos que se acercaban a la tienda más y más.

La cremallera de la tienda se abrió otra vez. Esta vez, Papá gateó hacia el interior de la tienda.

—Hazme un sitio, Carmencita —dijo mientras se tumbaba a su lado.

Ahora los cinco estaban tendidos en la tienda. Todos oyeron la música y los grillos.

Todos oyeron las puertas en la casa abrirse y cerrarse y abrirse y cerrarse. Entonces oyeron otro sonido de pasos acercándose más y más.

—Creo que sé quién es —dijo Carlos con una gran sonrisa.

—Yo también —dijo Carmen entre risas.

Mamá se abrió camino dentro de la tienda con un cesto de colada lleno de mantas y almohadas.

Y así, Mamá, Papá y Uncle Alex se acurrucaron con sus mantas al lado de Carlos, Carmen y Spooky. Era la perfecta gran sorpresa verde.

Inglés
al
Español

grilled meat – carne asada

Goodness gracious! – ¡Dios mío!

Mommy – Mamá

Daddy – Papá

What is it? – ¿Qué es?

surprise – sorpresa

also – también

Uncle – Tío

one more – uno más

that's enough – ya basta

Printed in Great Britain by
D. R. Hillman and Sons Ltd., Frome